Praise for *Walking the Labyrinth*

"Lisa Goldstein writes elegantly crafted novels and stories of magic realism, in which the familiar and the strange live not in separate realms but on the same streets. . . . With her deceptively clear style and her gift for creating natural-seeming characters, Goldstein seduces us into the labyrinth of her story."
— *Minneapolis Star Tribune*

"Goldstein's novel faultlessly conjures up the magic of past America. She reaches some remarkable new levels of insight in fathoming illusion's role in life. . . . *Walking the Labyrinth* shows Lisa Goldstein clad in a thaumaturge's mantle."
— *Asimov's Science Fiction*

"*Walking the Labyrinth* is full of enchantments and illusions, wonders and delights, and the mysterious connections of a family. A highly satisfying read!"
— *Fantasy & Science Fiction*

"A deft touch with the ways reality and magic swirl together at the edges and characters not easily forgotten."
— *Feminist Bookstore News*

"*Walking the Labyrinth* may be her most accomplished novel to date, because it combines all of Goldstein's style and poetry with a complex but satisfying plot and two strong heroes."
— *Starlog*

"A deftly woven, engrossing who-dun-what. . . . Goldstein's best outing since *A Mask for the General.*"
— *Kirkus Reviews*

WALKING
THE
LABYRINTH

LISA
GOLDSTEIN

A TOM DOHERTY ASSOCIATES BOOK
NEW YORK

This is a work of fiction. All the characters and events portrayed in this book are either fictitious or are used fictitiously.

WALKING THE LABYRINTH

Copyright © 1996 by Lisa Goldstein

All rights reserved, including the right to reproduce this book, or portions thereof, in any form.

This book is printed on acid-free paper.

A Tor Book
Published by Tom Doherty Associates, Inc.
175 Fifth Avenue
New York, NY 10010

Tor Books on the World Wide Web:
http://www.tor.com

Tor® is a registered trademark of Tom Doherty Associates, Inc.

Design by Nancy Resnick
Edited by David G. Hartwell

Library of Congress Cataloging-in-Publication Data

Goldstein, Lisa.
    Walking the labyrinth / by Lisa Goldstein.
        p.   cm.
    "A Tom Doherty Associates book."
    ISBN 0-312-85968-6 (pb)
    I. Title.
PS3557.O397W35   1996
813'.54—dc20   95-53142
                                                        CIP

First hardcover edition: June 1996
First trade paperback edition: February 1998

Printed in the United States of America

0 9 8 7 6 5 4 3 2 1

FOR CLAIRE PARMAN BROWN

WALKING
THE
LABYRINTH

PROLOGUE

When the show ended, when the stagehands came out to clear away the stars and streamers and glittering sequins, Andrew made his way down the aisle to the stage. He knocked at the door to the greenroom, which opened to a woman in a turban and a short green and silver kimono.

"I'm Andrew Dodd from the Oakland *Tribune*," he said. "Callan and Thorne Allalie told me to meet them after the performance."

"Ah," she said. "Callan's in the trap room. Do you know where that is?"

He shook his head. The woman gave him complicated directions and he walked down the stairs, then followed a maze of sloping corridors. The brown and off-white walls, the rough ceiling and bare bulbs, were almost a relief after the opulence of the theater. He came to the trap room and knocked.

"Come," a deep voice said. Andrew opened the door and stepped inside. "I'm Callan Allalie. You're the reporter, aren't you?"

"Is this part of the mind-reading act?" Andrew asked.

Callan laughed. He was, Andrew saw with surprise, fairly short; on stage, wearing a top hat and tails, he had seemed larger, more imposing. He was almost completely bald; that had been hidden by the hat.

"You were the only man in the audience not wearing a tie and tails," Callan said, indicating Andrew's white blazer and straw skimmer. "I saw you from the stage and I thought, There's the reporter. Sit down, sit down."

Andrew looked around. In one corner stood a piano covered with a cloth. Near it were several rolled rugs, then the ramp leading to the orchestra pit. Clothing racks hung with costumes took up another corner. Two men carrying a golden statue between them came through the door. So they had been statues, then. Andrew hadn't been sure.

He sat on one of the rolled rugs. Callan laughed again and sat next to him, stretching his legs. "Good, good," Callan said. "I like informality."

Andrew could smell the man's strong sweat. He fished a notebook and pencil from his blazer pocket. "So," he said. "Magic. Lead into gold, water into wine, that sort of thing."

"Gold into wine," Callan said.

Andrew looked at him, discomfited. He had had a good strong drink before the performance, thanking God, as he always did, that Prohibition had ended two years before. He hadn't thought anyone could tell, though.

"That dame who disappeared," Andrew said. "She went through the trapdoor, right?"

Callan put a thick finger to his lips.

"You don't give away your secrets, is that it?"

Callan's finger was still at his lips. No, Andrew saw—it was pointing upwards, to the ceiling. "The room under the stage is always called the trap room," Callan said. "But in this particular theater there's no trapdoor."

Andrew looked up at the unfinished ceiling. Pipes ran along it and down the walls; there was no room for anything else. "I love this theater," Callan said. "It's the most beautiful place in the world."

"So how did you do it?" Andrew asked.

"Trickery."

"Right." Andrew opened his notebook, glanced at the questions he had written there. "Is everyone in the act part of your family?"

A woman came through the door. Callan stood and they embraced. "What do you think?" she asked. "They loved us, didn't they?"

"Of course they did," Callan said. He turned her toward Andrew as if introducing her to an audience.

Andrew stood and doffed his skimmer. "Hello, ma'am," he said. "I'm Andrew Dodd from the *Tribune.*"

She held out her hand to him. "A pleasure," she said. "I'm Callan's sister."

Andrew took the hand, noticing the Allalie family resemblance. Both brother and sister were short, muscular, with gaps between their front teeth. But where Callan looked squat, like a frog or a gargoyle, the same features had somehow combined to make his sister almost beautiful. Her kimono was purple, with gold stars.

"And you're all one family?" Andrew asked.

"Oh, yes," the woman—she had to be Thorne—said. She leaned against the piano and lit a cigarette with a green marble lighter, fanning the smoke in front of her face.

"When did you get started? And how?"

"And why?" Thorne laughed.

More people were entering the trap room now, some still in costume, some in ordinary work clothes. A woman painted gold leaned over and kissed Callan, leaving a smear of gold on his cheek.

"Were you one of the statues?" Andrew asked her.

"Statues?" the woman said. She stood on tiptoe and kissed him as well, a touch as soft as soot on his face.

"I get it," Andrew said. "None of you guys are going to give me a straight answer, is that it?"

"Of course we will," Thorne said. "Callan, what have you been saying to this poor man? Tell him anything he wants to know."

"How many are you?" Andrew asked.

"It varies," Callan said. There was a cigarette in his hand too now, though Andrew hadn't seem him take it out. "Some stay home and study."

"Study? Study what?"

"The art—" puff "—illusion."

A young man with curly reddish-gold hair came into the room. He wore a capacious raincoat, though there had been no hint of rain that evening.

"Corrig!" several people called. He turned and grinned, showing the same gapped teeth as the rest. From his raincoat pockets he drew a bottle of champagne and several cut-glass goblets, and set them on the piano.

A woman brushed against Andrew. "Of course you'll have some," she said in a low voice. "You're our guest tonight."

Callan handed him a glass. The red-haired man popped the cork; it shot through the air and seemed to leave a purple trail behind it. He filled Andrew's glass.

Andrew took a sip, and then, surprised, sipped again. It was very good—he hadn't tasted anything as delicious in a long time.

"All right," he said. His notebook and pencil had somehow gotten back into his pocket. He set the champagne glass down and took them out again. "When did you people start touring together?"

"Centuries ago, really," Thorne said. "Well, not us, of course, but our family."

"Ah," Andrew said. This was something he could use. He took another sip of champagne, then finished the glass and held it out for more. Corrig filled it to the brim. "So your family has a tradition of performing."

The woman he had met in the greenroom came in the door. She still wore the green and silver kimono but the turban was gone and she had large black glasses, men's glasses, over her eyes. "Thorne!" Callan said. "Come help us. This young man is asking us all sorts of questions."

"Thorne?" Andrew said. "I thought you—" He turned to the woman with the cigarette. "I thought you were Thorne. Callan's sister, you said."

"I'm Callan's other sister," the woman said. "Fentrice."

A man carrying a trumpet followed Thorne into the room, then a woman with bells on her wrists and ankles. The small space was filling with people: a woman with a snake around her neck, a man leading a tiger. Andrew couldn't remember seeing that many on stage. Dozens of gold statues were propped up against each other in the corner; Andrew looked for the woman who had kissed him but couldn't find her anywhere. Someone was playing the piano, thumping the wooden top to keep the beat.

He turned, turned again. A woman smelling of jasmine and tobacco ran her scarf across his face, and for a moment the room turned gauzy green, as if seen underwater. He pushed it aside and tried to focus but could see only fragments: coins, jewels, stars. Two women danced in front of him. A voice sang,

> "Got a dog, got a cat,
>   Got a car, got a flat,
>   Got everything but you, my baaaby. . . ."

Where was Callan? He pushed his way through the crowd, past people wearing headdresses of feathers, circlets of flowers. A man in clothing a century old gripped the hilt of a sword.

Ahead of him stood the red-haired man, Corrig, pouring from another bottle of champagne. Callan was talking earnestly to him. "Callan!" Andrew said.

"Ah, there you are," Callan said. "Where did you go off to? Have some champagne."

Andrew took another glass, drank. When he looked up most of the crowd had gone; a single white feather floated through the air.

He cleared his throat. "How—how did you do that?" he asked.

"Trickery," Callan said.

"Illusion," Thorne said.

He turned. Where had Thorne come from? His notebook had gotten lost again. He patted his pocket, then looked up and saw Corrig holding it out to him. He took it, opened to the first page. It was filled with writing he couldn't read, eyes, triangles, suns. He turned to the middle.

"We've been touring all over," Callan said. "Boston, Philadelphia, Denver. Last month we were in England."

"England," Andrew wrote. He frowned. There had been something he had been about to ask but he couldn't remember what it was now.

He drank more champagne. The room seemed to contract down to the glass in his hand; everything else was spinning around that one still point. He looked up. The red-haired man was grinning at him.

The piano music started up again, joined by a trumpet and a clarinet this time.

"Devil take the car and flat,
    Hang the dog and shoot the cat,
    Don't want anything, babe, but you. . . ."

It was an effort to move his head, to raise pencil to paper. He closed his eyes.

He woke up on the trolley home with no memory of having left the theater. He got off at the stop nearest his apartment, climbed the stairs, and fell into bed without taking off his clothes and shoes.

The sun coming through his window woke him the next morning. He cursed; his editor would be expecting his article. He groaned, sat up, and rubbed his forehead. If he was lucky he would have written some of it last night.

He fixed a cup of coffee and drank it, then opened his notebook. "Lies?" it said. "Truth?" The rest was blank.

ONE
Magicians Dazzle

Sixty years later Molly Travers left an office building in downtown Oakland to go to lunch. As she stepped out into the crowded street someone called out, "Ms. Travers?"

Peter? she thought, though Peter would certainly never use her last name. Despite that, she looked around eagerly.

The man who had spoken pushed his way through the crowd. He was medium height, with curly brown hair and a pointed chin. His eyes were set too close together.

She stopped. "Yes?"

"I'd like to ask you a few questions," he said. "Can I buy you lunch?"

"Questions about what?" she asked.

"Your great-aunt."

"My *aunt?*" she said. "What do you know about my aunt?"

"Your great-aunt Fentrice Allalie." Several people left the building and pushed their way between them. "Can we go somewhere private?"

"Who are you?" she asked.

"My name is John Stow. I'm a private investigator."

"Oh," she said. "Well, I've certainly got nothing to hide.

Would the deli be okay with you? It's right down the street."

They stopped at a light. It was a sunny day, after months of rain; the long California drought was finally ending. John Stow squinted at the heavy downtown traffic. The light changed; a chirping sound came from the traffic lights to indicate to the blind that it was safe to cross. They started across the street.

"I should probably ask for some identification," Molly said.

Stow took out his wallet and opened it to a Xerox of his license. "Why are you so interested in my aunt?" Molly asked.

"It's a matter of an inheritance."

"An inheritance? Don't look at me—my aunt had barely enough to live on."

"She raised you, right?"

"You've done your homework."

"Could be she's owed money."

Molly laughed. "I can't imagine."

"Your aunt's brother—"

"Her brother?"

"Yeah."

"Her brother?" Molly said again. She slowed. "Her brother's long dead."

"Are you sure?"

"Of course I'm sure. He was my grandfather—he died before I was born."

"Well, it seems that someone related to this brother didn't get some money that was owed him."

"Listen, are you sure you have the right person? I don't think my grandfather had any relatives besides my aunt and my parents."

"Pretty sure. There aren't too many people named Fentrice."

"Yeah, but—Who are you working for, anyway?"

"I can't tell you that."

"Then I don't have to answer your questions."

"No, sure. Listen, did your aunt ever say anything about her time on the road?"

Molly hesitated. She had, of course, asked questions about

the family history, but Fentrice never talked much about the past. She wasn't going to tell John Stow that, though. "All she ever said was that she had had a pretty wild youth, but that she had given it all up and settled down. She was a touring magician or something."

"The Allalie Family."

"You seem to know more about it than I do. Why don't you ask her?"

"I might do that. I'd like to start with you first, though. She ever say anything about her brother? Your grandfather?"

"Hardly anything. His name was—let me think. Callan, something like that. Callan Allalie."

"Callan, that's right. Anything else?"

"Not that I can remember."

They went into the deli and ordered at the counter. When the sandwiches came they took them to a table by the window. Stow bit into his reuben and then set it down and reached into his jacket pocket. The jacket sleeves were worn at the elbows; it looked like something he had gotten at a thrift shop. Molly thought of Peter, his khaki jackets and open-neck shirts, of the way he seemed ready at all times to hop a plane and travel to some exotic destination.

"Here, look at this," Stow said, setting a piece of paper on the table.

It was a Xerox of an article from the Oakland *Tribune*, dated April 9, 1935. *"Magicians Dazzle at the Paramount,"* the headline said, and underneath, *"By Andrew Dodd."*

Molly began to read. " 'Audiences sat spellbound as a family of magicians took to the stage at the Paramount Theatre last night. The Allalie Family, consisting of Callan, Thorne, and Fentrice, and large numbers of their kith and kin, managed to engage, enchant, and amuse—and did it all as effortlessly as pulling a rabbit out of a hat.' "

She looked up. "Thorne? Who's Thorne?"

"I was hoping you'd know."

She shook her head. "Never heard of him."

"Keep reading," Stow said.

" 'Callan, the patriarch of this remarkable clan, caused his sister Thorne to vanish in full view of the audience. He made a number of predictions, telling a gentleman about a promotion awaiting him, a lady where she had misplaced her diamond and ruby watch, which, according to her, he described perfectly. There was a considerable stir in the audience at these prophecies. But even they paled in comparison with the last act, in which Callan conjured several gold statues and finally his sister Thorne, who reappeared to loud applause.

" 'The sister thus returned might have been Fentrice; I confess that to this reporter the various family members looked remarkably alike. Even when I went backstage to interview them I was subject to some confusion. I did discover, however, that the Allalie clan has a tradition of touring, which, according to Thorne (or Fentrice), goes back several centuries. Some of this enormous family stay home and study what they call the art of illusion while the others tour.

" 'Callan Allalie told me that the Paramount Theatre is the most beautiful place in the world. Because of this recommendation I turned to take a final look at its facade as I left. It consists of a tile mosaic several stories high featuring a man and a woman, each manipulating a number of marionettes which depend from their hands on strings—dancers, actors, athletes, animals. I felt a kinship with these figures; I had been manipulated as thoroughly by Callan, Thorne, and Fentrice Allalie. The difference was that I had enjoyed myself throughout.' "

There was a picture along with the article. It had not reproduced well; there were whole sections of shiny black where the Xerox machine had apparently given up in confusion. But Molly could make out a man standing at the front of the stage, two women somewhat behind him, a number of statues along the side, and what looked like a tiger at the back. Funny the reporter hadn't mentioned the tiger.

"Thorne could have been someone who joined them along the

way," Molly said. "Maybe they called themselves a family because it sounded better."

"The article says they all looked alike."

She peered closer at the photograph. Did the three performers resemble each other? She couldn't tell. The man wore a top hat and tails, the women long fringed dresses and beads. More to the point, did they look like her? She was short, with a wide face, curly light-brown hair, and blue eyes. Could it be she had a whole group of relatives she had never met?

Her heart began to pound. "I don't know," she said. "I never heard anything about these people."

"Maybe she had a falling-out with them." Stow squinted at the article.

Maybe. It was true that Fentrice rarely spoke of Callan. But she couldn't see why that should matter to Stow and his mysterious client. And there was something a little shifty about the investigator, with his shabby coat and his talk of inheritances. Would he look as sinister if his eyes weren't so close together?

She pushed the Xerox toward him. "No, no, keep it," Stow said. "I have another copy." He bit into his sandwich. There was a spot of mustard on his collar. "Did your aunt ever keep a scrapbook? Newspaper articles, things like that?"

"I don't know."

"Could you ask her?"

"I guess so," Molly said slowly. "How did you find me?"

"Paper trail. Colleges, taxes, that sort of thing. I nearly lost you in Oregon—you were calling yourself Ariadne Travers then."

"That's my middle name."

"I know."

"I thought that stuff was confidential."

"It is." She waited for him to go on, but all he said was, "What do you do in that office building, anyway?"

"Temporary work."

"Do you like it?"

"Not really."

"Why do you do it, then?"

"I don't like being tied down. Do you like being a private investigator?"

"Keeps me busy."

That wasn't really an answer. Stow must have thought so too, because he added, "It's the only thing I've ever done."

They spent the rest of the lunch in silence. "Here's my card," the investigator said when they had finished. "Give me a call if you remember anything."

Molly took the card, put it in her purse. She had no intention of ever talking to him again.

But all that afternoon, as she sat at her desk and worked at her word processor, she thought about John Stow, about her aunt and this person who claimed to be related to her grandfather. And in the evening, after she had gone to her small apartment and cooked and eaten dinner, she wondered if she should call Fentrice.

It would be an extraordinary step, she knew. They wrote to each other at least once a week, Fentrice with her chubby black fountain pen, Molly on the computer at work. Fentrice talked about her garden, the friends with whom she played bridge, the small midwestern town where she lived. Molly told Fentrice about her succession of jobs, though she was never sure how much her aunt understood. Fentrice seemed to live in an older, slower world.

But she had been a magician, a part of the Allalie Family. She had toured the country, hopping trains, staying in boardinghouses, carrying her trunk from town to town. Molly remembered the scuffed and battered trunk from her childhood; it was dark blue, with leather straps and gold studs and a large ornate gold lock that had reminded Molly of an ancient idol.

Were there other people in the family? It had been lonely growing up with just Fentrice and the housekeeper for company. Back then nearly everyone had had a mother and father and at least one brother or sister; Molly had felt strange, an outsider, unable to fit in no matter how hard she tried. And there had been more: whispered conversations in school that stopped when she walked up, phone calls that consisted of giggling and then a dial tone, a few mornings after Halloween when they woke to find their trees draped with toilet paper and the windows of their old car soaped.

As she grew older Molly came to understand that any old, single woman who wore black and lived in a small town would be called a witch. That didn't diminish her feeling of isolation, of difference, though. She developed a tough exterior, a reputation for saying what she thought no matter whom it would hurt, an armor of honesty that, most of the time, protected her from the jokes and insults of her classmates.

Now she moved to the phone and dialed her childhood number. It rang once, twice. Molly could picture the old phone in the alcove off the hallway, black, with a large round dial and a straight cord connecting the phone to the receiver. "Hello," Fentrice said.

"Hi. It's Molly."

"Molly? Is something wrong?"

"No. Well, I don't know. Someone was asking questions about you today."

"About me? What kind of questions?"

"Something about an inheritance. He wanted to know about your family. About your brother, and a—a sister."

"A sister?" Fentrice sounded honestly puzzled; Molly felt relieved to hear it. So she didn't have a secret life, a hidden past. "Who does he think we are—the Russian royal family?"

Molly laughed.

"Did he ask anything else?" Fentrice said.

"He wanted to know if you kept a scrapbook from when you were younger. Did you? Maybe if I showed it to him he'd go away."

"Tell him I have a scrapbook, and tell him I'm using it to write my memoirs. If he wants to know anything about my life he can read the book."

"Are you really?"

"I'm thinking about it. When are you coming to visit? You can help me work on it."

"I'd love to," Molly said, suddenly overcome with a desire to leave this city with its unexpected meetings, its unanswered questions, to set all her problems in her aunt's lap and forget about them. "I've got some vacation time coming—I'll let you know when I can get away."

"Wonderful."

"Good-bye, Aunt Fentrice. I love you."

"I love you too, Molly. Don't tell this person anything."

"I won't."

"Good-bye."   .

Her phone rang at work the next day. Peter, she thought, and reached for the phone quickly. "Listen to this," the voice at the other end said.

It was John Stow. "I have to say I admire your persistence," Molly said. "What is it?"

"I found a review of the family's performance in Los Angeles. That's where they went after Oakland. Listen: 'The Allalie Family, consisting of Callan and Fentrice and their numerous cousins . . .' " His voice trailed off.

"So?"

"So Thorne isn't mentioned. Don't you find that odd?"

"No."

"But the *Tribune* said she was part of the family."

"Maybe she was sick that day."

"All right. But I can't find her in any of the clippings after the Allalie Family plays Oakland. And in Los Angeles Fentrice disappears too."

"Fentrice told me she left. There's nothing mysterious there—she just got tired of the show. And Thorne could have been sick for a long time. They didn't have penicillin in those days. Or maybe she left the show too."

"My client thinks Thorne might have been killed."

"Killed! Why? Who the hell is this client, anyway?"

"You know I can't tell you that."

"Oh, right. So your client can make all kinds of accusations, but I can't even know who he is. Or she. Who does he think murdered her? My aunt, no doubt, for the inheritance."

"He doesn't know. But like I said, I haven't been able to find Thorne. She disappeared somewhere between here and Los Angeles."

"So what are you saying? Are you trying to hurt my aunt? She's eighty-seven years old—she doesn't need someone like you making trouble for her."

"Why do you think it would make trouble?"

"Oh, please. What else? Here's someone claiming to be related to us, claiming to be owed money—Well, my aunt doesn't have any. That's all I'm going to say."

"I don't suppose you asked your aunt about a scrapbook," Stow said.

"Good-bye," Molly said, and put the phone down.

After she hung up she took the article Stow had given her out of her purse. She turned it over, wrote *"Callan Allalie"* and drew a vertical line connecting him to her mother and father, Joan and Bill Travers, killed in a car crash when she was three. She drew another descending line from her parents' names, wrote *"Molly A. Travers"* under that. A horizontal line linked Callan to Fentrice; another joined him and Thorne. Molly thought for a moment, then put a question mark after Thorne.

She turned the page over, looking for the author of the article. Without stopping to think she picked up a copy of the Oakland phone book. To her surprise an Andrew Dodd was listed. She dialed the number.

The phone rang five times, and then a wavering male voice said, "Hello?"

"Hello," Molly said loudly. "Is this Andrew Dodd?"

"Nothing wrong with my hearing. Who is this?"

"My name's Molly Travers. I want to ask you some questions about an article you wrote."

"Which one?"

"The Allalie Family. The magicians."

"Allalie, is it? Say, that brings back memories."

"Can I talk to you about them?"

"Sure, why not? How about tonight?"

"Tonight?" Molly said. It would mean not being home if Peter called. *Hell, let Peter wait,* she thought. *Let him see how he likes it.* "That would be fine," she said.

After work she skipped dinner and drove to Andrew Dodd's apartment in her old Honda Civic. Dodd lived in a renovated building of yellow-gray brick in downtown Oakland, not far from the old *Tribune* building. A yellow sign in front of the apartment said SENIORS XING; over that was a lozenge showing a silhouette of a man crossing the street.

She found Dodd's name and apartment number and pressed the buzzer next to it. "Who is it?" a woman's voice asked.

"Molly Travers."

"Please register at the desk when you come in," the woman said. A buzzer sounded, and Molly pushed open the front door.

The registration desk was to her left, past a bank of mailboxes. She went over and gave her name and Andrew Dodd's, and the receptionist picked up the phone and punched a three-digit number.

Andrew Dodd seemed to be taking a great deal of time to get to the phone. Molly studied the lobby with its faded maroon carpets and plush worn couches, its round wooden table and wilting centerpiece. "Mr. Dodd says to go on up," the receptionist said finally. "The elevators are through that hallway."

She took the elevator to the third floor and rang the bell to Dodd's apartment. Nothing happened. She rang again, then knocked. "In a minute," Dodd's voice said. "In a minute." She heard something being dragged across the floor and then the door opened.

Andrew Dodd looked far older than her aunt Fentrice. His gray hair was sparse on top, long and uncombed over his shirt collar. He had white stubble on his face, and deep lines, almost like scars, running from his nose to the sides of his mouth. At least he had smiled once, Molly thought. The sound she had heard was his walker, which he leaned on heavily.

"Come in," he said. "I'd offer you something but all I have is club soda." The walker had wheels on its two front legs; he turned and pushed it toward the couch. "Sit down."

Molly took an old wooden office chair in front of his desk. He sat heavily on the red and gold couch. "Allalie, is it?" he said. "Funny what you remember. I couldn't tell you what I had for breakfast this morning but I can see those people as if it was yesterday. You look a little like them, come to think of it. 'Cept you don't have the gap teeth."

Molly tried not to show her surprise. Her aunt had insisted on braces to correct her teeth. "Fentrice Allalie is my great-aunt," she said.

He nodded. "That explains it. You going to disappear now?"

"What?"

"Your great-aunt — she was a tricky one. She made me think she was Thorne, or Thorne made me think she was her — I never did get them straightened out. They gave me the best champagne of my life that night, and you know what? The next day I stopped drinking for good. Thirteen years of Prohibition didn't do it, but they did. I'm getting thirsty just thinking about that champagne. Do you want a soda?"

"Sure. I'll get it if you like."

"No you don't, missy. I can still take care of myself." He held on to the walker and pulled himself laboriously to his feet, then moved to the kitchen.

A minute later he came back. The sodas rested on a tray attached to the top of the walker. "Give you a piece of advice, if you like," Dodd said. "Don't get old."

Molly laughed. Dodd didn't; perhaps it hadn't been a joke. "What do you want to know about the Allalies? Writing a family history?"

"Something like that. What do you remember about them?"

"You read the article?" he asked. Molly nodded. "Did you see anything strange about it?"

She shook her head.

"It was all bullshit—pardon my French." He grinned. Molly said nothing, waiting for him to go on. "My editor didn't notice either, luckily. I practically made the whole thing up."

"Why?"

"Why?" He took a sip of his soda. "You sure you're not going to disappear? I went backstage to the trap room after the performance, and they gave me the runaround. No answers to my questions, lots of confusion . . ." He shook his head. "Fireworks, and music, and people dancing and laughing . . . I can still hear that damn song they sang. Couple years after the interview I heard it at a club and nearly went crazy. 'Got Everything,' by King Oliver." He looked at her shrewdly. "That name means nothing to you, does it?"

She shook her head.

"I don't remember the end of the interview. I woke up on the trolley going home. The next day I had to write something. My notebook was blank—all the questions I'd planned to ask and the notes I'd taken were gone. They'd probably torn the pages out."

Molly nodded, encouraging him to continue.

"Never took a drink again," Dodd said. He sipped at his soda. "That Fentrice. Is she still alive?"

"Yes. She raised me."

"That must have been something."

"What do you mean?"

"She was a wild one. Smoking in public, wearing scanty clothing. Did you know there was a room at the Paramount where women would go to smoke, so the men wouldn't see them? I got the feeling there was nothing Fentrice wouldn't do."

"Actually she's very staid. She gardens, plays bridge. She doesn't smoke at all."

"Doesn't she? Hell, I shouldn't be surprised. What's one more disguise to that family?"

"Disguise?"

"That's what I remember from that night. The show didn't end when they left the stage. They put on another show just for me, for an audience of one. And your aunt did the same for you."

"Why would she do that?"

"Why did they do anything? Why did they take my notes? I could have given them damn good publicity."

"I think I know my aunt better than you do."

"I don't think anyone knew that woman. Well, maybe her family did."

"I'm her family."

"Right." He drank. "And Thorne and Callan? What happened to them?"

"Callan died. I never heard of Thorne until yesterday."

"Well. So they dumped their sister and she went off to live on her own. Raised a kid. Not the ending I would have guessed."

"What I want to know, Mr. Dodd—are you sure Thorne was their sister? Couldn't they have called themselves a family for the publicity?"

"They could have, I guess. But they all looked a hell of a lot alike. I wonder why she never told you about them."

"So do I. Did a guy named John Stow call you?"

"No. Why?"

"He's interested in my family for some reason. He's the one who showed me the clipping in the *Tribune*. If he does call, I'd appreciate it if you didn't tell him anything."

"Like I said, I don't know anything to tell. Hey, maybe I can help you look into things. I haven't done any reporting in a long time."

"Maybe," Molly said.

"Listen to her, so polite. And all the while she's thinking, How do I get rid of this old man? The last thing I need is him tagging along."

"I wasn't—"

The door opened and a woman in a blue dress suit came in.

Her hair was ivory-white, forming a soft cloud around her face, and she wore glasses which hung from a chain around her neck. She went over to Dodd and kissed him on the cheek.

"My wife, Bess," Dodd said proudly. He smiled, deep lines scoring his face. "Married her the same year I did that interview, as a matter of fact."

"Hello," Bess Dodd said. She turned to her husband. "Carolyn and the kids dropped me off—she's looking for a parking space."

Kids? Molly thought. She had thought Dodd alone and friendless, an anonymous old man who spent his days watching television or sitting on a bus bench. "I should be going," she said.

"All right," Dodd said. "Let me know what happens."

Molly took the elevator to the lobby. As she left the building she held the door open for a middle-aged woman, a younger woman, and two noisy children about five and nine. Grandkids and great-grandkids, she thought. Thinking of large families, she walked to her car and drove home.

TWO

The Drowned Cities of Atlantis

Do you want to go out for a drink?" Robin Ann asked Molly after work the next day.

"I shouldn't," Molly said. "What if—"

"Peter calls? I know. What if he does? That's why God made answering machines."

Molly and Robin Ann had come from the same temp agency. Molly liked Robin Ann, even though she usually ended up doing most of the other woman's work. Instead of filing and typing Robin Ann spent hours gossiping, asking Molly questions, telling her about her boyfriends, her poetry—she had been published in several prestigious small magazines—her plans for the future. Twice in the year they had worked together Robin Ann had disappeared for several days. When she came back to work all she would say was that she had had one of her nervous breakdowns, casually, as though it were a recurrence of the flu.

"It's just that I wasn't home yesterday evening," Molly said.

"Yeah?" Robin Ann waggled her eyebrows like Groucho Marx. "How come?"

"It's not very interesting. Well, it is, but not in the way you think."

"I think we'd better have a drink. I think you're going to have to tell me all about it."

"But if I'm not there he'll probably call someone else."

"When are you going to dump this loser?" Robin Ann asked.

Molly shook her head. She had tried, several times, to tell Robin Ann how she felt about Peter. How her heart pounded against her ribs like a monkey swinging against the bars of its cage whenever she heard his voice on the phone. How she would think, not once or twice but dozens of times a day, *Oh, I have to remember to tell Peter that,* sure that only Peter, of all the men in the world, would understand. How he even smelled different from everyone else, of airplanes and of shirts that had been professionally laundered because he was too busy to go to a laundromat and had never settled down long enough to buy a washing machine.

"Where is this paragon of virtue now?" Robin Ann asked.

"Las Vegas, I think. Interviewing some Mob boss."

"Ah."

Robin Ann even disapproved of the books Peter wrote. They were the kind that were rushed into paperback and sold in supermarkets, unauthorized biographies of troubled royal figures or wealthy men married to starlets.

If Molly tried she could remember a time when she had disapproved of them herself, back when she had first met Peter Myers through the temp agency and was typing his manuscripts. But it was getting harder and harder to keep things in perspective, to remember the person she used to be before Peter. In the ten years since she had dropped out of college she had traveled through the United States, had taken temp jobs to pay for her moves from state to state; she had been a clerk in a toy store and a cab driver, had worked in a fish-packing plant in Alaska. How had she ended up like one of those pathetic women she had met in her travels, the ones who did nothing but stay home and wait for the phone to ring? But she could not seem to break away from him; she felt that if she stayed she was being faithful to love, and that if she remained constant through all obstacles he would someday understand, and become faithful too.

"Forget Peter," Robin Ann said. "It'll be good for him if you're not home once in a while."

"Maybe."

"Definitely. Tell me where you were last night."

Molly laughed. "There's this guy," she said. "A private investigator."

"Great," Robin Ann said, impressed.

"No, it's not like that. He's kind of a jerk, really. He keeps asking me questions about my family."

"What kind of questions?"

"Who they were. What they did. What happened to one of them, a woman he claims was related to us. I never heard of her."

"Did you ask your aunt?"

"Yeah. She said not to answer his questions."

"Sounds like she has something to hide."

"Don't you start. He thinks this woman was murdered. Murdered—I ask you. Who would murder her?"

"Maybe you should visit your aunt. Find out what's going on."

"Yeah, I was thinking of that. Maybe I will."

When Molly got home after drinks with Robin Ann there was a blinking light on her answering machine. She played the message back.

"Hey, Moll," Peter said. She felt a rush of pure pleasure at the sound of his voice. "I'm in town, back at the hotel. Give me a call, maybe we'll have dinner."

She called his hotel, on Bush Street in San Francisco. No one answered. Who was he with now? No, better not to think of that. But all the names he had dropped so casually in conversation came back to her one by one, persistent as ghosts.

Dammit, she thought. *Robin Ann's right. I'm going to visit Fentrice. Let him see what it's like when I'm not in town.*

She picked up the phone again and made reservations.

* * *

In her black dress and necklace of large amber beads Fentrice stood out easily from the more colorful crowd at Chicago's O'Hare Airport. They hugged, and Molly smelled her aunt's familiar odors of perfumed soap and crinoline.

"Let me look at you," Fentrice said, holding her at arm's length. She wore a bracelet of onyx and tarnished silver; it had turned her wrist a little blackish-green. "I must say California agrees with you."

"How have you been?" Molly asked.

"Fine. Do you have any other luggage?"

"Just this."

"Good. Lila's waiting in the car."

They walked down the long airport corridor, Molly slowing as Fentrice began to lag behind. The familiar black Oldsmobile stood at the curb; Fentrice had had it for as long as Molly could remember. When Molly had gone away to college she had been amazed at how often people changed cars.

Chicago was far colder than California. Molly shivered and drew her coat around her and got into the back seat. "How are you, Lila?" she asked.

Lila looked in the rearview mirror and nodded. Molly grinned; the housekeeper was as taciturn as ever. Lila lit a cigarette and pulled away from the curb.

Fentrice lived in a small town a few hours' drive from Chicago. They talked about neutral subjects, Molly's jobs, Fentrice's garden. Now that she was finally here Molly found herself reluctant to ask questions. It was enough to be home, to be surrounded by the familiar sights and smells of home.

The road before them darkened. Lila switched on the headlights. Traffic had been heavy on the highway leading out of Chicago but was now starting to thin. Finally they left the highway; the streets here were narrow and tree-lined, their blackness relieved only by streetlamps and an occasional light or flickering television screen from the houses on either side.

Lila pulled into the driveway of Fentrice's house. Fentrice unlocked the front door and held it open for Molly while the housekeeper drove the car into the garage.

"Are you hungry?" Fentrice asked.

"No, I ate on the plane," Molly said.

"Why don't you get a good night's sleep then? We'll talk in the morning."

"I'm not tired. It's only eight o'clock in California. Aunt Fentrice, I wanted to ask you — "

"Well, I'm tired, dear. It's been a long drive for me."

"Oh! I'm sorry, I wasn't thinking — " Lila came in and set the car keys on Fentrice's desk. Even Lila was older, Molly saw with surprise. The housekeeper seemed to have grown smaller; she shuffled rather than walked, her shoulders stooped. "I'll let you go then. See you in the morning." Molly kissed Fentrice and went upstairs.

Her old room was as she had left it, the brass bed with its patchwork quilt, the small scarred wooden desk. Over the desk hung an old map of the world, now badly outdated; she used to study it instead of doing her homework, wondering what the exotic-sounding places were like. To the right of the desk was a bookshelf over-filled with her childhood books: *The Jungle Book, Hans Brinker, The Hobbit, The Phantom Tollbooth.*

She had spent whole afternoons reading in this room, she remembered. She had rarely invited anyone over, preferring instead to go to other kids' houses. Had she been ashamed of Fentrice? Or was it that she didn't want the kids at school to know too much about her and her aunt, didn't want to give them ammunition for their crude jokes and insults?

When Molly came into the kitchen the next day Fentrice had breakfast ready, pancakes and tea and slices of cantaloupe. "Real maple syrup," Molly said, delighted. "You can hardly find this in California."

Fentrice smiled. She sat opposite Molly at the round oak

table. Sunlight came in through the window. "How did you sleep?" she asked.

Molly added milk to her tea. "Wonderful," she said. "Listen, Aunt Fentrice—this man's been bothering me again."

"Which man, dear?"

"The one asking questions about you. He showed me a clipping about your family, about you and Callan and someone named Thorne—"

"Thorne! I haven't thought about her in years. Lila, dear, there's no water left in the kettle. You'll have to add some more before you turn the stove on."

Molly nodded to the housekeeper. "Morning, Lila. Was Thorne related to you?" she asked Fentrice.

"Oh no. She joined us somewhere along the way. I don't remember where now. And then she left us—Oh, it's all so long ago."

"The clipping said you were sisters. That you looked like her."

"Did it? How odd."

"Here." Molly took the Xeroxed article from her pocket and put it on the table between them.

"Andrew Dodd! Do you know, I think I remember him. Cocky young man, he was."

"He remembers you too."

"Is he still alive? Good Lord. Whatever happened to him?"

"He got married, apparently. Quit drinking. Had some kids, grandkids. Look, Aunt Fentrice—"

"Did you go to see him? Andrew Dodd? Why?"

"Because of all these—all these questions." Molly spoke quickly. "He said you were wild, that you wore scanty clothes, that you and Thorne played tricks on him."

Fentrice laughed. "He must have confused us with some other act." She turned the article over, saw Molly's attempt at a family genealogy. "Well, if you're interested in the family you should have asked me. Let me see . . ." She picked up a pencil. "Our parents were named Verey and Edwina Allalie. And our grandparents, Verey's parents, were—let me think. Neesa and Harry." She wrote those names on the page.

"Allalie?" Molly asked.

"What, dear?" Fentrice frowned and crossed out Thorne's name, then looked up at Molly.

"Were their names Allalie too? Neesa and Harry?"

"I think so. They were my father's parents, so—oh, I remember now. We changed our name when we came to the United States."

"Changed your name? Why?"

"Everyone did it then. We were immigrants, starting a new life."

"Where did the family come from?"

"Somewhere in England."

"What was the old name? Do you remember?"

"No. In fact I think I had another name in England, not Fentrice." She thought for a while, shook her head. "Well, it's gone now. I was two years old when we got here, I think. That's right— it was 1910. Callan hadn't even been born yet."

"Really? You were born in England? Why didn't you ever tell me?"

"There was nothing to tell, really. I certainly don't remember it."

"Why did the family come here?"

"Oh, I don't know. A new life, a fresh beginning. A lot of people did it."

"When did you start touring?"

"Our parents did it—it was in our blood, you might say. Callan took to magic right away, from when he was a small child." Fentrice frowned again. "I used to wonder if that was healthy for him. Towards the end it sometimes seemed that he couldn't tell truth from lies."

"The clipping said the family had been touring for centuries."

"Did it really? Oh, dear."

"Can I see the scrapbook?"

"Of course. Finish your breakfast and we'll have a look for it."

But though Fentrice searched in all her closets and even ventured down to the basement, she couldn't find the scrapbook anywhere. And then it was time for lunch, and after lunch Fentrice went out to work in her garden. The housekeeper had the afternoon off.

Molly wandered through the house, looking at the familiar paintings and vases, the spinet piano. On the piano was a black-and-white photograph of her aunt as a much younger woman, her light brown hair parted in the middle and drawn back in a bun. She had lifted her head and was smiling, eager, the gap between her teeth clearly visible. At her feet was the trunk Molly remembered.

The trunk. What better place to keep a scrapbook, mementos from the past? Molly went upstairs to her aunt's bedroom and found the trunk where she had seen it last, at the foot of the bed. She knelt and unlatched the large metal lock.

The trunk smelled of cedar, though it was not made of wood. Molly lifted out carefully folded clothes, necklaces and bracelets wrapped in tissue paper. Something hard and flat lay at the bottom. She pushed the clothing aside quickly and looked inside.

It was a small block of cedar. She took out the clothes and the block and felt around but could find nothing else. She sat back, disappointed.

The trunk seemed larger on the outside than on the inside. Could there be a false bottom, a hidden drawer? But what would her aunt have to hide? Damn John Stow anyway, him and his suspicions.

Almost without thinking she felt along the inside of the trunk. Her fingers found a hole at one of the corners. She pulled. The bottom lifted out.

She looked inside eagerly, excited. There was nothing there. She nearly shouted aloud in frustration.

She picked up the false bottom and started to put it back.

Something was taped to the underside, a large manila envelope. *Probably empty, after all I've been through,* Molly thought. But her fingers were trembling as she pulled it off.

She opened the envelope and took out a yellowing pamphlet. *"A History of the True and Antient Order of the Labyrinth,"* the cover said. *"A Lecture by Lady Dorothy Westingate, Adept of the Eighth Grade. London, 1884."*

The pages inside were filled with small, barely legible print. "I'd like to thank all those who provided me with this platform from which to disseminate the fruits of my years of research, in particular the Master of our Order, Lord Harrison Sanderson, and his wife Lydia," Molly read. "In this lecture I intend to prove the antient and legitimate ancestry of our Order, and to defend it against those quarrelsome members of other orders who claim for us an existence of only ten years."

Molly began to skim. Lady Westingate did not seem to think in paragraphs; each page was a solid block of type. "All around us lies the evidence of a race of labyrinth-builders," Molly read. "The Cretan Palace of Minos . . . the Druids, the age-old Masters of India, the inhabitants of the drowned cities of Atlantis . . . an aura of the most spotless blue . . . a task for which our souls have laboured through many lifetimes." The abbreviation of the name of order, "OotL," was always printed in boldface, and had smeared in several places.

Molly read on. "One proof, however, I am prepared to give, and that is the ineluctable fact of our magick. We of the OotL are able to create and destroy, to bind and to loose, to bend the world to our will. There is no other order in all of Britain, I daresay in all the world, that is able to do this. Our guides in the spirit realm, revealed to us by our guide upon this Earth, Miss Emily Wethers, have shown us miracles that no man can deny: we have all seen them. We alone hold the wisdom that has descended to us through the ages."

"Molly!" Fentrice called.

Only now did Molly feel as if she had intruded on something

private. She put the pamphlet in the envelope and taped the envelope to the false bottom, then put the bottom back and quickly replaced the clothes and jewelry. "Yes?"

"I've found the scrapbook," Fentrice said. "Where are you?"

Molly closed and latched the trunk. She stood. "I'm coming, Aunt Fentrice," she said, and hurried downstairs.

"Look at this," Fentrice said, sounding disgusted with herself. She sat at the oak table in the kitchen with the open scrapbook in front of her. "It was in with my cookbooks."

Molly sat next to her. "There—that's Callan, your grandfather," Fentrice said. "And this is me—can you believe I was ever so young?"

"And who's that?" Molly asked, pointing to a woman on the other side of Callan.

"Do you know, I think that's Thorne. Yes, it must be. I don't think we look anything alike—that young man Andrew must be seeing things."

Not so young anymore, Molly thought. "Where did you get the tiger?"

"The tiger—let me think. Callan rescued her from another act, I believe. That's right. They had mistreated her dreadfully—it took her a long time before she would trust anyone but Callan. Several people in the act wanted us to leave her behind."

Fentrice turned the page. Molly saw a candid black-and-white photo of her aunt sitting at a bench at a train station, a book in one hand and a cigarette in the other.

"When did you quit smoking?" Molly asked.

"A few years before you were born, I think. We didn't know smoking was harmful in those days—in fact, we believed it was good for us. I could never understand why it was so hard for me to climb a flight of stairs."

The next photograph showed an old woman bent over a table. It took a moment for Molly to realize that she was playing pool. "Ah," said Fentrice. "That's my grandmother. Neesa Allalie."

"She played pool?"

Fentrice laughed. "Toward the end of her life that's all she did. She seemed to have lost interest in everything else."

There were yellowed newspaper reviews on the next few pages, chips from their corners missing. *"Scintillating,"* the headlines said. *"Stunning."*

Molly stopped her aunt from paging ahead. "Look at this, a clipping from London. Did you play there? What was it like?"

"London, let me think. No, I can't remember. It was all so long ago. . . ." She turned the page. *"Magicians Dazzle at the Paramount,"* a headline said. "Hey," Molly said. "It's the article from the *Tribune.*"

"Why so it is," Fentrice said.

"He said he made it all up. Andrew Dodd. He said that he couldn't remember anything when he got home."

"Poor man. Drank too much, as I remember."

"He said he gave up drinking after he interviewed you."

"Well," said Fentrice, "I guess we did something right after all."

"There's another picture of Thorne. She must have been with you in Oakland."

"She must have been." Fentrice turned the page to a black-and-white photograph. "See this baby Callan's holding? That's his daughter, your mother Joan. He was so proud of that child."

"My God," Molly said, struck by several emotions at once, sorrow and love and curiosity and even anger at the mother who had died and left her.

"Here she is again," Fentrice said, pointing to a photograph Molly recognized. It showed a woman kneeling to talk to a child. "And that's you. You were two years old, I think."

"You know, I think I remember her. I can see her kneeling, just like this. But then I wonder if it's this picture I remember. You gave me a copy when I went away to college."

"That's right, I did."

✿ ✿ ✿

Fentrice's bridge group visited the next day. Lila got out biscuits and the china tea service and set them on the table, then retired to the kitchen. Fentrice poured the tea.

These women had come to play bridge for as long as Molly could remember. There were three of them, all unmarried like her aunt. Vivian and Lillian were sisters who dressed alike; as a child Molly had had trouble telling them apart. They used to hug her and pinch her cheek hard enough to hurt. "Oh, how sweet!" they would exclaim to each other, far too loudly. They smelled of face cream and too much makeup. Molly had quickly learned to keep her distance from them.

There had always been something odd about the third woman, Estelle. Now that she was grown Molly could see what it was: Estelle was a little slow, confused by the simplest things, flustered even by the ritual of pouring the tea. Her teeth were straight and perfectly white—dentures, Molly realized. Her dress was loose and shapeless, like a sack, but she was festooned with jewelry, dangling earrings, massive necklaces, rings that covered her fingers up to the knuckles. She had always worn heavy black glasses, the lenses growing thicker over the years; now they looked like goldfish bowls, the eyes swimming behind them. Estelle was also, Molly remembered, the best bridge player of the four of them.

"Goodness, Molly," one of the sisters said when they had settled to their tea. "Look how she's grown!"

"How sweet she looks," the other sister said.

"Hi, everyone," Molly said. She never stayed for the bridge games, had never even learned how to play. "I think I'll go out for a while, see how the town's changed."

"Be back by dinner," Fentrice said.

Molly stepped out the front door. Odd, she thought, that three such strange old women should all live in the same small town. Four, really, counting her aunt. Did the kids call the other ones witches too? She couldn't remember, recalled only the hurtful comments about her and Fentrice.

"Molly?" someone said. "It is you! Hey, Molly!"

She looked up. A woman pushing a baby stroller came toward her. "Christine?" Molly said.

"Hi! What are you doing in this dumpy old town? I thought you went to Alaska."

"I did, for a while. Then I moved to California."

"Sunny California. I wish I could go there." A strong wind blew down the street, rattling the bare branches of the trees.

Christine looked into her stroller. Molly followed her gaze, as she knew she was meant to. "Hey, cute. A girl, right?"

"Yeah. I ended up marrying Billy Foreman. You remember him, don't you?"

Christine had to be kidding. Everyone remembered Billy Foreman. He had been the most popular boy in school, tall and blond, a football quarterback who had his own sports car.

"Sure," Molly said. "Congratulations. What's he doing now?"

"Joined his dad's business. We closed on a house two weeks ago, up in Oak Knolls." Oak Knolls was the most expensive area in town. "Just another month and we'll be out of this dump. What brings you here? Visiting your aunt?"

"Yeah."

"Does she still have that spooky old black car?" Christine asked, though from where she stood she could no doubt see the car in the garage. "And that weird housekeeper? What was her name—Lily, something like that? Do you remember the Halloween when Billy and I soaped the car windows?"

"I didn't know that was you, actually."

"Oh, come on. It was all anyone talked about the next day."

"No one said anything to me."

"Don't tell me you're still mad. It was just a joke."

"A joke is 'Two guys walk into a bar.' What you did was vandalism."

"Oh, come on. You always were so serious about things. What are you doing these days?"

"Me? I'm a private investigator out in California."

Christine narrowed her eyes; for the first time Molly thought the other woman envied her. It was as good an exit line as any. "Gotta go. See you later."

"Yeah," Christine said, a little subdued. " 'Bye."

Molly continued down the sidewalk. The streets seemed smaller than she remembered, the houses shabbier. Naked oak trees, their branches ending in knobs like skulls or fists, lined the sidewalk, their roots buckling the pavement.

Without thinking about it she headed toward the high school. Even it looked less impressive, the paint peeling, the grass in front giving way to patches of weeds. A sign on the fence warned away drug dealers. Molly felt a little shocked to see it, though the drugs had been there in her day.

She looked through the fence, remembering how intense everything had felt back then, how certain she had been about things. Now the place seemed insignificant, a stopping point on the way to the rest of her life. She grinned, thinking of the conversation she had had with Christine. Christine was no doubt unused to envy.

By the time she returned to Fentrice's house the bridge group was leaving. "Good-bye," one of the sisters said. "So nice to see you, Molly," said the other.

Estelle's head jerked upward in surprise. "Molly!" she said. "I didn't recognize you. Look how you've grown!"

The rest of the visit went quickly, and a few days later Fentrice and Lila took Molly to the airport. Once on the plane Molly stared out the window, wondering why she had ever moved to the West Coast, why she felt compelled to change her address, her job, her life, every few years. The midwestern winters, of course, but there was more to it than that.

"What is the answer?" Gertrude Stein had asked on her deathbed, and then, receiving no answer, had said, "Well, then, what is the question?" Molly had heard that about Stein, an Oakland native, since moving to Oakland. *At least you learn things when you move around a lot,* she thought. *Useless trivia, most of it, but it keeps you going.*

She took out the family tree she and her aunt had drawn and studied it. All those names she had never known — Verey and Edwina, Neesa and Harry. She whistled softly. Harry. Lord Harrison Sanderson, Master of the Order of the Labyrinth. Could they have been the same person? Fentrice's grandfather, and her — she counted it out on her fingers — great-great-grandfather? Was that why her aunt had saved the pamphlet? But then who was Lydia, Harrison's wife in the pamphlet? Was that Neesa, the old woman who played pool?

"The Order of the Labyrinth," she wrote on the back of the article. *"OotL."* She had started to think of it as Ootle.

How could she find something like that out? Her aunt had forgotten most of it, or so she claimed. Maybe she could hire a private investigator. And hey — she even knew one, John Stow. She just didn't like him very much.

THREE
A Sheep in Capricorn

On her lunch break a few days later Molly stopped into Tangled Tales, a used bookstore near work with a large occult and metaphysical section. The store was dim, the bookshelves high, with books piled sideways two and even three deep. She picked her way through the narrow aisles, stepping around the leaning stacks of books on the floor. Dust covered everything. A white cat jumped soundlessly from a shelf to the floor.

A man stood behind the counter at the back of the store adding up a column of figures on a yellow legal pad. He wore a white turban, though with his fair skin he probably wasn't Indian.

"Excuse me," Molly said. The clerk continued to study his numbers. "I'd like some help, please." Silence from the clerk. "Listen—could you tell me if you have any books on the Order of the Labyrinth?"

The clerk looked up, blinking. The eyes under the turban were blue. "The Order of the Labyrinth? Where on earth did you hear about them?" he asked.

"I saw a pamphlet."

"Ah. Lady Westingate's lecture."

"How did you know?"

"That's the only piece of writing that's ever come down from the Order. Other people have written about them, of course, mostly rumors and attacks from rival groups." He paused. "The thing about the Order of the Labyrinth is that several eyewitnesses claim to have seen them work, well, magic. . . ."

"Do you have any books about the Order?"

The man shrugged. "There aren't any, other than bits and pieces in general histories of the occult. No one knows what happened to them. They seem to have vanished around the turn of the century."

"What about the lecture, the pamphlet? Do you have that?"

"It's fairly rare. The last time I saw one was, oh, three-four years ago. If you're looking to sell yours . . ."

"It isn't mine."

"Ah. Well, I can take your name and phone number and give you a call if I find one, but like I said I don't get them too often. It'll run you something like—oh, I couldn't let it go for under a hundred dollars."

"A hundred dollars!"

"People are intrigued by them. An order that worked real magic . . ."

Molly hesitated. She didn't want to give this odd man her phone number, and she didn't have a hundred dollars. The visit to her aunt had taken all her savings. Well, it was John Stow's problem, after all. Let his mysterious client pay for the pamphlet. She opened her purse and took out the card he had given her.

"Here's the person who's interested," she said. "Let him know if you find a copy."

The clerk looked at the card. "Private investigator," he said. "May I ask what . . . ah . . ."

Molly wished the man would finish a thought, complete a sentence. "I have no idea, really," she said, and turned to go. Tonight she would give Stow a call, bring him up to date. If he found anything out he could let her know.

✻ ✻ ✻

After she left another man stepped out of the back room of the
store. "The Order of the Labyrinth!" he said, sounding impressed.
He wore a flat racing cap. "I thought we knew everyone who was
interested in the Order."

"I guess we don't," the bookstore clerk said. His pale blue
eyes were still looking toward the door, though Molly was nowhere
to be seen. He held the card Molly had given him out to the other
man. "Follow him, would you, Joseph? See what he wants, if he
knows anything."

When Molly got home there was a message from Robin Ann on
her machine. "Hi, Molly," Robin Ann said. Her voice sounded flat
and uninvolved, and that, Molly knew, was almost always a sign
of trouble. "Look, I'm going crazy here. They gave me some weird
medication that's making my heart stop — I swear, I have to think
about it all the time to keep it going. I know I'm not going to sleep
tonight, and I think they're getting ready to fire me at work. Can
I come over?"

Molly called her friend. Five minutes later the doorbell rang.
That was quick, Molly thought, and buzzed to open the downstairs
door.

A minute later she heard a knock. "Listen," the person on the
other side of her apartment door said. The voice was deep, a man's
voice.

"Who is it?" Molly asked.

"John Stow."

"Dammit," she said. She opened the door. Stow stood there,
looking angry. "Dammit, dammit, dammit. Why don't you leave
me alone? I was expecting someone else."

"Why are you following me?"

"What?"

"Someone's been following me all afternoon. A small foreign
car, a Fiat or something. Stayed on my tail all the way home."

"Well, it wasn't me. I don't have a Fiat. Why the hell would I follow you?"

"That's what I was wondering."

The buzzer sounded. Molly pressed the button to open the front door and a moment later saw Robin Ann coming up the stairs. "You've got some nerve, assuming it was me," Molly said. "Don't you have any other cases?"

"No."

"What?"

"No, I don't." Stow didn't look at all abashed. "Things've been slow lately."

I shouldn't wonder, Molly thought. "I wasn't following you," she said again.

Robin Ann looked from Molly to Stow. "Not my friend," Molly mouthed to her behind John's back. "John, Robin Ann," she said. "Robin Ann, John. John was just leaving."

"I'll talk to you later," John said.

"Oh, please," Molly said.

She and Robin Ann went into Molly's apartment. "Was that the detective?" Robin Ann asked.

"Yeah. I don't want to talk about it. What about your medication?"

"My doctor prescribed something for my heart, but you know what it turned out to be? Nitroglycerin. Do you think that's a good idea? I mean, nitroglycerin—I'd feel like I could blow up at any moment."

"The bookstore!" Molly said. "That's who's been following him!"

"What?"

Molly ran down the stairs. "Mr. Stow!" she said. "John!"

The investigator was letting himself out of the building. He turned. "Listen," Molly said, running up to him.

She told him about the pamphlet, Tangled Tales, the business card she'd given the clerk. John took a small spiral-bound notebook out of his pocket. "The Order of what?" he asked.

"The Labyrinth."

"What were the names in the pamphlet?" he asked, writing. "Do you remember?"

"Lady Westingate. Lord Harrison Sanderson and his wife Lydia."

"And it was published when?"

"Oh, I don't remember. Sometime in the 1800s."

John pocketed the notebook. "I'll get back to you," he said.

"Okay," Molly said. She watched him leave, then went back upstairs to her apartment.

John called her at work a few days later. "Here's the thing," he said, once again without preamble. "Lord Albert Westingate was a very wealthy man who died in 1878 of tuberculosis. He was thirty-two. After he died his wife, Lady Dorothy Westingate, built herself this incredible house in Applebury, England, called Tantilly. She referred to it as a retreat, but people who visited called it a mansion, a castle. She didn't go outside for five years. She had everything delivered—neighbors said there was a steady stream of grocers and dressmakers. Tutors for her son—she wouldn't let him leave the house either. And plasterers and bricklayers and stained-glass artists, because she kept working on the house. Then somehow she discovered the Order of the Labyrinth, or they discovered her, and she started going out to their meetings. One of the sources I read said she was hoping to contact her dead husband through them—there was a craze for spiritualism in those days. Anyway, a few years after she started going to their meetings she began to have financial problems, which got worse and worse and finally ended in her having to sell the house in 1912. This same source thinks she donated money to the Order, and ended up making over her entire fortune to them. They made her an adept in return—I suppose it was the least they could do." He paused. "Hello?"

"I'm still here," Molly said. "I'm impressed. What happened to them?"

"I don't know. The Order of the Labyrinth broke up into different groups and factions — I didn't have time to research them all. Lady Westingate died in 1919. Spanish influenza."

"Where did you find all that out?"

"At the library. Books on the occult, on strange houses, on the British peerage. The question now is, what do we do with all of it? Where does it lead us?"

Us? Molly thought. "Well," she said. "I think this Harrison Sanderson was a relative of mine. Fentrice's grandfather. She said her grandfather's name was Harry, and that they changed their last name when they came to the United States. Hey. Do you think this has to do with the inheritance? Was Sanderson rich?"

"I don't know. Not as rich as Lady Westingate, that's for sure. All the books I read go into loving detail about her fortune."

"Did she lose it all?" *And to who?* Molly wondered. *To Lord Harrison Sanderson, Master of the Order of the Labyrinth? What am I going to learn about my family?*

"I think so," John said. "The house is still there, though. I guess that's where I should go next."

"To England?"

"Sure. Why not? My expenses are all paid."

"Your client must be as rich as Lady Westingate."

He laughed. "Not nearly. Listen — do you want to come with me? You're the expert on the family history, after all."

"I can't afford a trip to England."

"No, no, my client will pay for it. I'll call you my assistant or something."

Should she go? She didn't trust him, was annoyed by the outrageous accusations he had made about her family. And what about Peter? He hadn't called once since she had come back from the Midwest.

But she had never been to England. And if she went with John she might learn about her family's past, discover things Fentrice had never told her. What would Peter say then? Now she would be the one with exotic places to visit, intriguing questions to answer.

"Sure," Molly said. "Sure, I'll go with you."

She got a passport, bought a ticket to England with money John gave her. Her temp job came to an end. A few days before her plane left Peter called, and she drove to San Francisco to meet him for dinner.

The heavy spring rains had returned, slowing the traffic on the Bay Bridge. Someone honked and someone else cut in front of her, spraying her windshield with water. She cursed loudly. It was too bad she couldn't live in the peaceful world of Harrison and Lydia Sanderson, whoever they were, instead of with this dreadful modern traffic.

The snarls on the bridge made her late to the restaurant, but Peter wasn't there yet. Five minutes later he came toward her table, smiling his disarming smile. She had forgotten how handsome he was. He shaved once every three days, so that whenever she saw him he looked different from her last memory of him. He was on the third day today, with the stubble of a man who had more exciting things to do than shave.

"Hey," he said, sitting opposite her and shaking off his wet trench coat. Light glinted on his round tortoiseshell glasses.

"Hi," she said. "How was Las Vegas?"

"Las Vegas was the last trip," he said. "I've been to New York since then. Had a talk with my editor. They've moved up the deadline on my book—looks like the subject is hotter than I thought."

"Are you going to make it?"

"Oh, sure. What about you? How have you been?"

"I'm fine. Went to visit my aunt."

"Really? In Chicago?"

"Near Chicago. And then in a few days I'm going to England."

His eyes narrowed. Molly had learned to recognize his expressions; he was displeased. "England?" he said. "Why?"

"My aunt's family comes from there." He said nothing. "There's this guy, a private investigator. We've learned all kinds of things about my family. They were involved in the occult in the 1800s, with something called the Order of the Labyrinth. And with this woman named Lady Westingate, who lived in some kind of castle."

"And you think you'll find out more about your family?"

Suddenly Molly understood what was bothering him. She was poaching on his territory, traveling, asking questions. Her life had become as interesting as his own. "Sure," she said. "Why not?"

"Well, no offense, but you don't know anything about investigative journalism. A lot of people don't like to answer questions. Especially if they've been involved in something as shady as the occult."

"No offense yourself, but I am traveling with a private investigator. I think he knows a little about asking questions."

Peter raised a hand. "Sure, sure," he said. "When are you leaving?"

"Day after tomorrow."

"Well, then, we'll have to celebrate. We'll have some champagne, what do you say? You'll like England."

"Great," Molly said, relaxing. She had been wrong about him; of course he wouldn't be threatened by her. They spent the rest of the dinner talking about New York, about the places she should visit in England.

After dinner they went to his hotel room and made love. She was eager, insistent, trying to annihilate the weeks that had passed since they had seen each other, to spark the gap between them. He was slow, careful, taking his time. Afterward she ran her fingers through his hair, trying to memorize his face. "I'll miss you," she said.

"Miss you too," he said.

Two days later she took a shuttle to the San Francisco Airport. John was not at the gate where they had agreed to meet. *Great,* she thought. *Should I go on without him?* A man wearing glasses nodded to her.

She nodded back automatically. *Do I know him? And where is John?* Their plane would be boarding in fifteen minutes.

"You made it," the man said, coming over to her. "I was getting worried."

"John?" she said.

"Who else? Oh, the glasses. I usually wear contact lenses, but the air on the plane gets too dry."

"Flight fifteen sixty-three to London—" a voice over the intercom said.

"That's us," John said. "Let's go."

"—has been delayed," the intercom continued. "We will begin boarding at six thirty-five."

A chorus of voices in the boarding area rose in protest. "Half an hour late," John said, looking at his watch. "Do you want to get some dinner or something?"

"Sure."

They found a restaurant farther down the terminal. Molly sat and studied the man opposite her. "You look better with glasses," she said. "More trustworthy. Forget the lenses."

"You say what you think, don't you?"

"Sure, why not?"

"Because people like me, people who ask questions, might take advantage."

"I don't have any secrets."

"I don't believe that. Everyone's got something to hide."

"You certainly seem to. You've never told me a thing about yourself."

"There's nothing to tell."

"Oh, come on. You've got one of the world's most romantic-sounding jobs."

"It only sounds romantic. It's tedious, really—staying in one spot for hours and hours waiting for your suspect to do something, anything. Taking pictures when someone suing for whiplash goes out for a night on the town. That kind of thing."

"Do you have a girlfriend?"

John picked up his spoon, turned it over. "Look at this," he said. "Oneida silverware. Oneida was some kind of commune in the nineteenth century, practiced free love, had all their wealth in common, had children only when their leader said they could. Made silverware. Look at all the people in this restaurant calmly eating off Oneida spoons and forks—if only they knew."

"You're avoiding the question. I'm not applying for the position or anything, I'm just curious."

"You're right, I am. Okay. The truth is, I don't know."

"You don't know?"

"I thought I had a girlfriend. She's mad at me. I think."

"What did you do?"

"I don't know. Nothing."

"Nothing?"

"Well, something. Obviously. I just don't know what it was."

"Did you ask her?"

"I can't. She's mad at me." He took a deep breath. "Okay, your turn. Do you have a boyfriend?"

"I don't know."

John laughed.

"I'm in love with someone," Molly said. "I don't want to be, I just am. It's like malaria—it doesn't go away."

"Oh, shit," John said.

"What?"

"That man over there," John said quietly. "Don't turn around. Pretend you're looking for something, for the waitress. The guy sitting by the palm tree, wearing the flat racing cap. See him?"

"What about him?"

"He's the one who's been following me. The man in the Fiat, who's so interested in the Order of the Labyrinth. I got a closer look at him a few days ago."

"Are you sure?"

"Of course I'm sure. Don't turn around."

"Do you think he's on our flight?"

"I don't know. Probably. Shit. Well, maybe we can learn something from him."

The waitress came with their menus. They ordered, ate their dinner. When their flight was called the man in the racing cap stood, shouldered his carry-on bag and walked to the terminal. They watched him board the plane before getting in line themselves.

The plane stopped over in Chicago and landed at Heathrow Airport the next evening. They took the underground to the train station, the train to Canterbury, and a taxi to Applebury. At every stage of their journey John looked carefully at the people around them.

"Do you see him?" Molly asked once.

"He got a cab at the airport. It doesn't matter — if he knows about the Order he can probably guess where we're going."

They checked into a bed and breakfast in Applebury. "One room?" the proprietor asked. He had a surprising German accent, saying "vun" for "one" and nearly swallowing the "r" in "room."

"Two, please," Molly said.

John said nothing. At least that had been made clear between them.

John yawned as he signed the register, yawned again when they went up the stairs to their rooms. "God, I'm tired," he said. "I couldn't sleep at all on the plane."

"I slept great," Molly said. Peter had once said that an experienced traveler could sleep anywhere. *See,* she thought. *We are compatible.*

"I know," John said sourly. "Every so often I'd look over and see you fast asleep. I'll go back downstairs and call Tantilly after I unpack. And then I'm going to sleep for a long time."

"Tantilly?"

"The Westingate house."

"Who lives there now?" Molly asked.

"Someone named Westingate, oddly enough. Charles Westingate. Maybe they didn't lose the family fortune after all, though that's not what the books said. Well, we'll find out soon enough."

The next morning they had a full English breakfast, toast and jam and cereal and eggs and sausages and stewed tomatoes. Molly noticed, pleased, that John was still wearing his glasses.

The proprietor came around to pour them coffee. "I thought the English drank tea," Molly said.

"They do, most of them," the proprietor said. ("Say do," it sounded like.) "But I very much prefer coffee."

He went to serve another couple. John said, "Charles Westingate said to come over around ten. I told him I was researching the history of the house."

After breakfast they took a taxi to Tantilly, passing through winding lanes shaded by oaks. Soon they began to glimpse, between the boles of the trees, a huge lawn, vast and green as the sea.

A house materialized at the far end of the lawn. Another turn in the road and the house had vanished. As they drove closer the house seemed to be playing hide-and-seek, appearing and disappearing, always emerging in unexpected places and showing them different facets, chimneys, windows, gables.

The taxi left the trees and turned into the semicircular driveway. Now that Molly could see the house whole it looked both bigger and smaller than she had expected: bigger because she had not seen it complete through the trees, smaller because the drive had prepared her imagination for something far more grandiose. It had three stories, with an overhanging roof large enough for a fourth. Two wings of two stories each ran back from the front.

John paid the taxi driver and they walked to the door. John pushed the bell, which was made of brass and surrounded by brass leaves and flowers. A woman in her thirties wearing a tweed skirt and a worn cashmere pullover answered the door.

"I'm John Stow," John said. "We're here to see Lord Westingate."

"That's right, he's expecting you," the woman said. "Come on in."

There was something odd about the woman's speech, and after a moment Molly realized what it was: she was American. Except for overheard conversations at the airport and the bed and breakfast Molly had yet to hear a British accent.

The woman ushered them into the entryway, then through an arched doorway to a vast and drafty room. The ceilings were at least twenty feet high, with wooden beams separating panels of carvings. There was a carved marble fireplace nearly as tall as the room in one wall, and paintings in large gold frames on two of the others; the fourth was taken up by the doorway they had come through. Plush couches, heavy wooden tables, and huge porcelain figures and vases stood around the room. Several oriental rugs covered the patterned wood floor.

"Why don't you wait in the drawing room?" the woman said. "I'll go get him."

"Drawing room?" Molly said to John after she had left. "This is bigger than my entire apartment."

John sat carefully on a couch. Molly went to look at one of the paintings, a woman in green with long, thick black hair. An ormolu clock on one of the tables ticked loudly. "God, it's cold," she said, balling her fists in her jacket pockets. "Do you think that American woman was one of the maids? How on earth did she end up here?"

"I don't know," John said. "She's the one who answered the phone when I called, made all the arrangements."

"Hullo," someone said.

A tall young man, balding but not yet bald, came in through the arched doorway. He was wearing, Molly saw with surprise, a pair of tight leather pants. He had bright blue eyes, and small patches of stubble dotted his fair face, as if he had tried to grow a beard and been unsuccessful. He smiled, a hesitant smile that was at the same time somehow charming, and held out his hand toward John.

"I'm Lord Charles," he said, as John stood and shook his hand. He grinned. "You were expecting a tweed jacket or jodhpurs or some such thing."

Molly held out her hand and Charles shook it as well. "Sorry about not answering the telephone when you rang. I've a horror of the thing. You say you're writing a book?"

"That's right," John said. "We'd appreciate hearing whatever you can tell us about the house."

"Well, to begin with, Tantilly was built by an ancestor of mine," Lord Charles said. "Lady Dorothy Westingate."

John took his notebook out and started to write. "Dorothy was a bit of an eccentric," Lord Charles said, warming to his subject. "Mind you, she wasn't the only one. Money and eccentricity have produced startling houses all over England. Still, I daresay we're the only ones with a labyrinth in our basement."

"Labyrinth?" Molly asked. "Is that because of the Order of the Labyrinth?"

John gave her a look that said as clearly as words, I'll ask the questions here. Charles seemed startled, then laughed. "Where on earth did you hear about that?" he asked.

"We read the pamphlet," Molly said. "Lady Westingate's speech."

"Yes, of course. I'll show you the labyrinth later, or my wife will." The woman who had answered the door came into the room. "Ah, here she is now. My wife, Kathy."

"You're his wife?" Molly asked the woman. "But you're American."

John scowled. Lord Charles laughed. "Yes, of course she is," he said. "I met her on holiday in the States."

"We met at a magic show, believe it or not," Kathy said. "They called us both up to the stage."

"A magic show?" Molly asked. "Do you remember which one?"

"How could I forget? The Endicott Family."

Not the Allalies, Molly thought, disappointed. *Well, why should it have been, after all?*

"But I don't suppose you came all this way for my life story," Charles said. "What do you want to know about the house?"

"When was it built?" John asked.

"Dorothy started the house in 1878, with money she inherited from her husband," Charles said. "It took her five years. She added to it for years afterwards, of course. In this next room, for example . . ."

He led Molly, John and Kathy through the arched doorway into a hallway, and then to a room with a vaulted ceiling even higher than that of the drawing room. Marble pillars reached to arches which upheld the ceiling. Light shone through stained glass windows recessed beneath the arches.

"This is the Great Hall," Charles said. "See the windows? There are twelve of them, three to a wall. Most people assume they represent the zodiac and in fact they do, but they're also Dorothy's family. Aquarius, here, this man pouring a water jug—that's Dorothy's husband. This one here is her son, doubled for Gemini. Virgo is Dorothy herself."

Lady Dorothy seemed too ordinary to be immortalized in a window. She wore a hat and had the peering look of someone who had just taken off her spectacles.

"The account books say these windows were commissioned in 1885, when Dorothy was thirty-five," Charles went on. "Dorothy's son, in the Gemini window, was twelve. They were designed by Sir Edward Poynter." To Molly's blank look he said, "He later became president of the Royal Academy."

"Who are the rest of them?" Molly asked.

"I've no idea," Charles said. "Other relatives, presumably."

The sun shone through the eastern windows, deepening the blue water of Aquarius, sparkling the yellow and gold fish in

Pisces. One corner of the room was still in shadow. Molly could barely make out a young woman throwing a dark red shawl over her head. A lamb stood next to her. "Isn't Capricorn supposed to be a goat?" she asked.

Charles went on ahead; he seemed not to have heard her. They toured the smoking room, the breakfast room, the dining room, the conservatory. "I know it's absurd, all this space," Charles said. "We don't even entertain much. Most evenings we stay home and watch the telly, just as you do, probably." He shrugged. "The library is this way."

They entered a room filled with rows of books bound in red and brown and black. A wooden spiral staircase led up to a second story, a sort of mezzanine which was also lined with bookshelves. John took down a small pamphlet, holding it carefully.

"What have you got there?" Lord Charles asked.

"Lady Dorothy's pamphlet. 'A History of the True and Antient Order of the Labyrinth.' I was wondering if you had a copy." He glanced through the pages.

"It's quite fragile, really," Charles said, smiling his diffident smile. He held out a hand and after a moment John gave him the pamphlet. His hesitation was not embarrassment, Molly realized, but a way of keeping others at a distance, almost a form of rudeness. Charles returned the pamphlet to the shelves. Although he seemed proud of Lady Westingate's peculiar house it was clear that he did not want to discuss her later folly, the Order of the Labyrinth.

"Is there anything else you'd like to see?" Charles asked. "We've mostly bedrooms upstairs, and servants' rooms in the attic. They're not terribly interesting, I'm afraid. Princess Helena and her husband, Prince Christian of Schleswig-Holstein, stayed in the blue room once. She was a daughter of Queen Victoria."

"The labyrinth, if we could," Molly said.

"Yes, of course. Kathy, would you show them the basement?"

"Sure," Kathy said. "This way."

Kathy led them out of the library and down a long hallway.

She stopped before a door remarkable only for its plainness: unlike the other doors they had seen it was not carved or gilded or painted in any way. She opened it, turned on a light, and started down a flight of stairs.

The room at the bottom was filled with the clutter of generations: boots and broken mechanical toys, hunting rifles, chairs with three legs, a stuffed deer's head. Paintings leaned against the walls.

Molly looked closer at the paintings. They seemed to be stilted nature scenes. "Don't worry about hurting my feelings," Kathy said. "I know they're dire. We didn't paint them, thank God."

"Who did?" Molly asked.

"The last family that owned the house," Kathy said. "Dreadful people. Industrialists playing at being gentry."

"I thought the Westingates owned the house," Molly said.

"We lost it for a while," Kathy said. "Fortunately Charles was able to buy it back."

How? Molly thought. She was just about to ask when she felt John step on her foot. She looked at him, annoyed. How were they going to learn anything if they didn't ask questions?

Upstairs a bell rang, and was answered. More bells chimed in. "Tibetan music," Kathy said. "My husband loves it. And the acoustics in the Great Hall are fantastic. The labyrinth is this way."

They picked their way through the jumble on the floor and stopped before another door, this one open. A hallway lay beyond it; several feet down another hallway branched off at right angles to the first one. Kathy switched on the light. The walls were blue, lit by frosted white lamps placed at intervals along the corridor.

"Do you know how to get out?" Molly asked.

"I did once," Kathy said. "When we moved back Charles and I went exploring. I don't know if I'd remember, though."

They heard a tinny double ring upstairs, clashing with the Tibetan bells. "Damn, there goes the phone," Kathy said. "Charles won't answer that. Excuse me a minute." She hurried back through the room and up the stairs.

"Why don't you let me ask questions?" Molly said when she had gone.

"How long have you been a detective?" John said.

"I've got to start somewhere."

"Okay. You can start by letting me teach you something. Very few people want to talk about their money. If they do they'll bring it up themselves. Charles mentioned the family fortune a few times—he's the one I'd ask about finances. He wants to pretend all this means nothing to him, but you notice he keeps dropping names. Kathy wants to think she's British aristocracy."

"How do you know?"

"Look at her clothing. Nothing fancy, even a little worn. Reverse snobbery. And did you notice how sarcastic she was about the family who had lived here before? She has even less right to play at being gentry—at least they were British. My guess is that Charles married her for the money and she married him for the title. It's a common enough arrangement. That's probably how they managed to buy the house."

"But she said 'When we moved back.' "

"She was speaking figuratively. When we the Westingates moved back to our ancestral home. You can see now why they wouldn't want to talk about it."

"How are we going to find out, then?"

"Look into the sale of the property. Read the newspaper articles or the church registry about their wedding and then trace her through her maiden name. Hang out at the local pub."

Molly shivered. The basement was even colder than the drawing room had been.

"It's obvious they're trying to conserve money," John said. "I'll bet there's only one room in the entire house that's well heated. And did you notice they don't seem to have any servants?"

"So who keeps it clean?"

"They probably hire . . ." John paused. "Sheep!" he said. "Of course."

"What?" Molly said.

"I've got to check something out. Go into the labyrinth. Try to get lost."

She almost said "What?" again. But John had left, hurrying toward the stairs. She walked down the blue hallway and turned right at the first door.

This corridor led to another room. A man sat at a desk, his head bent over a newspaper. She nearly cried aloud. Then she saw that the figure was a statue, a mannequin.

She put her hand on her heart. Good Lord. Who would create such a thing, and why? Now she could see that the man was dressed in somber Victorian clothing, and that there was a thick layer of dust on his shoulders and hair. A tea tray with china cups and a silver teapot, also covered with dust, sat to the left of the newspaper. The desk held a blotter, several fountain pens, and a gilt clock. The newspaper was dated 1887 and said something about Queen Victoria's Jubilee.

As she left the room she glanced over her shoulder to make sure she hadn't imagined it.

The next rooms were just as odd, or odder. In one a hanged man dangled from a beam in the ceiling. In another a woman stood, holding a lion on a heavy chain; as Molly got closer she could see that the woman was blindfolded. A third room looked like a treasury, with a hoard of necklaces and rings and brooches sparkling in the light from the frosted white lamp. A man knelt on the floor and lifted a chain of jewels to his face, an expression of wonderment on his face.

Once she thought she saw the first room, the man at the desk, ahead of her. Relieved, she began to run; she had found her way to the beginning of the maze. But when she got there she saw that the scene was different: the newspaper had been opened to another page, and a dark stain covered most of it. She looked up and saw that the man had shot himself; the stain was blood. She hurried to the door and turned at random down a hallway.

The rooms opened out into corridors, or the corridors swelled to contain the rooms. The road was no longer straight but twisted, branching. There were bends in the labyrinth that revealed towers, gardens, grottoes.

In the weeks and months that followed Molly would sometimes wonder if she had ever left the labyrinth. It seemed large enough to contain forests and rivers, streets and signposts, even entire cities. Maybe all the strange and confusing things she was to encounter later were only more rooms in the endlessly forking maze, each a tableau cunningly arranged by whoever had invented this. Maybe everyone in the world—clerks and cab drivers, her aunt and all her friends and coworkers—was an allegory for something else.

"Molly!" someone called.

"Over here!" she said.

"Where?" It was John.

"Don't come in. Keep shouting—I'll find you."

She followed the sound of his voice. The hall grew straighter as she went. Finally she passed through a door and thought she saw the first room she had entered, the one with the man at the desk, across the corridor. But what if it wasn't? What if the John she had heard was different from the John she had come to the house with? She hurried to the room to make certain.

"I see you!" John said. "Molly! Where are you going?"

"Oh, dear," she heard someone else say. It was Kathy Westingate. "I should have warned you about the labyrinth."

"Molly!" John said.

Sure now that this was the same room Molly went back to the hallway and headed toward John. "Oh, dear," Kathy said as Molly joined them. "You're covered with dust."

"There are whole *rooms* in there," Molly said.

"It's not really safe to go in without a guide," Kathy said.

"Rooms with people, mannequins," Molly said. "Jewels. Flowers. Animals."

John looked at Kathy Westingate. "Is that true?" he asked.

"Animals?" Kathy said. She shook her head. "I don't—it was some kind of initiation, I think."

"For the Order of the Labyrinth?" John asked.

"I think so. I'm sorry—I should have warned you."

"I'm all right," Molly said. With every second that passed she felt more rooted in the present. She couldn't possibly have seen everything she thought she'd seen; she had become confused, disoriented. "Don't worry about it. It was interesting, actually. Did Lady Dorothy build the maze?"

"Yes," Kathy said. She led them back up the stairs to the ground floor. "Would you like to see anything else?"

"I don't think so," John said.

They said good-bye to the Westingates and thanked them for their hospitality. John called a cab.

When they were seated safely in the back seat of the cab Molly said, "Are you going to tell me what that was all about? Sheep?"

John drew a book out of the inner pocket of his jacket. It was bound in cracked and faded brown leather; there was no title on the cover. "Did you steal that?" Molly asked. "From the library?"

"Yeah."

"Yeah, he says. Calmly, like he's done it all his life. What on earth did you do that for? Is that why you wanted me to go into the labyrinth—so that if Lady Westingate got off the phone too soon you could tell her I was lost? Create a diversion?"

"Yeah."

"John—"

"Okay, okay. Do you remember the stained glass window of the woman and the sheep? When you said you thought Capricorn was a goat?"

Molly nodded.

"There was someone mentioned in the pamphlet by the name of Emily Wethers. A wether is a castrated sheep. When I realized that I remembered that this book had been shelved next to Lady Westingate's pamphlet, and that the books were alphabetical by author. So this could well be by Emily Wethers, or if not then maybe another book by Lady Westingate."

He opened to the first page. *"An Account of My Life, by Emily Wethers,"* it said. The handwriting was flowing, graceful. Molly turned the page.

"I was born in the country, around 1860," the same hand continued. "There are those who think that rustics are silly, untutored creatures, and so we are, some of us and some of the time. Yet we can learn. It is because I have learned that I am able to write this book. I owe it to you, my old friend, to tell you the truth for once, without deception and without art."

John closed the book. "We'll read it at the bed and breakfast," he said.

"Who was she?" Molly said. "I like her already. What did she have to do with the Westingates? Who is she writing to?"

"We'll find out."

"John? How did you know that—about the sheep?"

"I read a lot."

"Sounds like it. Sheep and silverware—what else do you know? Where did you learn to steal like that?"

John shrugged. "Here and there."

"Are you going to return the book?"

"Well, of course I am. We'll pay another call on the Westingates and I'll slip it back into the library. What do you take me for?"

"I don't know," Molly said.

FOUR
An Account of My Life, by Emily Wethers

I was born in the country, around 1860. There are those who think that rustics are silly, untutored creatures, and so we are, some of us and some of the time. Yet we can learn. It is because I have learned that I am able to write this book. I owe it to you, my old friend, to tell you the truth for once, without deception and without art.

My parents and brothers and sisters all had what we called the Gift, which had manifested itself in our family as far back as memories ran. It is the Gift that allows us to find lost hats and gloves, to guess what a man will say before he speaks, to make objects disappear in one place and reappear in another. The villagers would occasionally come to us for advice on stray sheep or matters of the heart; their parents, and their grandparents, and their great-grandparents had all done the same before them.

Harrison once asked me whether the villagers had thought of us as witches, and seemed startled when I laughed. The villagers had grown up with us, and thought our skills nothing untoward.

The Gift was strongest in me. My grandmother could remember her grandmother, a woman who lived in village memory as the one who had calmed the great storm of the last century. My grandmother said that with my brown hair and blue eyes and the gap between my teeth I looked very much like her, and that my talent was perhaps as strong as hers.

When I was seventeen or eighteen (our village did not keep track of such anniversaries) I went to work as a laundress in the great house. I was conscientious about my duties, and if it appeared that some item of clothing would not be ready in time I would use the Gift to see that it was cleaned. I did not do this often; I knew that I would be overwhelmed with work if the other servants had an idea of the extent of my talent.

The daughter of the house, Miss Sylvia, enjoyed taking her carriage to London, where she would spend a few days making the rounds of dressmakers and milliners and visiting her friends. She would generally take her maid, Henrietta, but on the day my life changed Henrietta had fallen ill. The housekeeper, a sour, squinting old woman named Jane, was given the task of finding a reliable girl to travel with Miss Sylvia, and as it happened her gaze fell upon me.

"You, girl," she said. "You've a level head on your shoulders. Can you take charge of Miss Sylvia's toilette?"

I said that I could, and we set off for London.

This was the first time I had been to London, and it appeared to me splendid beyond belief, a riot of sound and smell and colour. I had never seen so many people, nor carriages, nor houses jostling together side by side. We left our bags at the house of one of Miss Sylvia's friends and set off to the dressmakers' shops.

As we entered the first shop a couple was leaving. The man wore fashionable muttonchops and a high bowler hat; the woman had a pale face and astonishingly bright red hair which she had pinned tightly under her hat, almost as if she were ashamed of so much richness. He had tucked the woman's arm under his, and she was cradling her stomach protectively with her other hand.

So preoccupied was she that she very nearly pushed me back into the street. It was not this that aroused my ire, however, but the fact that the man raised his bowler hat and apologised, not to me but to Miss Sylvia.

"You don't need to be so careful of your wife," I said to him. "She ain't pregnant."

I think it was the word "pregnant," never used in polite company, that stopped him. "What?" he said.

"She ain't pregnant," I said again.

Lady Lydia looked at me hatefully, but the man, Lord Harrison Sanderson, seemed not to notice. "Who are you?" he asked wonderingly. "How could you possibly know such a thing?"

"Come, Harrison," Lady Lydia said. "We'll be late for the lecture." And Harrison raised his hat again, this time to me, and allowed himself to be led away.

It was easy enough for Harrison to find us again. He asked his friends, not of course about me but about Miss Sylvia, and his inquiries led to the great house in our village. I had had a premonition of his visit, and so I was not at all surprised to see his carriage coming up the drive a few weeks later.

He was not terribly clever, my Harrison, but he knew enough to spend a few hours in polite conversation before asking about a mere lady's maid. It was getting on towards supper before he was finally led downstairs to the laundry room.

"What is her name?" he asked.

"Em," Miss Sylvia said, and at the same time I said, "Emily Wethers, sir," and curtsied.

"Well, Em," he said. He was terribly earnest; he seemed always to consult some inner moral code before taking any action whatsoever. His hair and beard were wavy and black, almost blue in some lights, and he had deep brown eyes, concerned eyes. He wore a watch chain of heavy gold that draped across his stomach before disappearing into his vest pocket. He seemed anxious not to be thought patronising, and so, of course, I found him the most patronising fellow I had ever met. "How did you know that my wife—that we had hoped for the arrival of a child?"

"There's lots I know, my lord," I said. "I know that you're an adept of the Eighth Grade of the Order of the Labyrinth, but you want to be Tenth Grade. I know that you and your wife wanted a child for nigh on five years."

"How—"

"It's the Gift, my lord," I said. "We all have it in my family."

I knew this would intrigue him, and it did. I will not bore you with the details, but before nightfall I had a new master: Lord Harrison had taken me on at twice my previous salary.

The next day we set off for London. For several weeks, though, nothing seemed to have changed: I continued to work in the laundry, though now I worked for Lord Harrison and his household. I was introduced to Lady Lydia the day I arrived but fortunately she did not recognise me; she paid little attention to servants.

One day Lord Harrison made his way down to the laundry room, a serving girl in tow. It was the first time I had seen him since coming to work in his household.

"Em," he said. "I'd like you to get dressed. This girl here will help you. I'll be presenting you to the Order of the Labyrinth tonight."

I heard the excitement in his voice but did not know its cause. There were things here I did not understand, and I saw that I would have to pay close attention to what was about to happen.

The serving girl helped me wash and dressed me in a corset and bustle—the first I had ever worn—and bodice and skirt. She led me to the Great Hall and withdrew silently. I saw men and women dressed in finery—fox furs, watered silk, cravats, silver— and I wanted to follow the girl, to return to the familiar safety of the laundry room. What could these handsome, expensive people want with me?

"Good, we're all here," Lord Harrison said. "This is Em Wethers. She has a special talent, what she calls a Gift."

I looked around the room. To my surprise I understood that these people were no different from the villagers and servants I had known; I saw the same greed, love, envy, kindness, hatred, generosity. I was no longer frightened.

"We'll begin, then," Harrison said.

He gestured to a few of the others, among them a heavily rouged woman and a gentleman with a grey beard that forked in two, like a serpent's tongue. They began to trace a pentagram on the floor around the table. At each of the five points they paused to light a candle and to recite more invocations. Soon the room smelled heavily of wax and of some herb I did not recognise.

Harrison motioned us to the table. Someone lowered the gaslights while he lit candles set at intervals along the table. The lights rippled like water over our faces as we sat.

"Let us join hands," Harrison said, sitting. He closed his eyes, and everyone around the table followed suit. Everyone but me; I was eager to see what would happen next.

The woman wearing rouge spoke. "We are travelling through the turnings of the Labyrinth. Each turning represents an important event in our lives, a test successfully overcome. We turn now right, now left, and now right again. And now our guide, Arton, comes to meet us, clothed all in golden light. Arton, do you have a message for any of those present?"

The woman opened her eyes and looked around wildly. Her hair was dyed a flat black; she was tall and heavy and wore a skirt and bodice edged with black lace at her wrists and neck. Silver and garnet earrings dangled from her ears. "There is a message for—" Her face screwed in a frown. "—for Edward."

She fell silent.

I turned to my neighbour on my right, the gentleman with the forked beard. "Who's she, then?" I asked.

"Hush," the man said.

"Yes," the woman continued, less agitated now. "Arton bids me say that Edward's son is alive, and will return."

"Not soon, I'd bet," I said. "He's in India."

There was consternation around the table, expressions of shock, surprise, startlement. "Hush," the man next to me, Augustus Binder, said again.

But by far the strangest response came from the man I took to be Edward. "By George, and I'd give him ten thousand pounds to stay there, too!" he said.

I saw that Edward's son, who was also named Edward, had had to leave his college at Cambridge after a scandal involving a friend's sister and the sister's maidservant. I saw that he had lived riotously at Cambridge, and that his only communication with his father had consisted of requests for money. Before he left for India he had not seen his tutor in over a year.

"He'll come home to you," I said. "But in three or four years, and so different you won't hardly know him. You'll like him better then."

The rouged woman, Mrs. Frances, was looking at me with open admiration. She said, her voice low, "She speaks with Arton."

I saw that this woman had some small Gift, but that she needed the rituals, the candles, the invocations to focus it. "I don't know no Arton," I said. "I see Edward in India, that's all."

"What else does Arton say?" another woman asked.

I looked slowly around the table, gazing at each one in turn. What should I tell them? That this one would die, and that one prosper? That this one, so gently holding his wife's hand, would return tomorrow to the waterfront and the men he desired?

I needed time to think. "He don't say nothing more," I said.

After the meeting Mrs. Frances came up to me. "You have a great talent, young lady," she said.

"I know," I said. "We all have it in our family."

She laughed. It was a deep, gravelly laugh, beginning somewhere in her belly. "Immodesty becomes you, my dear. A word of advice, if I may. Don't fuck Lord Harrison, much as he desires you."

Not one of the fine men and women I had worked for had ever used that word, so familiar to me from my village childhood. It was as if, by not talking about it, they had managed to convince themselves that all the messy business of life did not exist.

"No, I won't do that," I said. "And he would never."

She laughed her strong laugh again and pressed my hand.

"So," she said, "there are some things that even you don't know."

The meetings continued. I was astonished, even a little scornful, when I learned what they would have me do. Rituals, incantations, invocations—they seemed like children playing a game, the rules of which they had not yet mastered. In vain did I tell them that none of this was necessary, that I learned all I needed from one look at their faces.

At every meeting, therefore, we drew the pentagram and lit the candles, spoke the invocations, held hands around the table. I would close my eyes and pretend to enter a trance, though I refused to speak the nonsense about the turnings of the Labyrinth. And then I would tell them what they most needed to know.

One woman had arthritis. I saw that this would worsen, but I saw also that the pain had woken within her a fear of death, and I was able to reassure her that her life would be long and, except for her illness, fairly happy. A man fretted over a new business venture, but I said nothing to him; I saw the business fail and his life along with it.

I can see today those meetings so long ago, the broughams drawing up the drive, the men entering and shaking the rain from their chesterfields, the women from their capes and mantles and boas. Beneath these outer coverings the men wore tailcoats with a flower in the buttonhole and bright waistcoats, the women crinoline bustles and trains trimmed with ribbons, frills, lace. Candlelight gleamed on silk, crepe, satin.

I must move forward a few months in my narrative and describe the members as I came to know them, before you, my dear friend, joined the Order. They were an odd group, even for their class. Colonel Augustus Binder, the man with the serpent's beard, sometimes slipped off his shoes and stockings when he came in the door and sat at our meetings barefoot; he thought that this allowed him to feel the nearness of the telluric currents. It was inexpressibly strange to see this careful man, with his neat tailoring and parted beard, walk towards the table on naked feet.

But he was not the most eccentric of them. A sharp-faced fellow named Jack Frederick brought a green cordial which he would sip at intervals during the evening; he claimed it would double or treble his life span, though I saw that it was nothing but distilled fish and hay. Another man had painted a third eye on his forehead and talked about his sexual exploits on the astral plane. But this proved to be too much even for our freethinking group, and it was made clear to him that his first meeting would also be his last.

After the first few meetings I saw that Harrison generally sat to my right, and that there was a kind of eagerness in the way he took my hand. I was not the only person to notice this; once or twice Lady Lydia pushed him aside and grasped my hand so tightly it hurt.

I did not want to cause Lydia pain. Furthermore I had seen, in both the houses in which I had worked, what happened to servants who aspired above their station. I tried to arrange the table so that I sat between two guests, Colonel Binder and Mrs. Frances, for example.

One day I went upstairs to put bedding in the linen room. As I closed the door I saw Lord Harrison coming towards me down the hall.

"Ah, Em," he said.

"Yes, my lord," I said.

He seemed at a loss. I did not need my Gift to see that he was drawn to me, and if truth be told I was drawn to him as well. I had tumbled one or two boys in my village, and had once spent a memorable night with Miss Sylvia's coachman, but I saw that Harrison was different, honest and gentlemanly. But it was just this honesty, I thought, that would ensure that nothing would happen between us.

"I wanted to tell you that I appreciate how hard you work," he said. "Both as a laundress and as an adept in our Order."

"Thank you, my lord," I said. As I went past him I felt the pressure of his arm against mine, and I continued to feel it at various times throughout the day. To be honest, I can recall that touch to this day.

A few days later Lydia received word that her father was dying. She packed quickly and left. The house without her seemed quieter, more peaceful. When I think of Lady Lydia today it is not her face or clothing that I remember, or even her remarkable red hair, but the fact that she wore what we called a chatelaine around her waist, an ornamental chain hung about with household objects. Scissors, button hooks, keys, containers of smelling salts — all these clanked together as she moved through the halls, so that there was ample time for the servants to hear her coming and seem to be hard at work.

While she was gone we held another meeting. Harrison did not sit next to me this time; I knew that he felt guilt because of his desire for me and that he would not take advantage of his wife's absence. I told one man where he had lost his tie pin, another that the woman he courted would be receptive to his suit.

The session ended. There were so many things to gather up at the end of an evening in those days, hats, gloves, scarves, canes, parasols. Our guests would put one down to pick up another and forget where they had placed the first, so that it often took them an hour or more to get out the door.

But after all the confusion and bustle Harrison and I were at last left alone. I made to move past him; he turned; his arms were around me before I realized it. He smelled clean and good, of macassar hair oil and strong male scent. I felt the hardness of his pocket watch, and that other hardness below it. "We must not," he said. "Dearest Em, we must not." But all the while he held me closer.

We kissed. A servant would come at any moment to wind the clocks and douse the candles. "Come," he said.

He led me upstairs, to one of the house's many guest rooms. We undressed, frantic in our haste: skirt, bodice, bustle, corset, undergarments, boots with their maddeningly small buttons. Finally, free of our clothing, we lay on the bed and caressed each other.

"Em," he said, kissing my mouth, my breasts, my stomach. "Ah, Em." His skin was white and smooth, with pale blue veins; he was the most beautiful thing I had ever seen. Next to him I was brown and coarse as a tree.

I thought that if he stopped I would not be able to bear it. I kissed him back. He entered me, fierce and hard and sweet. "Ah," I said. "Oh. Oh, my God!"

He stopped. "Em?" he said. "Dearest, what is wrong? Have I hurt you?"

"No!" I said. "Don't stop, fool!"

He began again, at first slow and wary, then faster and faster. This time when he felt my spasms he did not stop; I think he could not. He cried aloud once and was silent.

I had never met a man so ignorant of women. I wanted to talk afterwards, to caress him, to explore and laugh and taste and touch. Instead he rose and dressed without speaking. As he left the room he said, "We must never do that again."

FIVE
Rue and Ant

Molly and John had alternated reading Emily Wethers's book aloud. It had been John's turn to read about Emily and Harrison making love; as he read he spoke slower and slower, obviously tortured with embarrassment.

"Oh, please," Molly said. "Give me that." She took the book from his hands and continued to read.

I must now leap over several years, and so come to 1883. You, my old friend, must certainly be aware of the significance of the date; it was the year you joined our little group.

One day while I was in the linen room I overheard Lydia Sanderson talking to Harrison. "Lady Dorothy Westingate would like to join our order," she said. Her voice was low, intense; I saw that she valued the social cachet you could bring us.

"Lady Westingate? Where have I heard that name?" Harrison asked.

"You remember her, surely. Her husband died several years ago. She hopes we might be able to pierce the veil between our world and the other side, to receive messages from her husband."

"Receive messages from the dead? But we never have done. Our work is with Arton, a spirit—"

"Yes, a spirit. If we can reach him, surely we can contact the dead."

"Arton inhabits a completely different plane. He is not dead—he has never been alive."

"I've already invited her," Lydia said. "She'll be at our meeting next week."

"Well," Harrison said, "we'll see what Em makes of her."

This was my first encounter with Spiritualism, a popular—should I say sport?—in those years. Although I understood immediately what Lady Westingate would want from me, I did not think that I would give it to her. I know nothing of what happens after we are dead.

But when I met you, Lady Dorothy, my heart melted. You came to our meeting still dressed in black crepe, still mourning for your husband as Queen Victoria mourned for lost Albert. I saw that you had not left your house in five years, saw how lonely you were. And so when you asked me if your husband, also named Albert, had any messages for you, I closed my eyes and nodded solemnly.

"He says to tell you he is happy, very happy," I said. "He misses you and eagerly awaits his reunion with you. But your work on this plane is not finished, he says. You must learn more, understand more, before you are ready to join him."

This is how the deception started, with kindness. I learned everything I needed to know about your husband and your marriage just by looking at you, so the trick was not difficult. You remembered my every word in those days; sometimes you would even write them down in a little notebook you brought for that purpose.

As the years passed there were times when my inventions were insufficient to banish your melancholy. You would retreat to your house for months, where you would commission another painting or purchase another leather armchair. When you returned to our meetings I would outdo myself to provide a spectacle for you. Cymbals would clash, trumpets bray. A heavy scent of roses, Albert's favourite flower, would pass briefly through the room; sometimes a spectral hand would drop a few red petals into your lap. Mirrors would hang suspended in midair, and in them it would be possible to see a dim outline of your husband. All these things I took from your mind; they were all things you desired.

Shortly after you joined the Order you were absent from our meetings for several months. I travelled to your house in Apple-bury and found you sunk in misery. "When will I be allowed to join Albert?" you asked me plaintively. "He gives me his love, tells me all is well. But what is that to me if I cannot see him, or touch him? Have I done something, or failed to do something, so that I am being kept from him?"

It was then that I broached the idea of the Labyrinth. I swear to you, Lady Dorothy, that I meant nothing more than to create a diversion for you, to give you something that would occupy your mind and keep you from thoughts of your dead husband. It's true that I was remembering the ancient ruined mazes in the village where I was born, but at the time I had no idea of their significance.

You embraced the idea eagerly, excited at the thought of your house becoming a tangible symbol of our Order. Then and there you began to write to carpenters and bricklayers, stopping to sketch tangled mazes on your heavy embossed stationery. When you put your pen down I took it up again, elaborating on your drawings of the Labyrinth, straining to remember the twisting av-enues of stone I had played in as a child.

I lived with you, on and off, for several months over the course of that year. You kept busy in your basement, directing the labourers who worked for you. And I went there too, watching as the Labyrinth took shape. I walked it from its beginning to where the labourers had left off, and as I walked I felt myself growing stronger. And not just me—it was as if I were giving strength to the wood and brick and plaster around me.

It was then that I remembered something my grandmother

had told me long ago. "We give power to the places we live in," she said. "We make them magic. Why does our village have such fat sheep and cattle? Look at this apple — have you ever seen such a rich red? It's our doing, all of it."

The mazes focused the power — I saw that now. I had never understood that before, though I had seen my grandmother, and my mother too, walking those lanes of stone. Perhaps they didn't fully understand it themselves. It's strange, isn't it, Lady Dorothy, that Mary Frances should have stumbled on such a powerful symbol when she founded the Order. Or perhaps not — she had a vestige of the Gift, and perhaps she had learned this method of focusing it.

In 1886, several years after Lydia left, Harrison's fortunes received a severe blow. He had made a number of bad investments, and it was in this year that various notes came due and the managers of some of his ventures pressed him for more money to stay afloat. His banker, Mr. Griffin Patmore —

Molly looked ahead a few pages. "Molly?" John asked.

"Look at this — it's all about Harrison's finances. Lists of assets and deficits, pages and pages of it. I wanted to know what happened to Lydia."

"Does it say?"

"Nothing that I can see. Look at this."

John took the journal from her and they studied the columns of numbers together, the pluses and minuses. John paged to the end of the journal. The round, flowing hand reappeared; the narrative had apparently resumed. He turned back to the lists.

"Why on earth did she think this would be important?" Molly said. She glanced at her watch. "Good Lord, it's three o'clock. I'm starving."

"Now's as good a time as any to take a break," John said. "There's supposed to be a pub somewhere nearby. Want to see if we can walk it?"

"Sure."

They left the bed and breakfast. Outside John turned right and headed down a street lined with small shops, a grocer's, a post office, an estate agent.

"So," Molly said. "Emily's the one with the gap in her teeth, like me and Fentrice. Does that mean she's the head of this whole clan? Does that make her Neesa? Harrison is probably Harry in the genealogy. Do you think they got married?"

"Of course not," John said. "Lords didn't marry their laundresses."

"But if he's Harry he had children by her, or at least a child. Fentrice said her parents were Verey and Edwina, and *their* parents were Neesa and Harry."

"He still wouldn't marry her. It took money to run a household like the one Harrison and Lydia had. People married to join their fortunes, and Emily had to be penniless. Anyway, it wasn't so easy to get a divorce in those days. Harrison would have to prove adultery."

"Or Lydia would."

"But why would she want to? There would have been a terrible scandal. Besides, the laws were weighted toward men—a judge would have been much more lenient where Harrison was concerned. But he probably returned to his wife after this one lapse."

"But Emily says something about 'after Lydia left.' And she stayed in the Order for years, and somewhere along the way she learned how to speak better English. Who would she learn that from if not Harrison?"

"Anyone, really. She seems very resourceful."

"So they held hands at the meetings, exchanged steamy glances, and never said a word? Never made love again?"

"Probably."

"But she had a child, at least according to my aunt," Molly said. "I wish we hadn't stopped reading." She looked down the street. "Why does that building say 'Take Courage' on the side?" she asked. "Courage about what?"

"That's the pub," John said. "Courage is the kind of beer they serve. Some pubs here are tied to a specific brewery."

They went inside. Molly, remembering the sheep in the stained glass window, ordered a shepherd's pie. They took their food and went to sit down.

"How do you know all this stuff?" Molly asked. "Victorian divorce laws?"

"I read a lot."

"That's what you said before. I read a lot too, but I couldn't tell you what it took to get a divorce in the nineteenth century."

"There was a year when I didn't do anything but read."

Molly felt, very strongly, as if she had come to a fork in a labyrinth. She could ask him why, and he would tell her, and they would take another step toward friendship. Or she could change the subject.

"How come?" she said.

He sighed. "I was — I was in jail, actually."

"In jail! Why?"

"For being stupid. I was a clerk in a law firm. They made me a notary public, someone who would notarize all their documents. I just signed what they put in front of me, and it turned out that one of the partners was practicing fraud on a grand scale. Only all the documents had my signature on them, not his. So I got a year in jail."

"What happened to him?"

"Nothing. Like I said, I was stupid. I spent a year reading everything in the prison library. You'd be amazed at what they had, old books that no one wanted anymore, an ancient edition of the *Encyclopedia Britannica.* And I helped one of the guys figure something out about his case, where to find some of the evidence he needed, and he got off. So when I got out I became a private investigator. I was fed up with lawyers, and anyway no one would hire an ex-con — it was the only thing I could think to do."

"Good Lord." She remembered the ease with which he had stolen the book from Lord Westingate's library. So that was where he had learned how to steal, and other things too, probably.

"It was hard for me to get my license—I had to prove to the licensing bureau that I was rehabilitated. But they finally believed me."

"Hey, look," Molly said. "No, don't look. It's that man again, the one with the cap."

John turned around, pretended to study the view through the front window. "Damn. I was wondering when he would turn up."

"I'm going to talk to him." She stood.

"What? No!"

"Why not?"

"It could be dangerous. Molly!"

She went toward the other man. "Why are you following us?" she asked.

To her surprise he rose quickly and hurried out the door. "Come on," Molly said to John. "He's getting away!"

John followed her to the door. They watched as the man ran for a bus and climbed on.

"That's it," John said. "We'll never be able to find him now."

"Yeah, but we learned something. He's as afraid of us as we are of him."

"You're right about one thing," John said. "Emily must have been your ancestor. You both do what you like, and damn the consequences."

They finished their meal and walked slowly back to the bed and breakfast. As John put his key to the keyhole the door swung open. John stepped back quickly, motioning to Molly to do the same.

"Someone's been here," he said.

"Our friend in the cap?" Molly asked.

"Maybe. Maybe he was making sure we were out of the way while he looked around in our rooms. Don't come in."

Despite his prohibition she followed him inside and watched as he quickly checked the closet and under the bed. "He's gone," he said. "Why did he—"

"Damn!" Molly said. "Emily's book. He's taken it."

"Shit," John said. He went over to the table where they had left it. Nothing else had been touched.

"Damn," Molly said again. "Now we'll never know what happens next."

He looked at her sourly. "More to the point, we won't be able to return the book to the Westingates. We'll have to get it back."

"How?"

"I don't know."

"Well," Molly said, "I have a feeling we'll see Flat Cap again."

"Is this intuition?" The sour expression was back.

"You mean like Emily's?"

"Yeah. If everyone in her family had the Gift, and if she's your ancestor . . . What am I thinking now?"

"You're hoping we get the book back."

"Too easy. Of course I want the book back."

"Well, but there may be something to this. Aunt Fentrice always seemed to know what I'd done before I told her."

"That doesn't prove anything. Children are transparent that way. Can you tell who's stolen the book? Where they've taken it?"

Could she? She felt her way outward, saw John's tension, his dread of returning to prison. The book was . . . The book was . . . She shook her head. Something was blocking her, a fear of what she might learn. Some part of her felt relief that the book had been stolen, that the whole story of her family would not be told just yet.

"How much do you believe of what Emily said about this Gift?" John said.

"All of it," Molly said. "I was down in the labyrinth, remember. There was something there, some magic. Anyway, why would she lie?"

"To make herself more interesting. To get Harrison to marry her. To con all those wealthy lords and ladies out of their money. It's easier to believe that than to suppose she could actually read minds and predict the future."

"You really don't think much of my family, do you?"

"Look." John took a piece of paper and pencil and wrote *"Allalie."* Underneath that he wrote *"All a lie."*

"Good Lord," Molly said.

"Yes," John said.

With Emily's book gone there was no reason to stay in Applebury. They checked out of the bed and breakfast and went to London, looking for traces of the Order of the Labyrinth there.

In London Molly saw what John meant when he had called his work dull. They spent hours in the library, tracking down old books, running newspapers through a microfiche. In the evenings she wrote postcards to Peter and Robin Ann and other friends, sending off prettily colored pictures of tourist sights she hadn't actually seen.

"The trouble with secret societies," she whispered to John one day at the library, "is that they're secret."

In reply John pointed to the book he was reading, *A Brief History of the Occult in Great Britain* by Percival Swafford-Brown. "The Order of the Labyrinth appears to have been founded sometime in the mid-1870s by a woman named Mary Frances," Molly read. "Mrs. Frances either had some small psychic talent or the ability to tell people what they most wanted to hear; with this she was able to attract several wealthy and influential people to her seances.

"The only document to come down to us from the OotL is a pamphlet by Lady Dorothy Westingate entitled 'A History of the True and Antient Order of the Labyrinth.' Lady Westingate makes the usual extravagant claims for her Order, going so far as to give them a history stretching back into antiquity. With the aid of their spirit guide Arton, she says, they can predict the future, make contact with the dead, learn the lost wisdom of the ancients. Adepts of the Tenth Grade, she states, can enchant a man so that he does their bidding.

"In her pamphlet Lady Westingate credits Mrs. Frances with the central conceit of the Order, the labyrinth. Events in our lives, Mrs. Frances explains, are turnings in the labyrinth. If we understand these events correctly, if we pass the tests given us, we are allowed to continue on towards the next turning, the next test. Each turning successfully passed allows the adept to advance a grade in the Order. There are rumours of an actual labyrinth beneath the house of one of the members.

"The Order grew in popularity during the occult boom of the 1880s. One of the men who joined around this time, a Colonel Augustus Binder, is typical of a certain type of seeker after mysteries. From 1870 to 1876 he was stationed in a regiment in Bombay in India, where he became acquainted with Eastern religions, particularly Hinduism and Buddhism.

"Upon his return to England he subscribed to *Light*, a London spiritualist weekly; *The Theosophist*, edited by H.P. Blavatsky and Henry Olcott; and *The Religio-Philosophical Journal*. His niece and heir, Sarah Binder, in a letter to her sister Anna, mentions finding over twelve hundred books in his library after his death, among them *Modern American Spiritualism, Isis Unveiled, Atlantis: The Antediluvian World, Lights and Shadows of Spiritualism, People from the Other World*, and all five volumes of *The Vishnu Purana*, as well as Greek, Latin, Sanskrit, and Hebrew dictionaries. 'Oh, Anna,' she adds, somewhat plaintively, 'whatever shall I do with them? There is no bookshop here that will take them.'

"Even this very abridged list shows something of the breadth of Binder's interests, which included spiritualism, theosophy, and Eastern religion. We also know that he attended meetings at a spiritualist camp in Massachusetts, that he joined the London Lodge of the Theosophical Society, and that he was one of the founding members of the Society for Psychical Research.

"All this frenetic activity appears to have come to an end when he discovered the Order of the Labyrinth in 1879. 'I am very close to finding the answers I seek,' he wrote Sarah Binder in October of 1880. 'I have met a remarkable woman, Miss Emily Wethers, who seems to have true occult powers. I have been promised that I will know all when I reach the Tenth Grade of the Order.'

"Oddly, Binder does not mention the OotL in any subsequent

letters to his niece. Perhaps he had been told not to divulge the secrets of the Order, or perhaps he had not learned as much as he had hoped he would. Emily Wethers (about whom we know almost nothing) and Mary Frances must have satisfied him in ways that the other groups had not, however, because he remained in the Order until 1910.

"Another member, Lady Dorothy Westingate, joined the Order in 1883. Her husband, Lord Albert Westingate, had died in 1878. As far as we know, Lady Dorothy returned home after his funeral and did not leave again for five years. The first time she ventured outside seems to have been to attend a meeting of the OotL.

"Apparently a medium in the Order, either Mary Frances or Emily Wethers or both, professed to have contacted Lady Dorothy's dead husband. This marks a departure for the Order; they had never before claimed mediumship among their powers. (See Chapter 5, 'Ghosts and Guides,' for a comparison of occult groups which contact the dead and those which receive their wisdom from guides or masters on another plane. Madame Helena Blavatsky, whose masters or 'mahatmas' lived in the Himalayas, always spoke of mediums with a great deal of scorn.)

"It is difficult to see this new development within the OotL as anything but a desire for monetary gain. Lord Westingate had left his wife a very wealthy woman, though the precise extent of Lady Dorothy's fortune is unknown. It must have been considerable, however, because from the years 1878 to 1883 she did little but add to the house she had inherited from her husband. According to her record books she spent over £50,000 on this task.

"A gentleman, it is said, never discusses money. Yet gentlemen have money, a great deal of it, and this money must come from somewhere. Lord Sanderson's bank records, which were entered into evidence at his trial, show him in financial difficulties in the mid-1880s, though the ultimate cause of these difficulties is unknown. Perhaps he was caught up in the agricultural depression of the 1870s and 1880s, when wheat from the United States, newly strong after their Civil War, poured into England, causing the price of British wheat to drop. Perhaps he had industrial interests which failed when the industries of both Germany and Italy began to rival England's.

"But after these initial difficulties the fortunes of Lord Sanderson began to rise while those of Lady Westingate fell. At the time of his disappearance in 1910 he owned two houses in London and a majority share in a brewery, a shipping company, and a steelworks. In 1912 Dorothy Westingate, facing an acute shortage of funds, was forced to sell her house.

"Outright accusations of financial impropriety appear in 1910. On August 19 of that year Colonel Binder brought suit against four members of the Order, Mrs. Mary Frances, Lord Harrison Sanderson, Lady Dorothy Westingate, and Miss Emily Wethers, claiming that they had defrauded him of thousands of pounds. Why he waited thirty years before resorting to legal action is unknown.

"In the course of the trial Colonel Binder released several of the Order's secret documents and rituals, some of which were printed in the *Times* and other newspapers to widespread amusement and ridicule. One *Times* reader wrote, 'It is possible that there is a more foolish, more credulous man in all of England than Colonel Binder, but it is difficult to think who he might be. Any man who believed in "the spirit guide Arton, clothed all in golden light," has no business calling himself defrauded; he may as well have gone for advice to a conjurer at a county fair, or to a man who fries pancakes in his hat. One hopes that he has learned from the experience, and that he counts himself fortunate in having spent only a few thousand pounds for the privilege.' Binder's suit was dismissed amid a welter of accusations and counteraccusations.

"Lord Harrison Sanderson disappeared later that year. Rumours placed him in India, in Egypt, in America. Did he take Colonel Binder's money with him when he left? No one knows.

"Without Sanderson the Order splintered into various schisms. A small branch existed in London as late as the 1930s. In the 1950s the Order was revived in Los Angeles and a few years later a second American branch started near San Francisco. Very little has been heard from the OotL in recent times."

Molly got the London *Times* microfiche for August 1910, threaded it onto the reader, and wound it to August 19. She found nothing there, but in the next issue, August 20, she was rewarded. *"Colonel Augustus Binder Brings Charges of Fraud in Lesser Applebury,"* a headline said, and under that in smaller type: " '*The Order of the Labyrinth Promised Me Wealth, Power,*' He Says."

The story was the same as that in Swafford-Brown's history. Binder said that he had been promised an initiation into the secrets of the Order, that he had been asked for money totaling over five thousand pounds, and that finally, at the end of thirty years, he had received nothing but what he called "folderol." As proof he offered documents he claimed were rituals of the Order, which the *Times* reprinted in a separate article.

"Miss Emily Wethers, who was observed to bite her nails to the quick both on and off the stand, said that the Order had asked for nothing from Colonel Binder," the story continued. " 'We requested his presence at the meetings, nothing more,' she said. 'Where are the five thousand pounds he claims to have spent? I daresay there is no such sum missing from his accounts.' As her testimony came late in the afternoon the court recessed for the day."

Molly wound the fiche to the next day, August 21. "She seems awfully nervous," John said. "Biting her nails to the quick, it said."

"Maybe she bit them all the time," Molly said.

"She didn't mention it."

"Would you? If you were writing an account of your life would you put in all your bad habits?"

The librarian raised his head and scowled at them. "Okay, okay," John said. "Here it is." He pointed to the headline on the screen. *"Fraud Trial Continues in Lesser Applebury."*

"Colonel Augustus Binder, who claimed to have been de-frauded of 'over five thousand pounds' by members of the Order of the Labyrinth, received a blow to his case today as his banker, a Mr. Thomas Wheeling, took the stand. According to Mr. Wheel-ing, 'Colonel Binder has never withdrawn any large sums of money for which I cannot account, nor has he written cheques to the Order of the Labyrinth or to any of the four defendants.' Lord Harrison Sanderson's banker, Mr. Griffin Patmore, took the stand next and noted that Sanderson had never received money from Colonel Binder.

"The proceedings were interrupted by Colonel Binder, who shouted, 'You're a pack of liars, all of you. You've defrauded me, and Lady Dorothy as well,' and was suppressed."

There was nothing about the trial the next day, or the next. In the newspaper for the next week Molly and John found a brief note saying the suit had been dismissed.

"That seems to be that," John said. "I wonder why they didn't check Emily's bank account."

"Because laundresses didn't have bank accounts," Molly said, a little angrily. "Why are you so eager to think the worst of my family?"

"But was she still a laundress? The trial's thirty years after she joined the Order of the Labyrinth. A lot could have happened in that time. For one thing, she seems to speak like a lady now."

"She still has the same last name, though."

"Quiet, the both of you," the librarian said. "Another word and I'll have to show you the door."

"The letters!" Molly said. The librarian started toward them. "Sorry, sorry," she said.

She scrolled quickly through the fiche to the letters page. The *Times* had devoted far more space to letters about Binder's suit that it had to the suit itself. There were dozens of them, and the one Swafford-Brown had quoted was not the worst. "Lunacy," "folly," "extraordinary gullibility," some of the writers said.

"Poor Emily," Molly whispered.

On August 25 there was an answer from Lord Sanderson. "It is always easy to ridicule secrets and rituals that are incapable of immediate interpretation. Unfortunately it is far more difficult to understand these rituals with the proper questing spirit. We regret that these mysteries of our Order have been made public."

"Look," Molly whispered, pointing to the bottom of Sanderson's letter. "25, Sibylline Crescent," it said. "Could the Sandersons still be there? Eighty-five years later?"

John shrugged. "Maybe," he said.

She rewound the fiche and put it back. The librarian glared at them as they left. Molly blew him a kiss.

They bought a *London A-Z* at a corner shop and looked up Sibylline Crescent, then caught a taxi. Molly had expected a manor as imposing as the Westingates', but the taxi dropped them off in a part of town that reminded her a little of Berkeley. She saw small bookstores, record stores, take-out vegetarian restaurants, people wearing torn black clothing with their hair dyed in a dozen colors, blue, pink, purple, white. Loud reggae music came from a street market on the corner.

"Where are we?" Molly asked.

John looked at their map. "It's called Camden Town," he said.

"And the Sandersons lived here? It's not quite what I expected from Emily's description."

"It could have changed over the years. Or Emily could have made a lot of it up."

"There you go again."

John didn't answer. He walked to the corner and turned at Sibylline Crescent.

"Over here," Molly said from the other side of the street. "This is twenty-five. And look." She pointed.

She had stopped at a plain storefront. The front windows were soaped over, but three smaller windows above them were still clear. Two were blank. The middle one said:

RUE AND ANT

OF THE LAB

N BRANCH

"Rue and Ant?" John said.

"The True and Antient Order of the Labyrinth," Molly said slowly, working it out. "London Branch?"

"Or Camden Town Branch. Maybe they had branches all over—maybe they were bigger than we thought."

"I bet this is Harrison's second house in London, the one Swafford-Brown mentions. Swafford-Brown must have seen the address in the *Times* and didn't bother to go there himself. If he had he'd have known it was a storefront."

Molly went to the front door and knocked. No one answered. She turned the knob. To her surprise it opened. "Careful," John said behind her.

The shop was empty, dimly lit by the three top windows. The hardwood floor was scuffed and streaked with white paint. Dust circled in the wind from the doorway. "Hello?" Molly said. Her voice echoed in the bare room. "Hello!"

John moved to one of the corners. A light shone from another doorway. Molly went over to it.

A man lay slumped against the wall halfway down a corridor. Beside him was an overturned flat racing cap. Molly put her hand to her mouth.

"John!" she said.

"Don't touch anything," John said, coming over beside her. "He's dead."

"I know," she said, thinking of her days as a cab driver. "I've seen a dead person before."

"Go to a phone and dial nine-one-one. No, wait. It's nine-nine-nine in this country. I'll make sure no one disturbs him."

Molly went toward the body, reached into the man's pocket. "Molly!" John said. "What are you doing?"

She took out a small key and hastily stuffed it into her coat pocket. Then she went outside and made the call.

John was still studying the body when she got back. "How much do you want to tell them?" he asked tensely.

"What do you mean?" Molly said. "We didn't kill him."

"Do you want to tell them about the Order of the Labyrinth? About your family?"

"About the fact that you stole a book from the Westingates?"

"Well, yes." For the first time since she had met him Molly thought he looked a little embarrassed. "We could say that we were interested in the Order. That we traced it here, through the newspaper articles, and found this man dead. All of that's true, actually. And then there's the thing you took out of his pocket. Do you want to mention that? What was it, by the way?"

Molly looked at the dead man. She could not rid herself of the feeling that she was back in the labyrinth beneath the Westingates' house, that this man was made of wax like all the others. "He's the one who was following us, isn't he?" she said. "He's Flat Cap."

"Yes."

"Oh, God," Molly said. "I said I thought we'd see him again."

They heard the rise and fall of sirens. "Look," John said urgently. "I don't want to go back to jail."

"Okay," Molly said. "So we're—what? Students of the occult."

John relaxed. "Thanks," he said.

Two police officers, a man and a woman, came into the room. "Where's the body?" the man said. Molly pointed toward the hallway.

After a moment the woman came back. "Who phoned it in?" she asked.

"I did," Molly said.

"Can I see some identification?"

Molly and John took out their passports. "Yanks, are you?" the woman said. "We'll have to take your statements." She raised her hand as they started to talk. "Separately."

"You interview the woman," the other police officer said. "I'll take the man."

The room was too small for them to be interviewed separately. "We'll go outside," the policewoman said. She looked at the passport again. "Molly A. Travers, is it?"

"Yes," Molly said. She followed the woman out into the street.

It was easier than she had thought to stick to the story she and John had agreed on. They were students of the occult, come from America to learn more about the Order of the Labyrinth. No, she didn't know who the dead man was. They had come here after seeing the address in the London *Times*. No, she didn't remember the exact date of the letter in the newspaper, but she was sure John had written it down. She pointed to the sign on the window, explained what they had thought it meant.

More police cars and an ambulance drove up to the curb. People hurried into the store. The day was growing chilly. Molly shivered and balled her fists in the pockets of her coat. The key was still there, cold and hard. She closed her hand tightly around it.

"How long were you planning on staying in London?" the officer asked.

"I don't know. As long as it takes to do the research, I guess."

"Good. I'm afraid you won't be able to leave for a while." The policewoman paged through her notes. "I'll need you to show me your purse. And your pockets as well."

For the murder weapon, Molly thought. She handed over her purse and turned her pockets inside out. The woman saw the key but said nothing and wrote nothing down.

John and the other officer came outside. "They found his passport," the officer said. "Joseph Ottig. He's American as well. Interesting, that."

"Have you ever heard that name?" the woman asked Molly. "Joseph Ottig? Did you know him in America?"

Molly shook her head.

"We'll need your current address," the woman said, handing Molly her purse. Molly gave her the name of their bed and breakfast and the woman wrote it down. She said something to the man and they went back into the store together.

"I guess we're done," John said. They started walking back to the main street. "Don't leave town, they said."

"They told me the same thing. Do you know how he died?"

"He was shot, someone said. They looked at me when they said it, too. People don't tend to carry guns in England—it's not like America."

"Are we in trouble?"

"I don't know. I told them I'm a private investigator—they would have found out anyway, just by making a phone call. And then there's the fact that the guy's American. But they can't prove anything."

"Of course they can't. We didn't do anything."

"Well, I did steal the book. And you stole something, too. What was it?"

The street vendors at the corner market were packing up their wares, folding away awnings and tables. Molly took her hand out of her pocket, showed him the key. "It goes to a locker, I think," she said.

John nodded. "Probably from one of the train stations. Why did you take it?"

"That's where the book is. Emily's book."

"How do you know?"

"I just know. Like Emily would, or Fentrice."

"I bet it's his luggage," John said. "Half a dozen pairs of underwear, couple pants and shirts. Well, it's too late to check it out today."

A thin man with a sharp face watched them leave. First Joseph Ottig and now these two—would he never be free of these interfering Americans? But these interlopers were not nearly as dangerous to him and his associates as Ottig would have been.

Ottig was from the so-called American branch of the OotL, an upstart organization whose history only went back as far as the 1950s. The British branch had always kept a skeptical eye on the American heretics. As soon as they'd heard that Ottig was in the country the sharp-faced man had invited him to the storefront, insinuating that the two groups might be willing to put aside their differences and work together. And Ottig had had something, that much was obvious, an artifact or book from the first and nearly legendary Order. But he'd refused to say more.

The sharp-faced man frowned. He shouldn't have shot him, shouldn't have lost his temper that way. Then he smiled as a new thought came to him. The police suspected the two Americans of the murder. Lucky for him they had shown up when they did. *Let them interfere as much as they want,* he thought, patting the gun in his pocket. Maybe they would be able to find out where Joseph Ottig had hidden whatever it was he'd found.

The next morning Molly asked the owner of the bed and breakfast what the nearest train station was. "Charing Crustacean," she said.

"What?" Molly said.

"Charing Cross Station," she said, enunciating carefully, as if talking to a child.

They walked to the underground and set off for the station. John studied his notebook as the train trundled along the tracks. "All right, what do we know?" he said. "We know that Joseph Ottig probably belonged to the Order of the Labyrinth, and so did the man who killed him. Otherwise they wouldn't have been in the storefront. Maybe they'd arranged to meet—"

"But is there still an Order? It's been—what?—eighty-five years since Colonel Binder's suit."

"Flat Cap started following me after you asked about the Order in Oakland. And then he stole the book, and here he is, in a storefront that was probably used as their meeting place. . . . Even if the Order came to an end, say when Lady Westingate died

or Emily left for the United States, they might want to revive it."
He turned back a few pages in his notebook. "And why did Emily
and Harrison go to the United States right after the lawsuit? Were
they afraid of more scandal? Why did the family change its name?"

"Fentrice said that all immigrants did it. A new start, she
said."

"Only if they had a name that was hard to pronounce. Anyone could say Wethers. Or Sanderson, for that matter." He fell
silent for a moment. "At least we know why Lady Dorothy put the
stained glass picture of Emily in that dark corner of the room,
where it would never get any sun. She must have moved it when
she got Emily's journal—she must have been terribly disillusioned."

"I don't know," Molly said. "I just can't see Emily deliberately bilking Dorothy and Colonel Binder out of all that money.
Not the woman who wrote that journal."

"Emily admits to deceiving Dorothy."

"But she says she did it out of kindness, not for money. To
stop Dorothy from thinking about her husband, get her interested
in life again."

"Well, she would say that, wouldn't she? She's apologizing
to Dorothy. She's not going to say, Hey, I took all your money so
my lover and I wouldn't starve." John sighed. "I've never had a
case get away from me like this, go off in so many directions.
Occult groups and traveling magicians and laundresses and labyrinths . . . Maybe if we find out what's in the locker it'll start to
make sense."

But the locker wasn't at Charing Cross Station, or at the next
place they tried, Victoria Station. At Euston they found a number
that matched the key. Molly put the key in the lock and the door
opened.

"Emily's book," she said, reaching for it.

The book seemed thinner than she remembered. "Good
Lord," she said, opening it. "Someone's torn out some pages in the
middle. Three or four pages, looks like." She started to read aloud.

" 'And I should not have done what I did to you, Lady Dorothy. True, it was all meant for the best, but that is a feeble excuse when one considers the consequences. My children were right.' "

People were hurrying past the lockers, running for trains. The clatter of heels echoed in the vast space. A man in a business suit pushed them out of the way with his briefcase and opened the locker next to theirs. "Sorry," he said, not sounding apologetic at all.

"We can't read it here," John said. "Let's go back to the bed and breakfast."

"God," Molly said. "What if they tore out the part about Emily and Harrison? What if we never find out what happened?"

SIX
Emily Wethers, Continued

And I should not have done what I did to you, Lady Dorothy. True, it was all meant for the best, but that is a feeble excuse when one considers the consequences. My children were right.

Once again I will have to pass over a good many years, and so come to 1910. This was thirty years after Harrison first introduced me to the Order, and over twenty-five after Dorothy had begun to leave her house and come to our meetings. My two children were grown, and Henry had even married and had fathered children of his own.

The membership of the Order had changed greatly over the years. Most of the original group had been driven away by the scandal surrounding Harrison and myself, our Bohemian way of living. Augustus Binder, Mary Frances, and Jack Frederick had stayed on, but our meetings now consisted mostly of writers and labourers, artists and artisans, freethinking men and women, and what used to be called "women of easy virtue." (Among this last, of course, I would have to include myself.)

The day our troubles started we had travelled up from London to Tantilly, Dorothy's splendid house. The sun was shining through the Capricorn window, my window, and as always I smiled a little at Dorothy's pun on wethers and sheep. I remembered sitting for that window so many years ago, being sketched by that artist who was so famous, remembered too when the man had stopped visiting poor Lady Dorothy because, he said, the scandal had become too much for him. And I felt again the wonder and delight we had experienced when the windows had finally gone up and we had been showered in fantastic golds and greens and reds.

On the day of which I speak we were all present for what Dorothy insisted on calling a seance. Evening fell, drawing the brilliant colours from the windows. As always we sketched the pentagram, burned the herbs, lit the candles. We held hands, and as always Dorothy asked about her husband.

I closed my eyes and began to speak. Her husband was happy, I said, and sent his love. I had been practicing this deception for so long that it had become second nature to me.

I must say in my defence that my fictions seemed to have done her some good. Lady Dorothy had long ago left her house: she rode her horses, managed her estate, even sat on committees for charities. Still, I should not have done what I did.

My son Henry spoke next, telling us about a friend of his who had died this past week. Mary Frances said, "Your friend's death is the will of the powers that guide the Labyrinth. He was ready to explore the last turning of the maze."

"But is he happy?" Henry asked. "Has he a message for me?"

Mary looked at me. My mind was on something very different from the question he had asked. It shames me to confess it, but I was thinking of the sumptuous supper Lady Dorothy usually laid out for us after our meetings, the roasts and trifles and wines, the silver forks and cut-crystal goblets. I did not even wonder which friend it was who had died, and why I had heard nothing of this from my son before.

"Your friend is happy," I said, almost automatically. "He sends you his love."

"What is his name?" Henry asked.

"What?" I said, surprised.

"What is his name?"

I looked sharply at my son, and at that moment I saw many things. There was no dead friend. Henry was testing me, trying to catch me out, for reasons I did not understand. How different he was from his father Harrison, who would never seek to cause anyone embarrassment.

I looked at his sister Florence. She gazed back at me, her expression level. What were she and her brother playing at?

"His name is Bobo," I said. Bobo was a dog Henry had been fond of as a child. I stood rapidly, not giving anyone time to remark on such a ridiculous name, and said, "Arton has no more messages."

We ate supper and then retired upstairs. I followed Henry into his room. "What were you and Florence thinking of?" I asked angrily.

"Florence had nothing to do with it," Henry said. "It was all my idea."

"Really? And why, pray tell, did you ask such a stupid question?"

He smiled, showing the gap between his teeth. "Perhaps you need to explore a further turning of the Labyrinth," he said.

Rage rose within me, so strongly that I wanted to slap him. But he was a man now, over twenty-five. I could barely speak for anger. "You—you would ruin everything!" I said. "Don't forget that you and Florence are bastards, that you have no legal rights, no standing whatsoever. Everything we have we owe to Harrison's charity, and everything Harrison has depends on the Order."

"Does it?" Henry asked.

I could not trust myself to speak. I left his room, slamming the door behind me.

A few days later Harrison and I returned to London. King Edward had died a month before, and many of the people on the street still wore the crepe bands of mourning. It was not all heaviness and solemnity, though; Harrison and I went to the Savoy The-

atre for light opera, to the Adelphi to see Conan Doyle's *The Speck-
led Band.*

We held several meetings at our London house and I paid
close attention to my children, but neither of them asked any further questions. In the course of time we travelled back to Tantilly.

At our meeting there I spoke the usual comforting messages
from Dorothy's husband. I felt alert, aware; something was about
to happen.

There was silence when I had finished. Then Henry said, "I
have a message. A message from Arton."

I looked at him sharply. Only Mary and I received messages
from Arton; Henry had shown no trace of the Gift—though in
some of our family, I knew, the Gift appeared late.

"The message is from someone named—I can't hear it. Arton
says—he says the initials are L.S."

L.S. Lydia Sanderson, whose name had not been mentioned
at these meetings for nigh on twenty-five years. Old Augustus
looked up, his face shining with interest. "Lydia!" Dorothy said.
"What does she say?"

"She says—No, I can't make it out. Oak? Or woke? No, it's
gone."

He must stop, I thought. *He must.* I could hear nothing but his
voice, the rustle of his clothing, the loud ticking of the ormolu clock
on the mantelpiece. Harrison looked at me, shocked out of his im-
passivity.

Henry sat back. "No," he said. "That's all. Perhaps next time
it will be clearer."

There would be no next time, I thought angrily. I would
make certain of that. I stood, signalling that the meeting was at
an end.

Lady Dorothy went to the kitchen. Augustus turned to speak
to Henry. I cut him off. "We need to talk," I said to my son.

"You mean you need to talk," Henry said. "And I need to listen."

"Yes, that's exactly what I mean," I said, but Henry smiled

and moved toward the door. I hurried after him.

He made his way down the corridor. He was not running, but he was younger and faster than I was, and unencumbered by high heels. "Henry!" I called. "Listen!" He turned once and smiled again.

Finally he stopped at a door and pulled it open. I knew it well; he was heading toward the Labyrinth. I hurried after him down the stairs. "Henry!" I shouted, running into the maze. "Henry!"

A light shone from somewhere, but I could not see my son at all. I turned into a room and caught my breath. A woman and a man sat at a table; between them on the table were jewels, coin pieces, chains, goblets, rings, all piled so high that the two could hardly see each other.

I had travelled the Labyrinth many times, of course, but I could not remember ever seeing this room. I hurried away. Corridors seemed to melt and flow around me; I found myself in a room where a woman lay unmoving on the bed. Her long red hair fanned out like the reflection of the sun setting on the ocean. No, I have promised to be honest in this, my testimony to you, Dorothy, and so I will say what I saw at the time. It seemed to me that her hair was a pool of blood. I ran toward the door, nearly stumbling in my haste.

I do not know how long I traversed the Labyrinth, coming upon one sight and then another, each more dreadful than the last. The feeling of power growing and focusing around me had gone. I understood that there was someone stronger than I in the maze now, that I was following the course he had laid out for me. My son Henry.

Once I thought I had found the first room again, but as I drew closer I saw that the woman and man were now skeletons, their clothes rotting on their frames. The riches lay undisturbed between them.

In the next room I nearly fell over someone crouching by the door. I stepped back, trying not to cry out. The man stood; it was Colonel Augustus Binder.

"What the devil are you doing here?" I asked.

He put his hand in his waistcoat pocket. "Forgive me, my lady," he said. "I saw you run into the Labyrinth and I presumed to follow you. What a place this is! It's changed enormously since my initiation, become a cave of wonders. Was this always here, and I blinded to it by my ignorance? Have I reached the next grade in the Order?"

His babble maddened me. He would not reach any grade if we did not find a way out; we would become two more skeletons, an enigmatic tableau for the next visitor to the maze.

Someone called out and I hurried towards the sound of the voice, certain it was Henry. "Where are you?" I shouted. The voice came again.

"Is this a test?" Augustus asked me, quivering with excitement.

"Quiet," I said. I listened for my son but he said nothing more. I made a guess as to where I had heard him last and reached out with my Gift. The wall in front of us collapsed.

"What!" Augustus said. "How did — how did — "

"Quiet," I said again.

I walked over the rubble. The next wall fell back, and the next. I pushed out at one more wall, and then I knew where Henry was. I stepped through a doorway and saw my son.

"What have you learned?" Henry asked.

I did not understand him. He said nothing more, but went through the entrance room and climbed the stairs in silence. I followed, puzzled and angry, as he led the way to Lady Dorothy's panelled dining room. The servants had already begun serving the first course. Henry turned towards Dorothy. "You'll have to send more builders into the labyrinth," he told her. He was smiling again. "I'm afraid a few of the walls were knocked down."

Augustus drew something from his waistcoat pocket. He looked disgusted, and I knew that he had stolen what he thought was a jewel from the Labyrinth. "We give power to the places we live in," my grandmother had said. Henry had added lustre to the jewel, but away from the Labyrinth it had become just an ordinary stone.

I refused to allow Henry, his wife Edwina, or his sister Florence to attend any more of our meetings. I did not know what my son had in mind with these outrageous interruptions, but I would not allow him to jeopardize everything I had worked for.

When we returned to London I tried to continue as before. I took care of the household for Harrison, read more of the books he had recommended as part of my education, entertained visitors, went to operas and flower shows. I hired a new maid, though I knew she was pregnant; I remembered my own plight so long ago, and how I would not have survived without Harrison's kindness.

One grim overcast day in June I left the house to have tea with Lady Dorothy, who had ventured to London for the first time in many years. It was difficult to make my way through the noise and crush of carriages and motorized vehicles and safety bicycles, all the impedimenta of this dreadful modern world. I could well understand why Dorothy preferred to stay safe at home.

I thought of Henry and his recent behaviour. He had not been to visit me since we had come back to London, and I missed him deeply. I remembered him as a small boy, his curiosity and laughter. I wondered why he had turned away from me.

I crossed the street to the tea shop. A horse-drawn bus hurried past, spraying my shoes with mud from the recent rains.

Lady Dorothy was waiting for me at the tea shop. I sat at her table and said something light about the dreadful London streets. I knew she must be feeling distressed at the dirt, the crowds, the pervasive smells of coal smoke and factory smoke and horse dung, and I wanted to put her at ease.

We ordered our tea and cakes. "Augustus said something very odd to me the other day," she said, patting her white hair and fiddling with her spectacles. "He said that you were the one who knocked down the walls in the Labyrinth. Well, I said. She hardly seems strong enough. I'm certain old Gus did it himself, but I don't understand why he would put the blame on you. It's not as if I can't repair it."

Our tea and cakes came, and I sipped so as not to have to answer. "He's furious about something," Dorothy said. "I don't know what it is exactly. He seems to think that we're hiding things from him, that he's due to reach another grade. He says you worked magic down in the Labyrinth, and he wants to know how you did it."

"What did you say?" I asked.

"Well. I said that I knew you had powers, and that we would all learn your secrets in our own good time. That we'll advance to a higher grade when you find us ready, and not before. I hope I did the right thing."

I nodded. "And then?"

"He became angrier. He said that he had been promised these secrets since joining the Order, thirty years ago. That he had been given nothing in all that time. That he had been ready to leave the Order but had recently seen proof of your magic, and now he wants to learn more. He even went so far as to threaten us with a lawsuit. Well, I told him. The Order must be kept secret. You wouldn't dare break the oaths you swore to us all those years ago, I said."

"What did he say to that?"

"He laughed. Not a very pleasant laugh, either. He asked me where Lydia was. I repeated what you and Harrison had said, that she had lost interest in the Order. He laughed again. 'Then why did Arton bring us a message from her?' he asked. Here, you've gone quite pale. Let me pour you some more tea."

"I don't know that we did receive a message from Arton," I said finally. "My son's been very strange lately."

"Has he? I hadn't noticed."

"Well, I am his mother—"

"He seems wise to me. As wise as you are, possibly. Do you remember what he said the last time he visited? He asked, 'What have you learned?' Mary says that every time we turn a corner in the Labyrinth we have learned something new. I thought it was very clever of him to remind us."

Henry had put his question to me in the Labyrinth, before

we had both come to supper; she could not possibly have heard him. Had he talked to Dorothy since then? But she was still speaking.

"Lydia, though," Dorothy said. "It's strange that he should mention Lydia, don't you think? Perhaps she's died. Has Harrison had any contact with her since she left him?"

"No."

"Well, then. Perhaps she's made the final turning of the Labyrinth. I hope she learned what she needed before she left us."

She patted her hair again. Something strange was happening to it; it was growing longer, wilder, redder. She held it up so that it seemed pinned, the fashion that Lydia had used. Then she brushed her skirts with the other hand and I heard the clink of the chatelaine around her waist, the chain with its burden of scissors, keys, smelling salts.

I was nearly frozen with fear. "What?" I said. "How —"

The apparition — she could not be Lydia — smiled at me. Then she changed into my son.

I stood, knocking over my teacup. The apparition had gone. I looked around wildly. A serving girl hurried to my side.

"Did you — did you see him?" I asked.

The girl looked around her. "Your friend, you mean?" she said. "The old lady with the white hair? She's gone, ain't she?"

"I don't know," I said. The girl looked at me oddly. I paid for the tea and left.

The next few weeks were horrible. Wherever I went, whatever I did, I could never be certain what was real and what a phantasm sent by my son. Fishmongers and flower-sellers, shop clerks and passersby would stop in the midst of what they were doing and speak nonsense or strange oracular phrases. "Turn your spectacles around," one said, "and look at the backs of things." "Doubt nothing, believe nothing," said another. And another: "Close your eyes and see."

In the middle of a bleak rainstorm a cab driver drove me through a forest of green oak and aspen, and then out into the city again so quickly I could not be certain of what I had seen. Another driver took me past a woman who looked exactly like Lydia, but when I shouted at him to stop I saw the woman fade and turn to mist. Once when my beloved Harrison put on an unfamiliar expression I nearly ran from the room. It was as if I were back in the Labyrinth, stumbling on fantastic scenes with every turn.

I tried, of course, to battle the illusions, to use my Gift to see what was real. But they were too powerful for me. I was the strongest of my family, but it seemed that in this one thing my son was stronger still.

I began to spend more and more time at home, sending servants to get the things I needed. I became short-tempered, ghost-ridden, seeing phantasms out of the corner of my eye. I stopped holding meetings of the Order at our house, and did not attend them when they were held elsewhere; Harrison went and told me how the seances had gone, how much I was missed. Poor Mary Frances did her best, speaking the rituals and reciting the messages from Arton, but everyone agreed that she lacked my Gift.

Our troubles multiplied. One day Harrison came home to tell me that the Order was under siege. Colonel Binder had demanded to see me, insisting that I teach him what he called the secrets of the Order. He claimed that we had promised him much when he had joined the Order, and that we had delivered nothing.

At the next meeting, Harrison reported, Colonel Binder had threatened to see a lawyer. If I did not meet with him, Binder had said, I would have to go to court to testify. The thought filled me with horror.

"Come with me to a meeting," Harrison urged me. "Better still, let us hold a meeting here, let us show Augustus that we are hiding nothing from him."

Dear, sweet Harrison! His head was filled with abstruse notions—labyrinths, initiations, pure and abstract knowledge. He had never wanted power of the sort that I had, preferring instead to make his way though ancient books and manuscripts. Dorothy's elaborate history of the Order, her Minoans and Atlanteans, had been constructed with Harrison's help. Sometimes I think that it simply did not occur to him that anyone would want to leave the library and use real power in the world.

I shook my head. "I can't," I said.

"Why not?"

I had not told him about our son's dreadful actions; I did not want to worry him. "Augustus wants power," I said finally. "And I can't give it to him. But if he doesn't get it, he will continue to think that we're deliberately obstructing him. Perhaps it would be for the best if he took us to court. What can he prove?"

"What did you promise him?" Harrison asked. "Did you put anything in writing?"

But I didn't know, couldn't remember. It had been so long ago.

All too soon what we feared came to pass. Binder brought suit against us, claiming, among other absurdities, that we had bilked him of five thousand pounds.

And as I feared, I was called to testify. I sat on the bench, waiting my turn, wondering when the judge or the lawyers or the spectators would melt away like phantoms, when the court would be revealed as just another exhibit in Dorothy's Labyrinth. Several times I unbuttoned my gloves and bit my nails to the quick.

During a recess Binder caught at my arm. I was appalled to see how much he had changed. Gone was the dignified gentleman I had met thirty years ago. The forked grey beard was now snarled in impossible tangles, and had turned completely white. His usually impeccable clothes were rumpled and soiled. He looked tense, haggard; the whites of his eyes were a dirty yellow. Worst of all, he was barefoot, oblivious to the shocked eyes of the court turned upon him; his obsession with telluric currents had quite overcome him.

"Tell me the secrets," he whispered hoarsely. "Tell me all, and I'll drop the suit."

I pushed his hand away. "Don't be foolish," I said. "You aren't ready for that kind of knowledge—your bad judgement in forcing this trial shows that much. We didn't ask you for money, and you didn't give us any, and we can prove that in open court. Don't think you can blackmail me."

"But that's exactly what I intend to do," he said. "When this trial is over the world will know all the secrets of the Order of the Labyrinth, all its rites and rituals. They'll know how you, a serving girl with two bastards, tried to rise far above your station. You won't be able to hold your head up anywhere in England. Or lay it down on a pillow, for that matter." He smiled nastily, and I knew that he was referring to my liaison with Harrison. "Unless, of course, you tell me how to move to the next grade."

If I could have told him, I swear I would have done so at that moment. I saw the damage he could do to us. But my Gift was my own, and not something that could be taught. "You are not ready to be trusted with such power," I said finally, and returned to my seat.

Everything happened as Binder said it would. He lost the suit, of course, but the rituals of the Order were revealed in court and published in the newspapers to great hilarity. The *Times* did not print the rest of the allegations Binder made, about my virtue and my life with Harrison, but other newspapers were not so kind. We were hounded by the press, jeered at when we went out. Members of the Order fell away; soon only Harrison, Dorothy, and Mary remained to attend the meetings. And Lady Dorothy, Harrison told me, was once again beginning to waver, to doubt everything I had told her.

Ruffians gathered at our house, shouting our names, taunting us with coarse insults, sometimes flinging mud and less savory things at our doorstep. Harrison had by this time lost his membership in his club and was driven nearly mad by their din; he finally took a flat in far-off Camden Town to have some peace. This stratagem counted for nothing, however, when he insisted on answering the letters that ridiculed us in the *Times*. The newspaper would not print his reply without an address; he was forced to give them the address of the flat to draw attention from our house, and so the mockers assembled there as well.

He hired a guard for the flat and began to hold our London meetings there. Once again he tried to convince me to come with him. Now that Colonel Binder had left us, Harrison said, it would be safe for me to attend the meetings. And Lady Dorothy missed me.

Because he desired it so plainly, and because I missed Lady Dorothy as well, I ventured out with him one evening. But as our brougham passed fields and ditches and came to gloomy, ill-lit streets a sadness descended upon me, a sadness that grew stronger as we continued past railway halls and taverns and almshouses. The place had not even received the new electricity; a solitary lamplighter walked the streets, setting his ten-foot taper to the lamps. The gaslights shivered as they caught.

Even more distressing was the occasional reminder of better days: carved facades now chipped and begrimed by soot, a marble portico or stone terrace, a once-beautiful garden run riot. I was reminded of a lady who used to attend meetings of the Order, a woman fallen on evil times. She had tried terribly hard to keep up appearances, but she could not see well enough to notice that all her dresses had faded to grey. It would break my heart when I saw where her seams had pulled apart, revealing the original colour of the material beneath.

"Is this what we've come to?" I asked Harrison. "This meanness?"

"Hush, my dearest," he said, laying his hand over mine.

There were signs on several of the windows: MADAME SOPHIA WILL ANSWER ALL YOUR QUESTIONS, LADY FATIMA KNOWS THE MYSTERIES OF THE EAST. This was a street of charlatans, where wretched frowzy women studied their tense hopeful clients over glass balls, where cloth from India hid the mechanisms of wheels and wire that worked their tawdry miracles. And I would be counted as one of them — I, who carried within me the true Gift of our family.

Our driver let us off at a house as squat and dark as all the others. Harrison nodded to the guard posted at the door and we went inside.

I stayed that evening, spoke my piece and comforted those in need of it, but I did not return. I would never attend a meeting of the Order again.

Many nights Harrison and I lay in bed, holding each other and waiting for the storm to pass over us, wondering if it had done its worst or if there were other trials awaiting us. Through it all Harrison continued to trust me. He was a very simple man in some ways; he had given his love to me as he had never given it to Lydia, and he would not withdraw that love.

One day I received a letter from an old member of the Order, Jack Frederick. Frederick had deserted with the others, unable to bear the public ridicule. In the letter he intimated that he would be willing to return if I could satisfy him on a few points. He did not believe the accusations of that scoundrel Gus Binder—he knew from his own experience that we had never asked any member for money—but he wanted the answers to a few questions.

I wrote him back, saying that I would be pleased to see him. Harrison, I knew, would be happy to welcome him back to the fold.

It was strange to venture from my house after so many months of solitude. A thick yellow fog hung over the streets and covered everything but the carriage lights, which shone out like strange pearls. People emerged from the depths and then passed, and were absorbed once again by the veils of smoke and soot. Sounds were muffled, faces blurred.

Of course I did not see the three men waiting for me around the corner. One pinioned my arms behind my back while another pushed me into a carriage that had been standing at the curb. I was too startled to call out, let alone to use my Gift. When I came to my senses I saw that I had been abducted by Augustus Binder, Jack Frederick, and another man I did not know. Despite the cold weather Augustus wore neither shoes nor stockings, and his trouser cuffs were badly stained with mud. The third man was tall and heavily muscled, a servant of some kind.

I was not unduly frightened. By this time I was so used to strange sights, to discontinuities in what I had thought of as real,

that I was nearly certain this was just another performance con-
trived by my son. The men would next say something incompre-
hensible, I thought, and then melt away. I studied them dispas-
sionately, as though they were waxworks.

Augustus drew a pistol from his coat pocket. At that moment
I began to feel fear, and I reached out with my Gift. These men
were real enough, not sent by my son as I had thought. I had
never faced a pistol before, did not know if I could.

Augustus said, "I want the secrets of your power. I have
waited long enough."

"You are not ready for them," I said.

He waved his pistol threateningly. "We have formed another
Order," he said. "Jack and I, and all the others who are tired of
waiting. We will have your secrets, and we will teach them to anyone who asks."

I shook my head, feeling out cautiously with my Gift. If I
could turn the pistol away, opening the carriage door at the same
time . . .

"We have recruited your son, Henry," Augustus said. I
looked at him sharply, and he smiled. "Ah, that frightens you.
Your son has this power as well, doesn't he? He's told us that you
and he quarrelled bitterly a few months ago. Is it any wonder he
should want to join us, to come over to our side?"

I felt real terror now. My heart was pounding so loudly I
could barely hear him. Was it true that Henry had joined these
men? Why would he want to? But I no longer understood anything my son chose to do. Why did he torment me with phantoms?
Why did he oppose me?

If Henry had cast his lot with these men there was nothing I
could do. In many things he was stronger than I; he had proved
that in a dozen confrontations.

"Henry has promised to share his power with us," Augustus
went on. "Unlike his mother, who continues to use hers for her own
selfish ends. We will be able to work wonders, to gain temporal
power in England—no, in the world—and spiritual power in

Arton's realm. There's no end to what we can do, really. Take a good look at me now — in a few years I will be prime minister, at the very least. And you — you'll be in prison, or deported in chains."

In desperation I pushed out with my Gift. I flung Augustus against the side of the carriage and opened the door on my side. The pistol shot towards the roof. The other men in the carriage blinked stupidly with surprise. I hurried outside and waved to a passing hansom cab.

I retired again to my bedroom and spent several days in my bed, prostrated by fear and worry. During the long hours alone I turned over in my mind everything Augustus had said. Prime minister. I had little doubt Henry could achieve that for him, and with Augustus's selfishness, his mania, I knew that the world would suffer greatly at his hands if he did. And I myself in prison, or deported . . .

I had to talk to Henry. It was one thing for him to frighten me with phantoms, another to promise his aid to this monstrous man. I sent him a letter summoning him to my bedroom.

A knock came at the door two days later. I reached out and saw with surprise that it was my son; I had not truly expected him to answer. "Come," I said. I sat up, ready to match wits with him.

"I've been thinking about magic," Henry said without preamble, setting his hat on my vanity table. He took a deck of cards from the hat and made them pass from hand to hand without looking at them. They seemed to flow, to be one thing, like a river. "Not old Dorothy's magick, with that pretentious archaic spelling, but lies. Illusions."

"Illusions," I said. "I've seen more illusions than I like, these past few months. Why have you set yourself against me?"

He seemed not to hear me. "We could travel, you and I and Florence. We could perform magic shows all over England. People would flock to see us."

"You're mad," I said.

He thrust the deck of cards at me. "Pick a card," he said.

"No."

"Very well, then, I'll pick one. Now I'll guess what it is. Jack of spades. I'm good, don't you think? I even amaze myself sometimes."

"What are you doing? What do you want?"

"I want you to pick a card."

I took one, if only to silence him. "Two of hearts," he said.

"Of course. You or I could do that in our sleep. Florence too, probably."

"We could, but no one else can. People would pay, and pay well, to see us."

"I don't understand you. Why should we perform tricks for gaping fools? What is the meaning of these strange fancies?"

"Meaning?" he asked softly. He sat at my vanity table, studying his face in the mirror. Suddenly he pushed aside my silver-backed brushes and combs, my tinctures and perfumes, with his arm. He set his cards on the table one by one, some flat, some on their side. "Do illusions, do lies, have a meaning?" He balanced a card on top of a layer of others. "Sometimes they do, I suppose. The lies you tell Dorothy about her husband, for example."

"What of them? What harm have I done? You're too young to remember, but there was a time when Lady Dorothy refused to leave her house. If I can make her life a little happier —"

"And enrich yourself in the process —"

"Listen to me," I said. "I'm about to tell you some unpleasant truths."

"Oh, don't, please. I'd much rather hear pleasant lies."

I ignored him. "When Lydia left, your father lost a great deal of money," I said. I had never told him this, did not know how much he had guessed. "His finances have never really recovered — our life here has been more precarious than you ever supposed. Lady Dorothy has been extraordinarily generous, has helped us many times over. In exchange I give her messages from her husband. If she ever withdrew her support we might as well move to the poorhouse. We might as well travel like gipsies, performing that magic show you're so crazy for."

He smiled; I saw his gapped teeth in the mirror. "I ask for lies, and lies are what I get," he said. "Lydia didn't leave Harrison. And you've already admitted you never gave Dorothy messages from her husband."

"You have benefitted from what I've done as much as any. I was a laundress, and look at you—you've gone to away to university—"

"In America, since no school in England would admit a laundress's bastard." He set down another card. "And most people still snub us in the streets."

"In America, yes. What of it? If not for Lady Dorothy you would be in service by now, a butler or a coachman. And they snub us because of that madman Colonel Binder and his suit—"

"Binder's suit has nothing to do with it. They never spoke to us before that, because you were a serving girl and not even married to the father of your children."

"Why are you so quick to come to Binder's defence? He threatened me with a pistol, did you know that? And yet you see the justice of his position, and you won't see mine."

Henry looked up from the house of cards he was constructing and turned slowly towards me. I sensed that he was at a loss, and I pressed my advantage without quite knowing what it was. "I've lied to Lady Dorothy, yes," I said. "But you have done far worse by agreeing to help Binder and his friends."

"Have I?"

"Of course. What were you thinking of, promising Binder he would become prime minister? Don't you realise how much harm the two of you can do?"

"You've misunderstood my question. Have I agreed to help Binder?"

"Haven't you? He claims you did."

"But have I?"

I reached out with my Gift. For the first time in my life I could read nothing at all. Henry smiled infuriatingly. Had Binder lied to me? Why had I been so quick to imagine the worst of my son?

Could it be that he had not turned away from me after all?

"You haven't joined Colonel Binder and his friends," I said.

He nodded. He looked at me as a teacher might study an apt pupil, waiting for something.

"You haven't turned against me," I said. "Binder lied about you, to frighten me." He nodded again. "But then why did you send me all those apparitions? Why did you frighten me nearly to death?"

He set down a last card. "Lies," he said. "Lies and truth. And illusion, which can be used in the service of either." He pulled out a card from the bottom layer of the house he had fashioned. Impossibly, the house remained standing. He grinned, and the cards fell in a heap.

"I think I see," I said slowly. "Our house here, everything I have built, is based on illusions. Illusions I have created in the service of lies."

"The lies you told Dorothy about her husband," Henry said. "And the lies you told about Lydia." He paused. "A few months ago Father told me something about how Dorothy had helped us. After I left him I went over the account books without his knowledge. I was not aware that the deception had gone on for so long, or that it had involved such a large amount of money. If it continues Dorothy will lose her house, and everything she has. She may be in danger even now."

"So the illusions you created were in the service of truth, the truth about our position here," I said. "They frightened me, yes, but you meant them to make me think, to shake me up a bit." I laughed, a little breathless. "I have — I have explored another turning of the Labyrinth."

My son laughed too. He retrieved the cards, put on his hat, and walked out.

After he had gone I spent a long time thinking about the things he had said. I thought of the serving girl I had been, the brown innocent maid from the country. When had wealth started to matter to me, and position? I remembered the man and woman in the Labyrinth, their riches piled so high on the table between them that they could barely see each other, and I understood that they were Harrison and myself, that our money had become more important to us than the enjoyment of each other's company. And I remembered what had become of those two figures in the tableau, their bodies picked to skeletons.

I thought of lies, and of truth. At first I had lied to Dorothy in order to save her, to rescue her from her prison of brick and glass. But when Harrison had lost all that money I continued the deception in part because she was so generous to us—and I had done it without thinking, with my only aim that of preserving our fortune. Was it lying to tell Lady Dorothy the things she most wanted to hear? Was it lying to tell her those things for profit? She had made a thousand decisions based on what I had told her about her husband. Shouldn't those decisions have been made clearly, from truth?

And what of Colonel Binder? Had I truly promised him what he claimed in court, power and wealth? His presence at our meetings, a respected military man, had added to our prestige. Could I have offered him these things to urge him to stay, things I had no intention of giving him?

How had I changed so, over the years? Gradually, and without noticing it, I had become seduced by wealth, by position. This is my testament to you, Dorothy my friend, so you will have no doubt noticed how many times I referred to you as "Lady." And yet we were friends, with the friendship of equals. I was intoxicated by that word "Lady," as intoxicated as I was by Harrison's title. Lord Harrison. I even wrote, on scraps of paper, "Lady Emily Sanderson." Oh, I was seduced, truly I was!

Henry was right. Riches and power count for little. What matters lies beyond that: self-knowledge, self-mastery, a world outside our narrow lives here. I saw that this was precisely what I had tried to teach Dorothy when I had urged her to leave her house, and I understood as well that such things cannot be taught directly. They have to be shown, as my son had shown me, as I could show others.

In addition, our position in England was becoming intolerable. Colonel Binder and his cronies had not exhausted their store of malice; we were in very real danger from them. And Dorothy — I owed it to you, Dorothy, to tell you the truth.

I spent a long time alone with these thoughts. And at the end of it I decided on many things. I called my family to me, my son Henry and his wife Edwina, my daughter Florence, my lover Harrison. It was dangerous to stay here, I told them, faced with Colonel Binder's viciousness; it was always dangerous to offer power and not deliver it. Binder had waited thirty years to make his move, and that only because he had never been certain of the extent of my Gift. Foolishly, I had shown him what I could do that day in the Labyrinth.

We discussed various alternatives, and finally we decided to emigrate to America. We spent a giddy day choosing new names for each of us, making certain that Binder would never find us. I understood from the books Harrison had given me that America was an invented country, a state of mind. And so we picked invented names, the stranger the better: I changed into Neesa Allalie, Henry turned into Verey, Florence into Lanty. Henry and Edwina's daughters, who were then three and two, became Thorne and Fentrice.

I will send you money from America, as much as I can. When I first met you I was still, in many ways, an ignorant farm girl. I knew nothing of finances; I thought that lords and ladies had money and the common people had none, and that this was the way it had been and would always be. The only way I knew to get money for Harrison and my children was to accept it when you offered. I've learned a great deal since then. When you can see a little ways into the future, making investments becomes remarkably easy. I will try to give you back everything I owe you.

And I wrote this book, which I will have delivered to you, Dorothy, when I am gone. And I did the one last, necessary thing I told you of, and then we went to America.

SEVEN

Uncle Sam

Molly finished reading. "Wait a minute, wait a minute," John said, writing quickly. "Neesa, Verey, Lanty. Fentrice, Thorne. There, we found her—Thorne. But what happened to Callan? And Lydia?"

"Callan was born in America," Molly said, taking out the genealogy she had sketched on the back of Andrew Dodd's article from the *Tribune*. It had become smudged and torn, tattered at the edges.

"All right, but what about Lydia? Where did she go? Emily apparently saw her in the labyrinth, thought that her hair looked like a pool of blood. Was that her guilty conscience speaking?"

"What—you think she killed her? First you have my aunt kill Thorne, and now my great-great-grandmother kills Lydia? You really think we're a bloodthirsty bunch, don't you? I suppose Fentrice came all the way from Illinois to kill that man in the storefront, Joseph Ottig. I mean, she's only eighty-seven."

John held up his hand. "Of course not. But what did happen to Thorne? We have Emily's own testimony that Thorne and Fentrice were sisters."

Molly hesitated. "I don't know," she said finally.

"Could your aunt have lied to you?" John asked.

"Maybe. Maybe she did. But what do I do now? Go back and confront her? Maybe Thorne died, and if I asked Fentrice to talk about her death it would bring back unpleasant memories. She isn't young—she's—"

"Eighty-seven. You told me." He paged back through his notebook. "What was the one last thing Emily did before she left for America, I wonder?"

"But look how much we know," Molly said. She took a pen from her purse and added the names Emily had listed to her genealogy. She hesitated, wrote *"Thorne"* and a question mark. "The family left England because Emily had a change of heart, because she and her son wanted to use their talents to help others. That's why they became traveling magicians—not because they'd come down in the world, but because they wanted to teach. Look what they did for Andrew Dodd, for example—he stopped drinking after he interviewed them, married and settled down and raised a family."

"You're giving them an awful lot of credit," John said. "The way I see it, they left because Colonel Binder threatened them, and because they'd been ridiculed in the papers. And maybe because Dorothy stopped giving them money. Dorothy and Emily obviously had a falling-out—Dorothy moved Emily's window, the Capricorn window. In Emily's book she says you can see the sun shining through it."

"I bet she moved the window because Emily finally told her the truth—that she'd never gotten any messages from her husband. We know Emily managed to deliver the book to her because we found it in the library. Imagine how Dorothy must have felt when she read it."

"Angry at being duped, probably. Emily practically admits she did it for the money."

"But then she says that what she did was wrong. She apologizes, she offers to send her money—"

"And a lot of good that did after Dorothy squandered her fortune on Emily and her family."

"We don't know she squandered—"

"She lost the house a few years later. Maybe she'd had to bail out Emily and Harrison one time too many."

"Oh, I don't know," Molly said, suddenly angry. "I still think Emily was a good person. She hired that maid who was pregnant, for example, and she did try to help Dorothy, at least in the beginning. No one's perfect. I mean, look at you. You stole that book from the Westingates."

"Yeah, and we'd better put it back before someone steals it from us again. We'll Xerox it tomorrow and then invite ourselves back to Applebury and sneak it into the library. And let's hope no one notices those three or four pages are missing."

"Didn't the police tell us to stay in London?"

"What—you think they're going to follow our every move? We'll go up for the day, come back before they even have time to suspect we're gone."

That night, as Molly closed her eyes to sleep, she saw the wax figure of Lydia lying on the bed, her red hair fanning out from her face. What had happened to Lydia? Emily might have taken money from Dorothy, but she would never commit murder—of that Molly was fairly certain. But it had shaken her more than she would admit to John to see Thorne's name in Emily's journal.

John's plan worked better than they had hoped. He called the Westingates from London and set up an appointment, and they took the train to Canterbury and a cab to Applebury. During another tour of the house John excused himself to go to the bathroom; when he came back he nodded to Molly slightly. The book had been returned to the library.

They left Tantilly feeling giddy. "Oh, God," Molly said. "I can't believe we got away with it."

John reached for his notebook, stopped in the act of taking it out. "Don't look around. There's a man behind that hedge over there."

"Not Flat Cap again. No, it couldn't be—Flat Cap's dead. Who is it?"

"I don't know. Don't go after him — Molly!"

"Hey, it worked the last time," Molly called over her shoulder. But the man was leaving the safety of the hedge and walking quickly toward her. He had a sharp narrow face, a pointed nose. His right hand was tucked into his jacket pocket. Was he holding a gun?

"Hello," Molly said. "Do you want to talk to us?"

"That's right," the man said as he came nearer. He sounded almost cheerful, as if he was doing them a favor.

"Why?" John asked, coming up next to Molly.

"You returned something to the Westingates, didn't you? What was it? It looked like a book."

"What difference does it make?"

"None, really. Except that I think a man named Joseph Ottig had the book before you, and he's dead now. The police would be interested in that, don't you think? Your fingerprints over Ottig's, on stolen property? And then there's the fact that you were told to stay in London after Ottig's murder."

"Who are you?" Molly asked. "Why are you threatening us?"

"Well, for one thing I'd like to know what was in the book and why you took it. They didn't give it to you, that's for sure. Charles Westingate would sooner part with the family silver than let a book out of his sight. Odd, when you consider that he doesn't even read much."

"Why do you want to know?"

"I'm interested in the Order of the Labyrinth. The secrets of their power. I shouldn't like to resort to blackmail, but I thought it best to put my cards on the table before we begin. You tell me about the book and I don't go to the police."

"You and Ottig weren't working together," Molly said slowly. "He must have hidden the book for safekeeping and then wouldn't tell you where it was. And so — " She stopped. *And so you killed him,* she had been about to say, but it would be dangerous to let him know she knew that.

"Very good," the other man said. "Now tell me what was in the book."

"Why don't you just steal it yourself?" Molly said.

"Never you mind why."

"You tried something in Lord Westingate's house and he caught you at it. Is that it?"

"Never you mind, I said. You tell me what you know, or I'll talk to the police."

"Go to the police, then," Molly said. "I'll bet you have a criminal record. I'll bet your relationship with them isn't as cozy as you'd like us to believe."

"You'd bet that, would you?" the man said. "Would you bet a lengthy stay in prison on it? I'll give you a day to think about it." He still sounded cheerful; anyone watching them would have thought he had just concluded a tremendously profitable transaction. "I'll be waiting for you at the shop in Camden Town tomorrow. Bring your notes."

The cab they had called was pulling up to the circular drive. They hurried toward it and got in. Molly looked back and saw the man taking his hand out of his pocket. She braced herself for a noise, a shot, but the hand was empty.

John directed the cab to the train station. "God," Molly said. "Flat Cap wasn't the only one. We're still being followed. Are we going to see this guy tomorrow?"

"No."

"But then—"

"We're going to leave the country."

"Leave?"

"If he goes to the police they'll check Emily's book, find the torn pages. We're foreigners, Americans, who might have damaged historical British property. We'd be in trouble, especially since we were questioned in a murder investigation."

"But the police told us to stay. Won't they have our names on a list at the airport or something?"

"I'd rather take that chance than stay here. They may have our names, but on the other hand there's this crazy person with damaging information and a gun—"

"He had a gun, then. He was the one who shot Flat Cap."

"I'm pretty sure, yes."

"And then what? What do we do when we get home?"

"Go talk to your aunt. Fentrice."

"I don't want to bother—"

"Molly. She lied to you about her sister. She's got information I need. I'll have to talk to her sometime."

"Okay," Molly said suddenly. "Okay, I'll introduce you. On one condition: you let me meet your client."

"You know I can't do that."

"Fine. Then we're not going to see her."

"Don't you want to know what happened to your family?"

"Not badly enough to hurt my aunt. First I have to see your client, find out why he's pursuing this."

"I'll tell you what," John said. "I'll ask him. If he says yes then I'll set up a meeting."

"And if he says no?"

"Then I won't."

"Then you'll never meet Fentrice."

"Look. I can probably find the information I need some other way. It would just be easier—"

"You know, I haven't been too impressed with what you've done so far. You found Emily's journal, yes, but then you lost it again. You managed to get us involved in a murder, and you're more vulnerable than anyone else would be because you have a police record. Now we've got to leave the country before we're really finished here—"

"We're finished."

"All right. You call your client and get back to me."

"I will."

They woke hours before dawn the next morning. It was chilly, and the streetlights outside their bed and breakfast turned everything the same flat gray. They said very little to each other as they checked out and rode the underground to the airport.

A car bomb had exploded the day before, and lines at the airport moved slowly as inspectors checked through luggage and questioned passengers. To her surprise Molly and John were waved through without a second glance.

"I guess we don't look very suspicious," Molly whispered.

"Yeah. There's nothing less suspicious than someone whispering in front of a police inspector."

Molly said nothing. John was angry at something, she knew. The fact that he had not yet discovered the answer to Thorne's disappearance? The fact that she had placed conditions on introducing him to Fentrice? She didn't know, and she didn't much care. She had called Peter's hotel the night before and left a message with her flight number; perhaps he would be waiting for her at the airport.

But Peter wasn't there when they landed in San Francisco. She tried not to feel disappointed. He was probably busy or out of town—he had work to do, after all.

"I'll let you know what my client thinks," John said at the luggage carousel.

"Okay," Molly said. Her bag came around on the carousel and she reached for it, slung it over her shoulder. " 'Bye." It was an oddly unsatisfying end to what had promised to be an exciting adventure. She wondered if she would ever see John again.

The next day she went to the temp agency and signed up for new assignments. Peter's voice was waiting for her on the answering machine when she returned home. "Hey, Moll," he said. "I'm in town. Give me a call—we'll go out to dinner."

She called him back and then drove to their usual restaurant. His face was smooth; he was at the stage in his three-day cycle where he had just shaved. She kissed him and sat at the table. "What's new?" she asked. "How's it going?"

"Just got back from my publisher in New York," Peter said. "The latest deal fell through. I thought the idea was a natural, but they disagreed. Someone's doing an authorized biography, apparently, and they didn't want an unauthorized one."

"So what are you going to do?"

"Oh, I've got plenty of ideas. There's no shortage of celebrities out there, and no shortage of people with nothing better to do than to read about them."

Molly frowned. She had noticed this before, the contempt that Peter felt for his readers.

"How about you?" Peter asked. "How are you doing?"

"I went to England," Molly said. "Remember? I told you about that guy —"

"Right. The private investigator. How did that go?"

"Pretty good. I learned some things about my family, my great-great-grandmother —"

Peter wasn't listening. Put like that it did sound dull, like a home movie or something. How could she convey to him the strangeness of the trip, the feeling of moving down tangled corridors toward unexpected sights and revelations?

"There was this guy, a lord in a castle who wears leather pants and listens to Tibetan bells, has a labyrinth in his basement. And then I found a dead body. We were actually involved in a police investigation for a while."

"That doesn't sound very healthy. What do you know about this investigator, anyway? What's he been getting you into?"

"Well, it certainly wasn't his fault that someone got killed."

Peter raised his hand. Molly realized that she had spoken louder than she meant to; a few of the other diners were looking at her curiously. "Did you see his credentials?" Peter asked.

"I saw his license, if that's what you mean."

"Did you sleep with him?"

She should have been angered by the question. Instead she felt a rush of evil pleasure that she had roused him to jealousy. "No," she said levelly.

Peter looked down at his menu and said nothing. Molly cast around for something to say. "How long are you staying in town?" she asked.

"About a week, at least. I need to make some inquiries, send out some letters. Then I've got to get back to New York, pitch a few ideas."

There was another awkward pause. For the first time in a long while Molly remembered John and his strange bits of knowledge, the way he had discussed the Oneida commune and their silverware at the airport. She picked up her fork and turned it over. "*Stainless Korea,*" it said. She sighed.

Over the next few days the events in England receded, faded into memory. They seemed like something that had happened years ago, or to another person. She fought jet lag, found another temp job, went out to dinner and movies with Robin Ann and other friends. She wrote a long letter to her aunt and read the letter Fentrice sent in return, filled with chatty gossip about the garden and the strange things Estelle had done lately. She waited for messages from Peter, felt her heart race as she rewound her answering machine tape.

One day on her lunch break she went to the Oakland library for books on the occult. All the interesting-sounding ones had been checked out or lost, and she turned away from the computer terminal in frustration.

Well, but she and John knew, more or less, what had happened to the Order of the Labyrinth. It was when Emily and Harrison and their children came to America that the trail had disappeared. She typed in "Vaudeville," and the word conjured up dozens of books on the screen.

She went to the shelves and checked out a few of the likely-looking ones. That evening, waiting for Peter to call, she began to read.

The magicians known as the Allalie Family, like most vaudeville performers in the early part of the century, traveled on their own from town to town (she read). The act at that time consisted of Neesa Allalie and her children Verey and Lanty. They played fairgrounds, beer halls, civic centers, school auditoriums. As their fame spread their bookings grew, they began to get noticed by the local critics, and finally, in 1916, they signed on the Orpheum Circuit with E. F. Albee.

Magicians in vaudeville were not as popular as comedians or jugglers or even female impersonators. Harry Houdini, who started his career as a magician, soon found that it was his spectacular escapes that would draw the crowds. But the Allalie Family managed to succeed where others had failed. Perhaps it was their air of having come from somewhere else (other performers spoke vaguely of their "British accents"), perhaps the fact that they refused to condescend to their audiences.

From all contemporary accounts, though, the Allalie Family had more to offer their audiences than the run-of-the-mill sideshow. They never filmed their act for posterity, so at this late date we can only guess what the difference was. Alexander Woollcott, writing in the New York *World* in 1926, speaks of "the poetry of their performances, the sense that they are not acting but presenting a sonnet or sestina. There is an inevitability to their actions, so that when we watch we find ourselves nodding in agreement, not amazement. Of course the woman turns into a tree, of course the stars fall into the lake and become swans, of course, of course . . ."

"My father took me to see the Allalie Family at the Palace Theatre when I was ten," the actress Lucy Benham writes in her autobiography. "When the curtains closed and the lights came up I felt as though I had been rudely slapped, dragged from a world where I belonged into some pale, inferior copy. Wherever they came from, the Allalies, it was where I was meant to be, it was my true home. That was the afternoon I realized I would be an actress."

"They were from England, I think," Michael Claudine, another magician of the day, said. (There was a footnote here, and Molly, turning to the back of the book, read "Conversation with the author, May, 1971.") "They had that accent, anyway. There were a lot of them, more every time you turned around, fathers and mothers and aunts and uncles and cousins. They kept to themselves a lot — I don't think they even joined the Society of American Magicians. I never saw them at the society dinners, anyway.

"They were good magicians, though, I'll grant you that. One day I started rehearsing with them on the train ride out west. There wasn't much to do during these jumps—people would sit on those hard seats of woven straw and write letters or argue politics or practice their instruments or play poker.

"I held out my deck of cards and asked the guy next to me, the sword swallower and fire-eater, to pick one. 'You're holding a red card,' I said to him. 'No, wait, a black one. A face card.'

"All the time I talked I watched his eyes. Your eyes dilate when I guess the right card—you can't help it. All I have to do is ask a few questions, narrow it down.

"I did this with a few other people in the car and then turned to one of the Allalies, Verey I think his name was. And I could not get a fix on him, I could not guess what card he'd chosen. Well, finally he showed me how he did it. What he'd done was to bite down on his tongue, and that had kept his eyes dilated the whole time.

"We talked a bit after that. I remember mentioning the prize of $2,500 that *Scientific American* had offered for psychic phenomena produced under their control. This was in 1922 or thereabouts—that was a lot of money in those days. I wanted to claim that prize, get out of vaudeville for good. I thought I could work up some trick, hoodwink the muck-a-mucks at the magazine.

" 'And do you believe in psychic phenomena?' Verey asked me.

" 'Of course not,' I said. I'd never seen anything to convince me, anyway. One of the Allalie children was listening closely while I talked. Corrig, was that his name? Something like that, anyway.

"Well, in the middle of what I was saying this Corrig flew— I mean literally flew—out across the car, did a few somersaults, burst into flame, and then flew back. I couldn't believe it. I combed the passenger car for days, looking for wires, for mirrors, for some kind of explanation. Finally I even went against the protocol of the Society of Magicians and asked Corrig outright how he'd done it, but he just shrugged and grinned. Later, when we got to San Francisco, I cornered Verey and his sister Lanty and asked them. 'Trickery,' Verey said, and Lanty said, 'Illusion.' "

Even today professional magicians are at a loss to explain some of the tricks that were performed by the Allalie Family. In one contemporary newspaper account Verey Allalie steps on to the stage, takes off his top hat, and draws out stars, which he throws to the ceiling. Then he takes out a crescent moon, far larger than the hat itself, and hangs it from the sky, where it sheds a blue-white light. The moon tilts, becomes a jug; water pours to the stage. The water becomes a lake, lit by the moon and stars. Ripples appear in the water; a woman emerges from the lake and draws it around her shoulders like a cape. The stage is left completely dry.

Other newspaper articles speak of people becoming statues, statues becoming tigers. Dancers changed their shapes as easily as they changed their places, turning to animals, chairs, pianos, and cellos. And all of this was done, not hidden behind curtains or in-side boxes, but out in the open, in the light, and in full view of the audience.

The Allalie Family differed from the rest of the vaudeville acts in other ways as well. "Everyone wanted to play Albee's Palace in New York," said Claudine. "That was the pinnacle, the top of the profession. But the Allalie Family didn't seem to care. Some acts would say they'd already played in palaces in Europe, before real royalty, that it didn't matter to them what Albee thought. We kept waiting for the Allalies to boast about something like that. If you could believe it of anyone you'd believe it of them, with their high-class accents. But like I said, they kept to them-selves pretty much. And they did make the Palace — they got there before I did."

In the twenties and thirties Neesa Allalie's grandchildren joined the act, and musicians and stagehands were hired as needed. But like so many others in vaudeville the Allalie Family could not compete with talking motion pictures, and they performed their last disappearing act sometime in the 1930s, leaving the stage for-ever.

* * *

John called a few days later. "Hey, John," Molly said. "Good to hear from you."

"Is it?"

Molly laughed. "I guess we didn't part on such good terms," she said. "But I was just thinking of you. Did you find out anything new?"

"Yeah. It looks like I owe you an apology."

"Great. For what?"

"Someone in England was able to find me proof of Lydia's death. She died in 1913. Emily and Harrison were in the United States by then—they immigrated in 1910."

"So they didn't kill her."

"No. She must have left the Order, just as Emily said. Emily probably felt guilty over taking Harrison away from her, nothing more."

"I knew she wasn't a bad person."

"I wouldn't go that far. She still bilked Dorothy out of a lot of money—Well, let's not get into that."

"Did you ever find the missing three pages from the journal?"

"No. I had an idea Ottig might have mailed them to himself, so I tracked down his last known address. Nothing. And my contact in England looked all over for them, too. Searched the storefront from top to bottom, checked out all the places Ottig had stayed—"

"Too bad. I have a feeling we'll find all the answers if we just find those pages."

"Another feeling? Well, that's not why I called. What I wanted to tell you is that my client asked to talk to you."

"Your client? That's terrific. Can you tell me more about him?"

"Yeah. Are you sitting down?"

"Yeah, why?"

"You've got more relatives than you thought. Your grandfather, Callan, had two children. One was your mother, Joan. The other was a man named Samuel Allalie. Your uncle."

"Oh my God. Uncle Sam?"

"Yeah. He wanted to know what happened to Joan, his sister. She apparently left him and her parents, disappeared off the face of the earth as far as they knew. I traced her to Fentrice and then found you. He'd never heard of you."

"I never heard of him either. So the inheritance—"

"Callan had apparently always told Sam that Fentrice had taken some money, but that wasn't the important thing. He wanted to know what happened to Joan, what happened to Fentrice and Thorne. I couldn't tell you about him so I used the inheritance as a reason for digging into the past."

"You knew—you knew I have an uncle, and you never told me? Does he have any kids?"

"Two. Your cousins."

"Cousins. And you never told me."

"I couldn't. Professional ethics. You can see that, can't you?"

"You're a cold man, John Stow. Didn't you at least want to say something?"

"A couple times, yeah. So when do you want to meet him?"

"As soon as I can. Tomorrow's Saturday—what about then?"

"All right. He wants to meet you too. Your place?"

"Sure."

"Okay. Bye."

"Hold on," Molly said urgently. "Tell him to bring pictures of his kids!"

"All right. See you then."

She hung up. An uncle. An uncle and cousins. She smiled to herself.

It was only when she had gotten into bed that she wondered why he had lost touch with her mother, and with Fentrice. Did they have some sort of falling-out? And why had Fentrice never said anything?

* * *

Peter let himself into his hotel room. He sank wearily to the bed, resting his head against the wall and putting his feet up on the covers, and took the phone into his lap. He hesitated a moment and then dialed his editor in New York.

"Listen," he said when the editor answered. "Listen, I think I've got something. That famous actress in the thirties, Lucy Benham, she had an illegitimate child. And here's the thing: the kid became an actress too. Only no one knows they're related."

There was silence on the other end.

"Don't you see?" Peter said. "I could write about both of them. It's two books in one, really. And the kid's still alive. I've found someone who knows her, says she's ready to talk."

"No one remembers these people, Peter," the editor said.

"Sure they do. They're on TV all the time, on cable."

"Okay, they remember them, but no one cares about them. An illegitimate child? Everyone has one or two nowadays—it's no big deal."

"Yeah, but I could recreate the atmosphere of the thirties in the book, show what a big shock it was at the time."

"I don't think I'd be interested, Peter."

"But—"

"Now if one of them murdered someone, that would be something," the editor said. "That's what sells books these days."

They talked a little more and then Peter hung up. If one of them murdered someone, he thought, shaking his head in disgust. Wait a minute. Who was it who had told him about finding a dead body recently? Molly, that's right. Molly was on to something in England. Peter reached for his legal pad and pen on the nightstand and began taking notes.

EIGHT
Disappearing Acts

Molly's first thought was that Samuel Allalie had the family look she had come to recognize. He was short and muscular, and when he smiled he showed the same gapped teeth they all seemed to have. He transferred the backpack he was carrying to his other shoulder and shook her hand warmly.

"I'm Sam Allalie," he said. "I'm glad to meet you, Molly. Finally."

"So am I," she said, showing him and John into her apartment. "Sit down, please. Would you like some tea? Or biscuits?"

He smiled again. "My grandparents used to offer guests tea and biscuits. It's a British custom, I think."

"My aunt Fentrice does it. Not that she gets very many visitors besides her bridge club."

"Aunt Fentrice. So she's still alive."

Molly blinked in surprise. "Very much so. Didn't you know?"

"No. She left the family and never said a word to anyone after that. We looked for her for years — " Samuel turned to John. "Our family's very good at finding people, but she seemed to have disappeared completely. How did you find her?"

"I'm very good at finding people," John said.

"John—" Molly said.

"I know how to use a computer, and how to tie into databases across the country," John said. "Driver's licenses, social security cards—"

"Aunt Fentrice never learned to drive," Molly said. "Lila does all her errands. And I don't think she ever got a social security card either. She started working long before you needed one."

"No, but you know what she does have? A credit card."

"A credit card?" Molly said, amazed. "Fentrice?"

John laughed. "That's right. Uses it pretty heavily, too. I got her address and phone number from that and tried calling a few times. She wouldn't talk to me, so I decided to go after Molly here instead."

"Well," Samuel said. "So Fentrice is still alive. But John told me that Joan and Bill died in a car accident. I'm sorry, Molly."

"Thank you. You're her—you're my mother's brother, aren't you? What was she like?"

"A lot like Fentrice and Thorne, I gather. Wild, determined to go her own way. And she left the family just like Fentrice did, though I never knew she had had a child. Or that she found Fentrice. I wonder how."

Samuel looked at John, who shrugged. "There's a lot about this family I don't know," John said.

"Like what happened to Thorne. Like why Joan left the family—or why Fentrice did, for that matter."

"I'm going to interview Fentrice next."

"Great," Samuel said.

"Don't get your hopes up," Molly said. "Fentrice doesn't see too many people. I said I'd ask her if she'll talk to John, that's all."

"I'll wish you luck," Samuel said. "Oh, and I brought this. Maybe it'll help." He opened his backpack and drew out a large leather book, brown and stained with ink and coffee cup rings. "This is my father Callan's journal."

"*Callan's* . . ." Molly said. She reached for the book, held it reverently. The cover, she noticed, was made of imitation leather and cracked in several places. "Was there anyone in this family who didn't keep a journal?"

Samuel laughed. "I never have," he said.

"Did you know about this?" Molly asked John.

John nodded.

"I told him," Samuel said. "I wasn't sure I wanted anyone else to read it, but now I think it might help."

"What else are you hiding from me?" Molly asked John.

"Nothing," John said. "We all know each other's secrets now. Unless there's something you haven't told me."

"I don't have any secrets," Molly said.

She opened to the first page. There were no ruled lines on the pages; it looked like an artist's sketchbook. Callan's writing, unlike Emily's, was sharp and spiny. " 'January 2, 1935,' " she read aloud. " 'Thorne gave me this book for Christmas.' " She looked up at Samuel. "This is wonderful. Thank you so much."

John held out his hand for the book.

"I'll start reading it right away," she said.

"You —" John said.

Molly smiled as sweetly as she could. "I am a member of the family, after all." She turned to Samuel. "Did you bring pictures of your children?"

"Yes, I did." Samuel took out his wallet and opened it. "That's Kate, and that's Elizabeth," he said, pointing to a photograph. "And this is my wife — she's also named Elizabeth."

"They're beautiful," Molly said. "Didn't you want to name them something stranger? Like Verey and — what was it? — Lanty?"

Samuel smiled. "Read the book," he said.

January 2, 1935. Thorne gave me this book for Christmas. I think she intended for me to draw costumes and stage settings for our shows, but I've always wanted to keep a diary. Our life seems very unsettled, compared to the lives of the people we play for — we move constantly from place to place, from theater to auditorium to county fair. After a while the cities and towns seem as alike as the rows of planted corn we see from the train, each succeeding the other in fanlike waves. I hope this book will give me a way of fixing places in my memory.

My father Verey thinks this is a bad idea. We shouldn't leave traces for anyone to follow, he says. He's become almost obsessed as he's grown older, thinking constantly about the old business with Dorothy Westingate and the Order of the Labyrinth.

I tell him not to worry. All that happened in another country, and before I was even born. He looks at Grandmother Neesa, but she is busy playing pool and says nothing.

I'm glad for that. If she'd joined in, my diary would have become the subject of another loud and argumentative family meeting, what Verey and Lanty call a row. They pronounce it to rhyme with "how" — it was years before I realized that this was a British expression and not an American one.

January 3, 1935. The words I wrote yesterday were prophetic. Today at the family meeting there's another row, this one brought on when Thorne and I broach the subject of making a motion picture. The live theaters are disappearing one by one, we can all see that. Only a remnant is left of the old vaudeville circuits Verey and Lanty knew. But Aunt Lanty says that no one would believe in magic on film — there are too many tricks that can be done with a camera. We need that excitement from the audience, their gasps and shouts of surprise. But what will we do when there are no more live theaters? Thorne asks. Even the Palace in New York has started showing motion pictures. Verey tells us not to worry.

It's strange to watch the family from the point of view of an outsider, of someone who is recording their actions in this book. Thorne and I were on the same side, with Fentrice supporting us. Our father and Aunt Lanty were against the whole thing. But ten minutes later, when we began to rehearse, Fentrice had a long and heated argument with Thorne over whether she was being given enough to do. Neesa did not express an opinion either time, and Corrig, of course, said nothing.

January 7, 1935. Boston. It's snowing and we saw several

breadlines as we came into the city, but there's a crowd at the theater nonetheless. Maybe Lanty was right—maybe nothing will keep people away from a good magic show, not the Depression or motion pictures or the bitter cold. We're an escape for these people, a way to get beyond their limited lives.

The show went well, I think. Corrig did his new trick, the one where he takes a violin from his coat pocket and plays it while the violin grows smaller and smaller. The music continues as the violin disappears, and then suddenly changes to the sounds of a jazz piano. The audience cheered and applauded. Someone audible even from the stage said, "Must be a phonograph." Corrig just grinned.

Then it was my turn. I asked for a volunteer from the audience. Many people raised their hands eagerly, but I picked someone who hadn't, a man with worried brown eyes and a mouth just beginning to turn down. I saw that he was working ten or twelve hours a day, six or seven days a week. He was afraid of losing his job like so many others, but I knew he was invaluable to his boss, who would never fire him.

When he came on stage I opened our box and had him step in. I left it open, turned it around once. When the box faced the audience the man was gone. I turned it again and he reappeared. "What did you learn?" I asked him, repeating Verey's old formula.

He blinked. "I was outside, in the falling snow. But there was some kind of room, with a fire burning in the grate, and I went in. I had nothing to do there but sit by the fire and read the Sunday paper. A memory, I think. Or a dream." He brushed snow from his shoulders absently.

I took his hand and led him to the front of the stage—quickly, before the audience became restless. I bowed, still holding his hand. He bowed as well—very few of them can resist the spotlight—and then left the stage to loud applause.

Would he change now? Would he begin to spend more time with his family? I studied him as he returned to his seat, saw a future where his second son died in the coming war.

It's strange, this talent for glimpsing the future. Strange, and in a lot of ways unpleasant. I see bits of things, and most of the time not at all what I want to know. Will motion pictures drive us from the stage? Are Verey's fears of pursuit from England justified? Grandmother Neesa knows, I think — Neesa's the most powerful of all of us. But she says little since Grandfather Harry died, just smiles and lines up her shots on the pool table.

Anyway, as I said, the show went well, though a few things still need to be worked out before we open at the Palace in New York. For the first time we'll be sharing the bill with a motion picture. Can we compete? Does the sophisticated New York audience still respond to magic and wonder?

January 8, 1935. Reading over what I wrote yesterday I see that my father, for once, might have been right. If anyone were reading this book he would now know a little about what we do, the ways we use our magic and power. We cause people and objects to appear and disappear, we show people dreams, we foretell the future — all things my father and my aunt warned us against revealing.

Well. On the other hand this book is mine and mine alone, one of the few things that is in our crazy communal life. When I write in it I can finally hear my thoughts over the din of Thorne's arguments with Fentrice, Fentrice's arguments with Verey. And who am I kidding? No one will ever read it. I'll keep writing, and keep it out of my father's sight.

January 14, 1935. Philadelphia. Show went badly. Thorne was supposed to reappear on stage but Fentrice appeared as well. With the two women on stage everyone in the audience was certain he understood how the earlier tricks had been done — we had simply substituted one for the other. Coughs and restless murmurs from the audience — the sounds every performer dreads hearing. I made a few predictions, settled them down. After the show Fentrice complained once again that she did not have enough to do.

January 15, 1935. Philadelphia. Show went well. When Fentrice appeared on stage again Corrig turned her and Thorne into golden statues. Afterward Fentrice was furious, but Thorne wants to use it in the act. She's already arranged to have several statues made. It's hard to tell what Corrig thinks, or even if he'll do it again. I said earlier that Neesa was the strongest of all of us, but now I wonder if that could be Corrig. Perhaps fortunately, though, he's the one least interested in power.

I once talked to Aunt Lanty, Corrig's mother, about him. Even she doesn't understand him, she said. He never speaks, though the doctor she took him to could find nothing wrong with him. When we were children, moving from town to town, our parents tried to give us lessons over the long train trips. Corrig never showed the least interest. I don't even know if he can read or write. But we've never had a problem understanding him.

January 22, 1935. Philadelphia. The statues came today, mannequins painted gold. All week we'd been rehearsing the new bit that would feature them. Tonight, with the props finally here, we tried it for the first time in front of an audience.

The curtain rises to show five golden statues grouped in a semicircle. Corrig walks on and sees them. Greed shines in his eyes. He goes up to them carefully, knocks on the one closest to him (the audience hears the ring of solid gold), takes it and puts it over his shoulder. As he walks off the statue (who is of course Thorne) comes to life and breaks away from him.

Corrig takes a clarinet out of his pocket and begins to play. The woman moves toward him—it seems that she is giving in, charmed by the music. She resists, goes forward another step. Suddenly she realizes that Corrig has trapped her, that he is turning her back into a statue. She freezes in the act of pulling away, joins the other four around her once again. Corrig reaches for her.

The others come alive now and surround Corrig. His music grows faster and faster, more and more frantic. Suddenly there is silence. The five women step back to show that Corrig is gone. They freeze into immobility as the curtain drops.

The audience applauded wildly. I was watching from the wings and it seemed to me that every detail worked, everything went perfectly. The audience thrilled to the idea of so much gold in the middle of a depression, was just a little shocked by the suggestion of lust as Corrig moved toward Thorne. I felt very proud. This is what our family does best, despite all our arguments.

After the show a man came back to the greenroom with an offer for us to play in London. Thorne and Fentrice and I were excited, Verey and Lanty cold. Poor man—he had no idea of the kind of wounds he'd opened. We told him we'd think about it.

"Look," Fentrice said when he'd gone. "Our dates in Chicago have been canceled—the theater there went over to motion pictures like everyone else. We have a month free. And if we get good notices in England we'll really draw them in when we open at the Palace."

Verey was shaking his head. "No," Aunt Lanty said. "Far too dangerous."

"Dangerous!" Thorne said. "What kind of danger? From whom?"

"You know what kind," Lanty said. "The members of the Order of the Labyrinth haven't forgotten us."

"The Order—" Fentrice said scornfully. Her face had gone very white, the tip of her nose pink, the way it does when she gets angry about something. "The Order died when Grandmother and Grandfather came to America."

"You've heard the rumors, the same as I have," Verey said. "There's a new group calling itself the Order of the Labyrinth in London, and the children of some of the old members are part of it. They've even gone so far as to buy our father's old flat in Camden Town and turn it into a meeting place."

"Well, what of it?" Fentrice asked. "We've got power and they don't."

"I agree with Fentrice," I said. "What on earth can they do to us? And it would be fun to go to England, an adventure."

"You can show us the village where you grew up, Grandmother," Fentrice said. "And Grandfather's house, and Lady Westingate's."

"Don't you dare, Mother," Verey said quickly.

"Why not?" Fentrice asked.

Neesa said nothing. She studied us as if we were brightly colored balls on a pool table, each of us bouncing and colliding into the other. "Because we're on very shaky legal ground here," Verey said. "They could take us to court. Certain things might come out. . . ."

"After twenty-five years?" Fentrice asked.

"You don't know these people," Verey said. "They're very bitter. They were promised power and didn't get it—they still think they're owed something."

"All right, we won't do any sightseeing," Fentrice said. "Though I don't see why—you told me yourself that Lady Westingate lost the house, that a stranger lives there. But I still think we should go to England."

"I agree," Thorne said.

"There!" Fentrice said triumphantly. "Three to two."

"Mother hasn't voted yet," Verey said. "Or Corrig."

"Corrig never votes," Fentrice said. In fact, as we now realized, Corrig was no longer in the greenroom. None of us had seen him go.

We all looked at Neesa, who nodded. "Four to two," Fentrice said. "We're going."

I should explain something here about my family. Maybe putting it down will give me new insights, the way writing down our arguments helped me understand a little how our family works.

Our mother Edwina doesn't travel with us. She stays at the family house in California with Lanty's smaller children while we tour. Lanty, like Grandmother Neesa, had never married. Unlike Neesa, however, she has several children by different fathers.

(It's funny. I'm sure that my father would not object to my revealing the family skeletons like this, even though I've just called him a bastard. His greatest worries are about things that happened decades ago.)

Thorne, the oldest of us, will take over when Verey and Lanty decide they are too old to tour. Fentrice, the second oldest, resents this. I know how she feels. As the baby my opinion is almost never asked. I have a lot of ideas about improving the show — I even have some thoughts about a motion picture we might do. They let me design stage sets because they know I'm good at it, but I don't do too much else.

When Fentrice said "Three to two" she was being ironic, I think. We're not a democracy. The younger members suggest things, but the older generation makes all the final decisions. It was when Neesa nodded that we knew we were going to England.

After the meeting Thorne, Fentrice, and I stayed in the green-room and talked about how fearful the older generation is, how threatened they feel about things that can't possibly hurt them. Grandmother Neesa came back to pick up a shawl she had forgotten. I'll swear she didn't hear what we said, and I'll swear she smiled exactly as if she did. Worse, her smile said, clearer than words, that she knew something we didn't.

January 25, 1935. Now that we have a commitment in England we're working harder, rehearsing more. Everyone comes to rehearsals except Neesa and Corrig. Neesa no longer performs, of course, but I hope Corrig hasn't lost interest in the act, something he's done once or twice before.

In last night's performance, when we did the bit with the statues, Fentrice came alive and held her hands out to Corrig, and he froze her again. It happened very quickly, but one man in the audience had noticed and began to heckle us. "Hey," he said. "Let's see that dame again, the one on the left. Does she do anything else? Come on, baby, shake that body."

People on either side hushed him, but he wouldn't shut up. Finally I quieted him. He watched the rest of the performance with an expression of perfect idiocy.

I don't like to put people to sleep this way. For one thing, their companions might notice and begin to talk. But for another it seems like cheating. We're troupers — we should be able to handle an audience without resorting to our powers. But he was his old belligerent self after the show — I have no way of influencing people if I can't see them.

Afterward Thorne and Fentrice had a huge row. Thorne told

Fentrice never to do that again, and Fentrice complained that she wasn't being given enough to do.

February 5, 1935. Aboard the *S.S. Homeric*. Haven't written for a while because we've been so busy with rehearsals and our regular performances. We've decided to take a break for now, until we reach England.

Corrig had insisted on traveling first class. I worried a little about what he had planned, but when he came to dinner he was dressed very well, for him — white shirt and tie, dark brown pants and matching jacket. Over that, though, he had on the long bulky coat he wears on stage, with the enormous pockets that people think he hides his props in. The gentleman sitting next to him wore an evening coat and starched shirt. The man turned away in obvious disgust.

Corrig did nothing to annoy Starched Shirt until he passed him the fish. Shirt looked down at the platter Corrig handed him, and one of the fish winked. Shirt started up out of his chair. He sat back slowly and stared at Corrig, who looked at him with an expression of the purest innocence. When Shirt reached for the platter again a breaded tail waved at him. He excused himself and went to his room.

February 15, 1935. London. As usual everything went wrong in rehearsal and wonderfully well on stage. There was some unpleasantness with a woman calling herself the Première Danseuse, who insisted she be billed in the choicest spot, the one before the closing act. We had been promised this spot, and after some shouting and brandishing of contracts we got it.

The critics were lavish in their praise. I left Thorne happily cutting out clippings for her scrapbook and went out into the city.

February 23, 1935. Fentrice is gone. She didn't make it to the show last night, and when we looked in her room this morning we saw that her bed had not been slept in. We can work around her, of course, but I'm still worried. Is this what Verey and Lanty were afraid of?

February 26, 1935. Fentrice back. She refuses to tell us

where she went. But this afternoon I overheard her and Grandmother Neesa talking, and I think Neesa guesses or knows where she was.

"Did you walk the labyrinth, my dear?" Neesa said.

"What—what do you mean?" Fentrice asked.

I was in the theater, walking through the backstage corridors to the stage, hoping to come up with a way to improve a bit of business in the show. Neesa and Fentrice were in the greenroom and I stopped to listen, to eavesdrop perhaps. In my defense I can only say that this is how we live, all of us on top of each other; we have little privacy left.

"I think you know, dear," Neesa said.

"I went off to be by myself, that's all," Fentrice said. "I had to get away."

"Did you?" Neesa said. "Let me tell you something, a story. A long time ago I did what you are doing now. We have such power, and sometimes it's such a temptation to use it. . . . But I was wrong, very wrong. I've come to forgive myself, come to realize that no one can be perfect, that we are not saints. But I've lived with pain and sorrow and regret for many years—I live with it now, in fact. I don't want to see you make the same mistake I did."

"What mistake?"

"The best use we can make of our power," Neesa said, "is in the service of nothing at all. Corrig understands that—he seems to have understood it from the day he was born. I sometimes think he's the wisest of us all."

"I haven't the faintest idea what you're talking about," Fentrice said.

Neither did I. Neesa had never seemed to regret a thing. Was she thinking of her treatment of Lady Dorothy? But she made amends for that, long ago. And what had she meant by that odd question about the labyrinth?

I had a feeling Fentrice knew some of it, though. She ran from the room, nearly colliding with me. "How long have you been standing there?" she asked angrily.

I held up a placating hand. "Just walking through," I said. "Why are you acting so guilty?"

She stormed off down the corridor.

March 2, 1935. Last show in London. Tempers were high and nerves frayed, but we managed to pull it off. At the end Corrig showered us with confetti and sequins and streamers — we were knee-deep in the stuff by the time we bowed off. Afterwards we broke out the champagne, and toasted ourselves and the success of the show.

March 5, 1935. Sailing home. Fentrice has disappeared again, but at least this time we know where she is — every so often we see her in second class. She comes back with a trumpet player, Tom somebody.

March 31, 1935. Traveling west — Minneapolis, Kansas City, Denver. We're excited about seeing Edwina and all the cousins in California. Tom is with us — Fentrice has somehow convinced Verey and Lanty that we need a trumpet player.

April 2, 1935. Denver. An act called Bob Jones and His Savage Animals appears on the bill before us. The savage animals — a lion, a tiger and a panther — are thin, mangy, riddled with fleas. Like all traveling performers we put pots of oxalic acid under our bedposts, but these are mostly good for keeping ants away and in the morning we wake up covered with flea bites.

Today I spend some time watching Bob Jones rehearse. He works the animals hard with his whip — by the end of the rehearsal the tiger is bleeding. After Jones leads them to their cages I ask, "How much would you let the tiger go for?"

"You're kidding," Jones says. "I had to go to India to get Jewel — bargained with a maharajah for her. He didn't want to let her go, but in the end I discovered that he had a fondness for emeralds."

(Later today I learn, unsurprised, that Jewel is actually an African tiger.)

"Fifty dollars," I say.

He pauses in the act of locking the cages. "You deaf? I won't let her go for any price. She's been to Europe, played before the crowned heads."

"Fifty dollars, and I won't tell anyone why you had to leave Philadelphia in such a hurry."

He stops, leaving Jewel's cage unlocked. Red blood streaks her flanks, mingling with her stripes. "Who are you?" he asks. "You the cops?"

"No."

"You really want her? No tricks?"

"Yes."

"Well. I couldn't let her go for under seventy-five."

"Seventy," I say.

"Seventy, okay," he says.

I go to my room, check the money in my grouch bag. I have seventy-two dollars. It's only after I've paid him that I wonder what Verey and Lanty will say.

April 3, 1935. The family approves—everyone agrees that the tiger will add something to the act. We rehearse the bit with the statues again, and this time Thorne turns into the tiger Jewel before becoming a statue.

April 7, 1935. Oakland. In the morning we had a terrific reunion with the rest of the family and then moved to the boardinghouse to be closer to the theater. I'm excited to see everyone again, excited too to be playing the Paramount, my favorite theater in all the world.

I take the trolley to the theater, watching the streets as it pushes its way through the dreadful modern traffic. When I finally get there it feels like visiting old friends. The lobby with its green ceiling, its fountain of yellow lights, its frieze of golden women on the walls. The auditorium is more cavernous than I remembered, paneled with women and vines and warriors on horseback. Above the stage Poseidon flies out of the ocean, surrounded by stars and horses and waves. And over everything the amber light that seems to glow only here, in this special place.

I leave the auditorium and go out into the corridor, nodding to the cleaning staff. A woman vacuuming the floor plugs her hose into the wall—one of the staff once told me that the hoses all connect to a great vacuum in the basement of the building. I go backstage and find Jake trying to get Jewel settled.

"You guys never had a tiger in the act before, did you?" he asks.

"No, she's new."

"Beautiful," he says, admiring her. She's filled out a little in the short time we've had her, and her wounds have started to heal.

"Want to go for lunch?" I ask.

"In a minute. I have to make out the deposit for last night's take first."

Because of the Depression theaters all over the country have had to let some of their people go, so Jake acts as stagehand, usher, and bookkeeper all in one. Sometimes he even takes a turn at carpentry or plumbing, if the problem is simple enough. Like a lot of guys these days he's happy just to have a job, and he works long hours for very little pay.

I follow him to the office. He goes toward a painting of a woman putting down the mask of Comedy and lifting that of Tragedy. He swings this to one side, revealing the safe set into the wall.

I watch him as he twirls the dials on the safe and pulls open the door. "Shit!" he says. "My God. Shit."

"What is it?"

He can barely speak for fear. "The money. The money's gone." His face is very pale.

"What?"

"I put it here last night, I swear. It's gone. I'll lose my job for sure."

"Maybe you put it somewhere else."

"I remember putting it here. Right here. Oh, God, they'll have my job. They'll think I stole it."

"What about backstage?" I ask. "Maybe you left it there."

It's an absurd suggestion, of course, but by this point Jake is willing to grasp at anything. It's easy enough to lead him back-stage and, once there, to start searching. We rummage through all the strange things people have left over the years, boxes of books and costumes, a false mustache, a guitar pick, a cloth flower, a glass eye. Jake finishes one box and goes to another, closer to Jewel the tiger.

"You must dig deeper, Jake," the tiger says. "Deeper than you've ever gone before."

Jake looks up wildly. "Callan!" he says. "My God — the tiger said something."

"I didn't hear anything," I say.

"The tiger —" he says again.

"Your jewel lies hidden in the dirt," the tiger says.

"Callan!" he says. "Didn't you hear that? Am I going nuts?"

"You'll be fine," I say.

"I'm going home," Jake says, unsteadily. "I feel terrible."

"That might be the best thing," I say. I watch him for a mo-ment as he leaves, seeing what will happen to him, and then head back to our boardinghouse.

Fentrice is in her room, putting on makeup. She sees me in the mirror and beckons me inside. I sit on her bed, watching her.

"I'm going out with Tom tonight," she says. She's been more excited, more open, since she started seeing him.

I realize I haven't seen Tom all day. "Where is he?" I ask.

"He's staying in San Francisco with his family," she says. "We're going to Playland at the Beach."

"Have a good time," I say.

"Oh, we will," she says.

April 8, 1935. Fentrice has started to confide in me for the first time since we were children. It reminds me of the times we hid in the bathroom on the train, when she would tell me about her petty struggles with Thorne. And then, I'm ashamed to say, Thorne would closet herself with me and tell me about Fentrice. It gave me a feeling of power that my two older sisters would put themselves into my hands this way.

This time, though, that feeling is gone, and I listen with nothing but pleasure to Fentrice's account of her date the night before. Because of our old closeness I can even see her as she and Tom ride the roller coaster and explore the House of Mirrors. I watch as Fentrice expands to twice her size and Tom shrinks down to nothing but a head and two feet. I hear with them the hideous Laughing Sal, a huge and awful mannequin whose unstoppable laughter peals out continuously across the playground.

Later I see them go out for dinner, and listen as Tom tells my sister his plans. "I don't want to be in the two-a-day the rest of my life," he says to her earnestly. "I'd like to join a big band somewhere, play some hot jazz. I need monnney," he says, caressing the word like a lover.

He's a bit too superficial for her, I think. Too preoccupied with the surface. There's even a hint that he might be using her, using the Allalie Family, to get ahead. I begin to wonder how I might change that, and then shake my head. This is my sister's boyfriend, after all, not some man who has paid to sit in the audience and see wonders.

Perhaps because of Fentrice's newfound happiness the performance this evening goes better than ever. When Tom plays she dances to his trumpet as if he and she were alone, the only people in the vast auditorium.

Later a newspaperman comes to interview us in the trap room and we put on a second show just for him. Even Thorne and Fentrice cooperate. For once I see clearly what will happen to the man: he will quit drinking, get married, raise a family. And near the end of his life he will become involved once again with the Allalies—but the vision goes dark here.

April 9, 1935. Oh, little brother, it was nothing at all like that. Yes, this is Fentrice, who's just discovered your precious diary and read it all the way through. Does my nose really turn pink when I'm angry? You should see how you look when you join the fray.

Tom and I took the ferry to San Francisco, and then the streetcar to Playland. There was no room in the car so we sat on the cow catcher in back, where the conductor couldn't reach us. I held him and he held me and I wished the ride would never end; I wished we could sit with our arms around each other like that forever.

Yes, we rode the roller coaster, and yes, we went into the dark of the House of Mirrors and came out into the bright lights and distorting mirrors. And we walked through the rotating barrels and spun on the carousel (he had the ostrich, I the lion), and we climbed the stairs and slid down the huge wooden slide. And Sal laughed and laughed, but she wasn't at all hideous but somehow wonderful, as if she expressed my joy.

You've never been in love, have you, little brother? You say Tom is superficial but that's because you're superficial, you haven't taken the time to get to know him. He's an artist, a serious musician. Of course he wants something better than the daily grind of vaudeville. You love the magic act and the sense you have of playing God to these people — look what you did to that poor newspaperman last night, for example. But Tom and I walked the streets two nights ago, the stars shining down on us, and we both talked about our dreams, our futures. Can you see into the future for us, little brother? I don't think we'll be in the act much longer.

April 10, 1935. I thought of a hiding place for this diary that Fentrice will never discover. And then I went looking for her, angrier than I've ever been.

But when I finally find her I see that something is dreadfully wrong. I know what it is, of course, at least part of it, but I ask her anyway. "What's the matter?" I say.

"Tom's not at home," she says. "His mother says he's out on business, but what business can he have that doesn't involve the show, the Allalie Family?"

Another woman, I think, someone he knew before in San Francisco. I know that Fentrice is thinking this as well, and that she's trying not to, trying to persuade herself that she's the only one he sees. Unbidden, the names of other women he's mentioned come to her mind.

April 11, 1935. Things at the boardinghouse are tense, and so I go for a walk during the day, find out how Jake is doing. When I come back I see all the signs of another family row — Fentrice is screaming, Verey and Lanty are trying to placate her. Her face has gone white again, and yes, the tip of her nose has turned pink.

"He was supposed to — She — That miserable bitch — "

"What is it?" I ask Fentrice. "What's happened?"

"Oh, it's all right for you to talk," she says bitterly. "She doesn't envy you. It's just me she takes it out on, because I'm better looking."

I had never thought of one sister as being prettier than the other. "What did Thorne do?" I ask.

"You won't believe it. Tom was supposed to pick me up tonight — we were going to go to a movie. But when I got here I found out that he's been and gone. Gone with Thorne, who changed to look like me."

There was a time when Thorne and Fentrice would trade places, would each turn into the other by some magic I don't entirely understand. Normally they don't look very much alike, but at first their illusion was enough to confuse even members of the family. Later, of course, we found ways to distinguish them, and they stopped playing the trick on us. Or so we thought.

"Verey and Lanty just stood there, watching them go," Fentrice said. "Didn't even try to stop them. I'm so sick of this family — "

"We didn't realize, dear," Lanty said.

"You didn't realize," Fentrice said sarcastically. "You must have suspected something. She's not that good."

"We had no idea," Lanty said.

April 12, 1935. Thorne returns this morning, looking happy and smelling of sex. The minute she sees her Fentrice begins screaming. I leave quickly, take another walk.

April 13, 1935. Thorne's gone. Verey is angrier than I've ever seen him — he says that he's about to give up on the whole pack of us, that he's ready to retire and let us bicker among ourselves. He's convinced that Fentrice had something to do with Thorne's disappearance, but Fentrice hotly denies it. She says that Tom the trumpet player is also gone, insists they must have run off together. Verey calls our mother, asking her to send us someone to replace Thorne, and to let us know if Thorne shows up.

Our performance tonight goes well despite all the tension.

April 14, 1935. We left for Los Angeles today. We waited as long as we could at the freight yard where we board, stowing away our bags and boxes, the statues and musical instruments and tiger's cage, but Thorne never arrived. She knows our itinerary — maybe she'll catch up with us later. We hope so, anyway. No one has the slightest idea where she could be.

April 15, 1935. Los Angeles. Fentrice is certain Thorne isn't coming back. That might be wishful thinking on her part — if Thorne stays away she'll be the one to take over when Verey and Lanty retire. I truly hope this won't happen. I like Fentrice well enough, but she has always had this bitter rivalry with her sister, and now that Thorne's taken Tom it's grown worse. Fentrice sees Thorne's disappearance as her chance in the limelight, and she could ruin a lot about the act just to give herself more to do.

April 16, 1935. Los Angeles. Last night Fentrice took Thorne's place in the sketch with the statues. Although the bit is a pantomime, she began to cry out when Corrig chased her — "No! Stop! Please stop!" At one point she looked truly afraid. Stage fright? I thought. It didn't seem likely with all her experience.

This morning she asked me how I thought it went. "I don't think you should say anything," I said. "It destroys the mood."

"That's all right for you to say — you get to talk every night when you do your fortune-telling number. Do you realize I don't speak once in the entire act? I might as well be mute, like Corrig."

"Well, bring it up in rehearsal. The act works — don't take it upon yourself to change it."

She started to say something. I didn't need to be a fortune-teller to know what it was — she was sure Verey and Lanty would never change a thing. And it's true that we've been doing some bits ever since Grandmother Neesa first set foot on the stage. Still, they work—that's the important thing.

"I'll tell you what," I said, interrupting her. "When you come to life you can do a little dance. I've seen you dance—you're good. Show the audience how happy you are to be free. Then Corrig plays the clarinet, trying to enslave you again, and you and he struggle. You become a tiger to escape him, but he freezes you and starts to take you away. And then the other statues close in on him. The whole thing can work as a dance."

She nodded eagerly. "Great idea," she said.

"Rehearse it first, though. Give Corrig some idea of what you're going to do."

"Oh, Corrig knows everything anyway," Fentrice said.

April 17, 1935. Los Angeles. I hadn't seen Fentrice and Corrig rehearse, but the pantomime went off as smoothly as if they'd done it for years. Another minor crisis averted.

April 18, 1935. Los Angeles. Fentrice is gone again. I don't understand it—I thought she was happy now that Thorne's left, excited about having more to do in the act. We spend a frantic day rehearsing with the cousins Edwina's sent us. The show tonight goes better than I expected, though of course we still need a lot of work.

Molly skimmed through the rest of the diary, curious whether Fentrice had ever returned. The Palace Theatre closed in September of 1935, two months after the Allalies played there. More theaters around the country closed or showed only movies; the family toured less and less.

When the United States joined World War II in 1941 Callan and some of the others traveled around the country entertaining the troops. Callan quit the next year. "I look into a crowd of uniforms and I see that this one will die, and the one sitting next to him will lose his arms," he wrote. "It's all too much for me. I can't face it anymore. Verey and Lanty will come out of retirement and visit army camps with Corrig and some of the other cousins."

While touring Callan met Mathilda Dunstone, a dancer in the chorus line of another show. "She's beautiful — I'm very much attracted to her," he wrote. "Would I be as attracted if I didn't see us in the future, see our house, our children? The first child will be named Joan, I think, and the second Samuel. The fashion in our family for strange names has passed — we don't need to hide any longer."

Molly read the paragraph over. The first mention of her lost mother. She wanted to cry, and angrily told herself to stop.

Callan and Mathilda were married in 1943; Joan was born in 1945. Molly turned the page, realized with surprise that it was the last one. Surely Callan hadn't fit the rest of his life into one page. When had he died? She didn't know.

The last entry was dated February 10, 1946. "Joan sat up by herself today. Mathilda had gone to do the shopping. When she came home I told her about Joan's progress. She didn't believe me, and Joan refused to do it again."

The light outside had faded while Molly read the diary. She sat in the darkness a while. Callan must have written more books, books that continued the story. Joan grew up, married, left the family. Did Samuel have the rest of the journals?

Statues becoming women, women becoming tigers. People who disappeared on stage, and then disappeared in life, the final magic trick. Streamers and music and stories . . . What a time it must have been, in spite of all the arguments. She wished she could have been there.

One mystery at least was solved, had turned out not to be so mysterious after all. Thorne had run off with Fentrice's boyfriend, Tom the trumpet player. Fentrice left the act soon after, angry with Thorne for stealing Tom and disgusted at not being given enough to do.

John was going to be disappointed, Molly thought. He had been so certain someone had been killed. She grinned and reached for the phone to call him, to tell him that he could read the book now.

The scrapbook, she thought. Her hand was still outstretched; she returned it to her side. Callan had said that Thorne had cut out the clippings for the scrapbook, and yet somehow it was Fentrice who had wound up with it. And the last clipping was . . . She was pretty sure it was Andrew Dodd's review of the performance in Oakland. The last show that Thorne had attended, but Fentrice had gone on to Los Angeles. How had Fentrice gotten Thorne's scrapbook?

Molly shook her head. Thorne might have left the book behind when she went. Or Fentrice might have had a scrapbook of her own; Callan hadn't mentioned one but that didn't mean it didn't exist. And clearly Fentrice had been eager to leave Los Angeles. She wouldn't stop to cut out clippings.

Everything made sense now. Fentrice had never mentioned her sister for any number of reasons: Thorne had had far more to do in the act, Thorne had stolen her boyfriend. Callan had written the story from his point of view but it seemed to Molly, reading between the lines, that the family had treated Fentrice shabbily. It was easy enough to understand why Fentrice had cut off all ties with them.

NINE
Dig Deeper

John's phone was busy. Molly waited half an hour and called again, and once more fifteen minutes later. It was nine o'clock. Who the hell could he be talking to? He'd said he didn't have any other cases.

She was eager to talk over what she had learned. She looked in her phone book for his address, then grabbed her coat and the diary and went outside to her car.

John turned out to live fairly close by. The neighborhood had flirted with gentrification in the last decade, but during the real estate slump it had settled back into its former shabbiness. A house painted pink with blue trim sat on a well-maintained lawn next to a peeling house with a broken washing machine out front.

John's place was a duplex. She rang the bell. No one answered, and she rang again. *He's got to be home,* she thought. *Unless he's taken the phone off the hook, but why would he do that?*

She tried the bell a third time. A black woman opened the door slightly but left it on its chain.

"Does John Stow live here?" Molly asked.

"Yes, he does," the woman said, a little suspiciously. "Who are you?"

Oh my God, it's his girlfriend, Molly thought. The one who was mad at him. "I'm working on a case with him," she said. "I brought a book he wanted to read. My name's Molly Travers—maybe he's told you about me."

"He doesn't talk about his cases," the woman said. She hesitated, then slipped the chain and opened the door. "Well, you might as well come in. We can wait for him together. My name's Gwen."

Molly went into the front room and looked around curiously. It contained a battered sofa, a television set, a table with two chairs, and a bookshelf. The TV was on; the table was set with two plates, but only one of them held the remains of a dinner. There were no posters, no plants, nothing except the books to give any indication of personality. Did Gwen live here too? Molly would bet that she didn't.

Gwen motioned her to the sofa and sat next to her. Her hair was straight and cut short, framing her face. She had high cheekbones and large, slightly upturned eyes. "Can I get you anything?" she asked.

"No, thanks," Molly said. "Look, I'm sorry to barge in this way, but the phone was busy—"

"I took it off the hook."

"Why?"

"Why? Listen, I don't know you—I'm not about to tell you the story of my life."

"When do you think John will be back?"

"I really couldn't say."

"Then why did you invite me in?"

"It seemed a better idea than having you wait out on the street."

Something exploded on the television screen; someone fired several rounds into a burning building and then drove away quickly.

Gwen stood. The noise from the television had covered the sound of the door opening. John came in. "Sorry I'm late," he said. Then, seeing Molly, "What the hell are you doing here?"

"Visiting you," Molly said.

Gwen looked from one to the other, smiling a little. She seemed to enjoy the sight of John at a disadvantage. "What do you want?" he asked, unfreezing slightly.

"I brought you the diary. I finished it."

"How was it?"

"Pretty interesting. I think I know what happened to Thorne."

"How could you? Samuel's read the entire thing and he has no idea. That's what he hired me for."

"It was pretty obvious to me. She ran off with a trumpet player named Tom."

For once John had nothing to say.

"Sorry," Molly said. "Fentrice didn't have anything to do with it."

"Then why did Fentrice lie when you asked her if she had a sister?"

"For any number of reasons. Here—read the book."

John took the diary. "What about visiting Fentrice? Did you ask her if I can talk to her?"

"I haven't had time. I'll call her tomorrow. But I really think you'll have to try another approach on this thing."

"Thanks for the diary," John said.

"Sure," Molly said. "See you around. Nice meeting you," she said to Gwen.

John frowned, no doubt wondering what the two women had talked about while he was gone. "Yeah," Gwen said. She sounded a little warmer this time; perhaps she considered Molly an ally in the battles she fought with John.

Serves him right, Molly thought as she went to her car. He'd obviously missed dinner, and he hadn't even called to tell Gwen where he was. But he couldn't have called, she remembered; Gwen had taken the phone off the hook. She shrugged. Maybe she shouldn't have gotten involved. There didn't seem to be any right and wrong here; probably both of them were at fault.

* * *

She called Fentrice the next day. "Hello, Molly," her aunt said. "What a pleasure."

"I have to ask you a favor," Molly said.

"Of course, dear."

"Do you remember that man I told you about? The private investigator?"

"Oh, dear. Don't tell me he's still asking questions."

"I'm afraid so. And he still wants to visit you. It might not be a bad idea—you can tell him you had nothing to do with Thorne's disappearance and he'll go away."

"I doubt it. That type never does."

"Look," Molly said quickly. "We found Callan's diary. We know that you and Thorne were sisters, and that Thorne ran away with your boyfriend Tom. I know the whole story now. Don't worry—I'm on your side. I won't let John badger you."

Fentrice said nothing. The line was silent for so long that Molly wondered if they'd been disconnected. Finally Fentrice said, "Tom?" She sounded confused, as if the subject had changed too abruptly for her.

"The trumpet player. Callan said you met him on the ship back from England."

"Tom! Of course I remember Tom."

"Thorne left the act with him. Remember? And then you disappeared too. You were angry with the whole family. I can't say that I blame you."

"You don't?"

"No, of course not."

"But I never told you about her. You deserved to know about your family."

Molly caught her breath. Fentrice was close to admitting that Thorne was her sister; all the lies were coming to an end. She felt a sudden resentment that the deceit had gone on for so long but she pushed it aside, hoping her aunt would continue talking.

"I think you had good reason to be angry with them," Molly said. "I don't think they treated you very well."

"No. Not very well at all. Oh, Molly—you don't know how guilty I've felt all these years, not telling you about the family. I was too stubborn to go back, and then by the time you were born it was too late. I wish I could have introduced you to Callan, at least. You would have liked him."

"I wish so too," Molly said. "What about John? Will you let him visit you?"

"Will you come with him?"

"Of course. How about next weekend? I can't afford to take any time off from my job."

Silence again. "All right, dear," Fentrice said finally. "You might as well."

Molly had told Fentrice not to pick them up from the airport; she and John would rent a car. When they got to Chicago Molly directed him away from the airport and onto the freeway.

It was late when they arrived at the house. Fentrice showed John to the guest bedroom and then she and Molly said good night.

Back in her old bed, in her old bedroom, Molly found she couldn't sleep. She worried about what Fentrice would think of John, what new revelations she would make. She woke late, confused by jet lag, convinced that she had gotten only two or three hours of sleep. She showered, dressed, and went downstairs to the kitchen.

Fentrice and Lila were already there, making breakfast. "Would you like some tea?" Fentrice asked.

"Coffee, please," Molly said.

"Sit down, dear," Fentrice said. "I'll get it." She turned to the stove. "So that's your private investigator," she said, her back still toward Molly. "I can't say I think very much of him. His eyes are too close together."

Lila made a strange choking noise. It was a laugh, Molly realized, surprised. She couldn't remember ever hearing Lila laugh before.

"He's not my private investigator," Molly said.

"No," Fentrice said. "No, I can see that."

John came downstairs, yawning and running his hand through his curly tangled hair. "Good morning, Miss Allalie," he said.

"Good morning," Fentrice said. "We're making eggs for breakfast. Would you like some?"

"Sure. Thanks."

Molly watched them with interest. She had had very few chances to see her aunt interact with people other than her bridge club. Already she admired the way Fentrice had sidestepped the question of what she would call John, while not correcting his formal "Miss Allalie."

After breakfast John took out his notebook while Lila cleaned up. "Could you tell me a little about your time in vaudeville?" he asked. "About the Allalie Family? Who was in the act?"

"Oh, dozens of people. It varied from year to year, you know. Dancers, musicians, assistants in the magic act . . ."

"But the family consisted of . . ."

"Well, my father, Verey Allalie. And Lanty—that was Verey's sister, my aunt. If you want to go all the way back there was Grandmother Neesa. She started the act, you know, in 1910."

John wrote in the notebook. "Yes. And Verey's children?"

"Lanty's children? Aunt Lanty had a son named Corrig—that was my cousin, you know. And there were others—oh, what were their names?"

"What about Verey's children, Miss Allalie? Did you have brothers or sisters?"

"Well, of course. My brother was Callan—that's Molly's grandfather." Fentrice looked at Molly. She was seeking reassurance, Molly thought, surprised. She wasn't as confident as she sounded. "And I had a sister," Fentrice said. "Thorne."

"Thorne disappeared, didn't she?"

"We both did."

"I'll get to you in a minute, Miss Allalie. But Thorne—"

"Callan would wave his wand and we'd disappear from sight, just like that. The audience loved it."

"What I mean is, Thorne left the act without telling anyone," John said. "Didn't she?"

"That's right. It was while we were in—was it Los Angeles?"

"Oakland."

"Well if you know, why are you asking me?"

"Because I don't know where she went. Or why she left."

"Well, I certainly can't tell you. I never saw her again."

"Didn't you speculate?"

"Of course I did. The whole family did."

"Why do you think she left?"

Fentrice hesitated. "I can give you an answer, but it's not very flattering to me. I had a boyfriend, Tom. Thorne ran off with him. Surely you can understand why I wasn't anxious to see her again."

"And then you left the act in Los Angeles. Why was that?"

"I was sick of the whole thing. With Thorne gone I was the oldest of our generation, but no one listened to me. I was supposed to wait until Verey and Lanty retired, and then I could take over the act. I guess I was impatient."

"Why didn't you ever tell Molly any of this? Why didn't you tell her you had a sister?"

"Molly?" Fentrice looked at her again. For the first time she seemed old, as worn out as if John had been questioning her for hours.

"It doesn't matter, Aunt Fentrice," Molly said softly.

"It's all right, Molly. I owe you an explanation. I suppose I hated Thorne for a while, and then when I'd made my peace with the whole thing it was too late. I thought if I brought it up you'd resent me for not telling you earlier, and I don't think I could have borne to lose you. You're the only family I have left. I'm sorry, Molly."

"And Samuel?" Molly asked. "Why don't you ever talk about him?"

"I don't know who he is, dear."

"My uncle. My mother's brother."

"Oh my God. Joan had a brother?"

"Yeah."

"Oh," Fentrice said. "Oh, dear. I—I had no idea."

Fentrice looked a little faint. *Should I not have told her?* But it was too late for secrets. Molly pushed on. "He wants to meet you."

"Does he?" Fentrice said. "I don't think I'm up to more revelations at this late date."

John paged through his notebook. "How did you meet up with Joan?" he asked.

"Now there's an interesting thing," Fentrice said. She was on surer ground here, Molly saw. "Lila drove me to town for my doctor's appointment, and there Joan was at the bus stop. With her husband Bill, and a baby. That was you, Molly, that baby. They had escaped from her father Callan—"

"Escaped?" John asked.

"Oh, you know."

John shook his head. "No, I don't, Miss Allalie."

"We're a hard family to get along with. Callan wanted her in the act, and she wanted to settle down, raise a family. They'd been hitchhiking since the day before, and someone had dropped them off here that morning."

"Quite a coincidence," John said dryly.

Fentrice shook her head. "I don't think it was. I think they knew somehow to come here, just as I knew immediately who they were. I took them in, of course. Bill was a teacher at the city college, until he died in the crash."

John wrote something, turned a page. "I guess that's all," he said. "Thanks for your help, Miss Allalie. Can I ask you more questions if I think of anything else?"

"No."

John looked up, surprised.

"My bridge club is coming in fifteen minutes," Fentrice said. "And you're leaving tonight, Molly says."

"Well, maybe I'll call you."

"Maybe you will," Fentrice said. "Did we frost the cake yet, Lila?"

The doorbell rang. "Goodness, that'll be Estelle," Fentrice said. "That woman's always early."

Lila went to open the door. Estelle followed her into the kitchen, her eyes looking puzzled behind her thick black glasses. She wore the heavy jewelry Molly remembered, chains of necklaces and earrings that pulled at her lobes. "I thought you went back to California, Molly," she said.

"I did," Molly said. "I came back again."

Estelle sat down at the kitchen table, flustered, as if the concept of two separate visits had overwhelmed her. "This is John Stow," Molly said. "John, this is Estelle. She's an old friend of my aunt's."

"Hello," John said. "Listen, can I ask you something? Did you know Miss Allalie when she was a magician in vaudeville?"

Estelle looked at her hands, festooned with rings, and said nothing. "No, of course not," Fentrice said. "All that happened a long time before we met."

"No," Estelle said, shaking her head. Her earrings chimed.

"Now you're going to tell me which parts you didn't believe," Molly said when they were on the plane heading home.

"You know, the funny thing is that I do believe her," John said. "Even the part about how she met Joan. Those kinds of coincidences do happen. I really think she told us everything."

"So what do we do now? How are we going to find Thorne?"

"I'm out of ideas. This looks a lot like another dead end."

They were still discussing the case when the plane landed and when they walked into the airport at what the flight attendant had cheerfully informed them was five in the morning, local time.

"Oh, God, it's Monday," Molly said. "I'm going to have to call in sick at work, spend the day sleeping. What are you going to do?"

"I don't know," John said. "I just don't know where to go

from here. It's hard to believe that all that work we did was for nothing."

Gwen was waiting for him at the gate. John kissed her and continued his conversation. "The trip to England, all that research," he said. "That stuff's got to tie in somehow."

"Hello, Gwen," Molly said.

"Maybe you missed something," Gwen said. "On the trip to England."

"What do you mean?" John said, surprised. It was clear that Gwen rarely interfered in his cases.

"When you left for England," Gwen said, "what day was it?"

"How can this possibly be relevant?" John asked.

"What day was it?" Molly asked Gwen.

"March 16," Gwen said.

"Why is that important?" Molly asked.

"Ask John," Gwen said.

John looked toward the ceiling, exasperated. "God, I don't know. It was—" He stopped. "Shit. It was your birthday, wasn't it?"

Gwen nodded. Molly put her hand to her mouth and coughed.

"I forgot your birthday," John said. "No wonder you were angry. Shit. I'm sorry."

Molly's coughs had turned to laughter. "What's so funny?" John asked, irritated.

"The great detective," she said. "You told me she was mad at you at the airport. And you had no idea why."

"I was thinking about other things."

"Obviously. Look—if you're going to be in a relationship you have to think about the other person once in a while. Remember anniversaries. Take her out on Valentine's Day."

"Valentine's Day? That's my busiest day all year. Everyone wants to know who's sneaking off with whom."

Molly looked at him. "Well, at least tell her if you're not going to make it for dinner," she said.

"How did you know—" John asked. "Did she tell you I'd promised to be home for dinner that night you stopped by?"

"John," Molly said. "There were two plates on the table, and she said something about waiting for you. Hey—maybe I'll be a detective too. It's not as hard as it looks."

John stared at her. "So long," Molly said. "I'll take the shuttle back."

Peter came to town the next day, and for a while Molly forgot about John and the investigation. "When do you have to leave?" she asked him after they had gone to his hotel and made love.

He sat up, scratched his day-old beard, and reached for his glasses on the nightstand. "Actually I think I'll stay here for a while," he said. "There's not much action in New York these days."

"Great," Molly said.

Peter frowned. "Whatever happened with that case you were working on?" he asked. "You find out anything more about your family?"

"Not much. I met an uncle I never knew about."

"Was he involved with the occult too?"

"The occult? Oh, no—that was a couple of generations back. Did I tell you what the family did after they left England?"

Peter shook his head. She hadn't brought up the case at all, she realized; she had just assumed he wasn't interested. Now she told him about the family's vaudeville act, their grueling jumps from town to town, the statues, the tiger. He stopped her a few times to ask questions. Molly had never seen him at work as an interviewer, and she thought how intelligent his questions were, how good he was at his job.

"You know, the Paramount in Oakland is still there," he said when she had finished. "I think they give tours on weekends. Do you want to go?"

She moved closer to him on the bed. What had happened? He had never expressed so much interest in her life, and he had always spent his weekends working—he'd said that the people he needed to interview were more likely to be home then. Had he finally understood how much she loved him? Would all the waiting, all the pain, turn out to have been worth it after all?

"Sure, that would be great," she said. "I'd love to tour the Paramount."

It was overcast and windy the next day, one of those days when it seemed that summer would never come. Peter looked up occult bookstores in the phone book and took the BART train to Oakland and Tangled Tales.

"I'm interested in the Order of the Labyrinth," he said to the clerk, a pale-skinned man wearing a turban. "Do you have anything on them?"

"The Order of the Labyrinth," the man said. "Everyone seems to want to know about them lately."

"Everyone? Who else was asking about them?"

"I'm afraid I can't exactly . . . What do you want to know about the Order?"

"Anything you can tell me. Who they were. What they did. I met a woman who's related to them somehow."

"Did you?" the clerk said softly. "Did you really? What's her name?"

"Why don't we trade information? You tell me what you know and I'll tell you who she is."

"The Order of the Labyrinth," the clerk said. "Well, it was started sometime in the 1870s —"

"I know all that," Peter said impatiently. "What I want to know is what happened to them."

"Well, it's difficult to say. Lord Sanderson disappeared in 1910. And a woman disappeared with him, someone named —"

"Emily Wethers. I know her great-great-granddaughter."

"You're joking," the clerk said, amazed.

"No, I'm not."

"Whatever happened to them? We've been searching for years . . ."

"Go on," Peter said. "We're trading information, remember?"

"Yes. Well." The clerk made an effort to pull himself together. "Some of the members continued meeting after Sanderson and Emily left, but it wasn't the same without them. They kept going for a long time, though, losing purpose, becoming involved in ridiculous fads. They still meet today—a few of them are even descendants of some of the original members.

"In 1953 a group of us in the United States split away from them. We thought they had lost sight of the Order's original purpose, which was to be guided through the Labyrinth and finally obtain enlightenment. There were arguments, accusations, even a libel case brought to court. . . . Well, you don't want to hear all of that. Suffice it to say that if you want information about the Order you've come to the right place. We are the true descendants of the founders, spiritually if not biologically." The man hesitated. "We're meeting next week. Would you like to come? I'm sure the group would be delighted to initiate you into the First Grade. And bring your friend, Emily's relative—she'll be very welcome too."

"She wouldn't be interested," Peter said. "But I'd like to come. Where is it?"

The clerk wrote down a time and an address on the back of a bookmark. "Great," Peter said. "I'll be there."

He left the store, went to the phone booth on the corner, and called the Paramount Theatre. Tours were given on alternate Saturdays, a helpful voice at the other end told him. The next one would be in ten days.

He thanked her and hung up. Wind blew down the street and he pulled his trench coat around him. Things were coming together, he thought. He felt excitement building within him, the way it always did when he was on the scent of something big. He called Molly and made a date for the tour.

They waited with a small group of people in the theater's anteroom. The tour was late starting; people murmured to each other and two children ran in and out of the crowd playing tag. Finally an old white-haired man came through a door, still speaking to someone in the other room.

"This is the third tour Joe's missed," the man said. His name tag said *"J. Polanski."* "I don't mind substituting for him, but you tell him I need more notice if he wants to go on vacation. It's hard just getting out of bed these days."

He greeted the group and led them into the lobby on thin, trembling legs. They stood a moment and gazed at the ceiling of metal spiderwebs and green light, the yellow fountain, the frieze of golden women along the walls, the lush jungle of the carpet.

"The ceiling here is seventy-five feet high," J. Polanski said.

It was, Molly thought, like stepping into the jewel box of a rich and slightly vulgar woman, where diamonds and sapphires mixed with tin buttons and glass beads and mold-green pennies. The fountain of yellow light rising to the ceiling, the women dancing along the walls, the leaves and vines twined underfoot on the carpet—all of it was undoubtedly beautiful, but somehow everything seemed at odds with everything else. It overwhelmed the senses.

"Tacky," Peter whispered.

She frowned. This was the theater of Callan's diary, his favorite place in all the world. Here, in a way, was her inheritance. "I'd say exuberant," she said. "Ornate."

"The Paramount opened in 1931," Polanski said. "It was in use almost continuously from the thirties to the seventies, as a theater, a movie house, a concert hall. In 1972 the great work of restoring it began."

He led them under the black arch of the stairway to the theater itself. The huge auditorium was as Callan had described it: more friezes and grillwork on the walls and ceiling, gods and warriors and stars and waves. The amber light he had mentioned was here too, turning everything to a deep dull gold. Blue exit signs, like turquoise inlay, shone brightly in the near gloom.

They went from there to the maze of bare rooms and sloping hallways backstage. Polanski pointed out the laundry room, the wind machine that powered the organ. They ended in the room beneath the stage, what the guide called the trap room.

Andrew Dodd had said he had interviewed Fentrice and Callan and Thorne in the trap room. Suddenly Molly thought she could feel them all around her, the music, the confetti, the throng of costumed men and women.

The guide paused for questions. "Do you know anything about the Allalie Family?" she asked. "They played here in the thirties."

Polanski looked at her sharply. "The—what was that name?"

"The Allalie Family. The magicians," Molly said.

"Never heard of them," Polanski said. "Though I suppose they could have been here—hundreds of acts came through back then."

"Are you sure?"

"Of course I'm sure. I was an usher here in the thirties."

The audience murmured in confusion, clearly wondering why he hadn't mentioned that earlier. This was just the sort of thing they wanted to hear.

More hands were raised, more questions asked. Polanski took a few of them, then hurried the audience back to the lobby and outside. Books and postcards were on sale from a table in the entranceway, and several people clustered around looking at the souvenirs. More stood talking to Polanski, seemingly unwilling to let the enchantment of the tour end.

J. Polanski, Molly thought. It could be. She joined the group hovering around him. He turned away from her, pointing to a young girl who had asked a question. When he finished with his answer Molly raised her hand, but he continued to ignore her, nodding instead to an old man at the back of the crowd.

"What are you doing?" Peter asked, coming up next to her and whispering harshly. "He said he doesn't know who they are."

"I think he does," Molly said.

"Oh, fine. So now you're an investigative journalist."

"Just wait a minute," Molly said.

Peter frowned; she could tell he was displeased again. She turned away from him, and at that moment the guide met her eyes briefly. "Hey, Jake!" she said, as loudly as she could.

"Yes?" he said. Then he scowled, obviously angry with himself for giving so much away.

"I thought so," Molly said. "Tell me about the Allalie Family."

"You should know," Jake said. "You look almost exactly like that damned woman. What was her name? Fentrice, that was it."

"Fentrice is my great-aunt. What did they do to you that was so terrible?"

"They stole from me. Stole from me in the middle of the Depression. I nearly lost my job."

The people buying souvenirs looked up at that, left the table, and began to cluster around him. Everyone fell silent, waiting for the story to continue.

"What did they steal?" Molly asked.

"The day's take, that's what. I was supposed to add it up, take the deposit to the bank. I opened the safe and it was gone. Nothing."

"Well, but why do you think they stole it? Couldn't it have been someone else?"

"Callan was there when I opened the safe, that's why. Callan Allalie, your—what? Great-uncle?"

"My grandfather, actually."

The crowd drew closer. This was better than the tour. "Your grandfather," Jake said. "Did he teach you to lie, cheat, and steal too? He made some ridiculous suggestion, that we look backstage for the money, something like that. And then that damned tiger, Jewel—Well, never mind."

"The tiger spoke to you."

"How did you know that? I *thought* the tiger spoke to me, which is a completely different thing. I was overworked, under a lot of stress. I went home early that day, weeded the garden."

Suddenly Molly knew the rest of the story. "And you found

the money there, in your garden. The tiger told you to dig deep."

"Did Callan tell you this story? Yeah, it was there. I pulled the bundle out and something tore—roots had already started to grow around it. I remember counting it—my hands were shaking so much I had to do it two or three times."

"So Callan didn't steal the money."

"It was his idea of a practical joke. Throwing his voice so I thought the tiger was talking, stealing the money, and then burying it in my backyard—I ran back to the Paramount for the bankbook, made it to the bank with no time to spare. I don't know why he did it, but I didn't think it was very funny. You can tell your grandfather that for me."

"He died a long time ago."

"Well. I suppose I'm sorry. All right, I'm sorry. But the joke wasn't very funny, all the same."

"Maybe he wanted you to think about things. To wonder at how strange the world is. To dig deeper into yourself."

Jake looked at Molly suspiciously. "Why on earth would he do that?" he asked.

The Paramount was near Molly's last temp job, near the deli she had gone to with John. When the tour ended she led Peter to the deli and they ordered lunch. Peter looked different, more open somehow, and after a moment she realized why: she had rarely seen him in daylight. Even when she'd worked for him he had come by in the evening to collect the pages she had typed.

"This is great," Molly said. "So the Allalies traveled the country, changing people's lives. Showing them there was more to the world than what they knew. Performance art, almost."

"I like the magic angle," Peter said. "The older generation performing their tricks for the British aristocracy, the younger generation more democratic, traveling through American cities and towns . . . People would find them sympathetic, but there's this almost sinister edge to them that's fascinating in its own way."

"Look at all the people they met. Andrew Dodd, Jake Polanski, some of the people who volunteered from the audience . . ."

"And then there's Thorne's disappearance. The mystery angle."

Molly became aware that they weren't talking to each other but at each other, each pursuing a completely different subject. "Peter," she said.

He said nothing for a while, lost in thought. Then it seemed to Molly that he ran the conversation through his mind, realized that she had spoken his name. "Yes?" he said.

"You're not going to write a book about them, are you?"

"Why not? It's a great story."

"Because it's my family, that's why not. Think of what it would do to Fentrice—she's too old for this kind of publicity. And what about Samuel Allalie, for that matter? He trusted me with Callan's journal when he barely knew me—I can't repay him this way."

"You can't think about those things when you're doing a book. The truth is always going to hurt someone."

"Sure, when you're doing an exposé or something. When someone's lying, and the public good is served by the truth coming out. But no one's been harmed by my family—they're just a bunch of performers, for God's sake."

"How do you know that? Didn't you say they blackmailed Lady Dorothy? Hey—there's another angle, the money angle."

"Oh, please. She helped them out a few times, gave them some of her fortune. That's a far cry from blackmail."

"Well, you'd have to research it, of course—"

"Peter. Don't do this." She took a breath, summoning all her courage for what she was about to say. "I'll have to stop seeing you if you're going to write a book about my family."

Peter held up his hand. "Hey. I was just thinking out loud, that's all. This is my job—you can't blame me for trying."

"Okay," Molly said. She smiled at him. "Great. Thanks."

"Sure," Peter said. He took a bite of his sandwich, chewed it thoughtfully. They said very little for the remainder of the meal.

✻ ✻ ✻

She woke in the middle of the night with the strong feeling that she was close to an answer. What was it, the answer she had found? She lay still, reaching out for it.

Callan had said that the family had bought property in California, that his mother Edwina stayed there with the children too young to tour. He'd mentioned a family reunion when they'd got to Oakland. And Samuel, Callan's son, probably lived in California; it had been easy enough for him to meet with her the day after she'd requested it. Lived in Oakland, maybe, or nearby. Was he still on the old family property? And did others in the family, Lanty's children and her children's children, live there too?

In the morning she dialed John's number. The line was busy. *Gwen's taken it off the hook again,* she thought impatiently. She dressed and drove to John's apartment.

John answered the bell when she rang. "What is it?" he asked suspiciously.

"I've got a question for you," she said. "Where does Samuel Allalie live?"

"You know I can't give you that information."

Molly sighed. She told him about the conclusion she had come to the night before. "When Samuel gave me Callan's diary you said that now we all know each other's secrets," she said. "I know yours, and you know mine, but maybe we don't know everything about Samuel. He could be holding out on you."

"Why would he do that?"

"I don't know. I just wonder what happened to Lanty's children, to the rest of the family. They might all be living together. I just don't know where."

"Well, I'm certainly not going to tell you."

She studied him a minute. "You don't know, do you?" she asked.

John said nothing.

"Samuel gave you a phone number but no address, right?" she said.

"Look," he said. "Gwen's left me. I've been on the phone to her all morning, I'm neglecting my work, but she won't come back. She says that the night you came over she started to realize I was mistreating her. You can understand why I'm not exactly delighted to see you this morning."

"Just give me Samuel's phone number and I'll go away."

"I can't do that. It's privileged information."

"Is it? Aren't we working together on this?"

"Not anymore we aren't. I don't need you coming in and ruining my life."

"I didn't do anything to your life. If you'd paid a little more attention to Gwen she wouldn't have left you. Sooner or later she would have realized how much you ignore her. I just happened to be there when she did."

"Just go away."

"What about the case?"

"I'll let you know when I have something."

Molly walked back to her car and sat behind the wheel. *What now?* she thought. Someone in a late-model Buick drove up to John's house and got out of his car. Samuel.

She ducked down, nearly certain he hadn't seen her. *Fine,* she thought. *If John doesn't want my help I'll do it myself.*

Samuel stayed in John's apartment for fifteen minutes and then left. When he pulled away from the curb Molly started her car and moved in a few lengths behind him.

He headed for the freeway and went west, toward the San Francisco Bay. The morning commute had just ended, and traffic at the entrance to the Bay Bridge moved smoothly. She dug a dollar out of her purse while driving and stopped at the tollbooth to hand it over.

She let Samuel stay a little ahead of her on the bridge. When he got to San Francisco she followed him south, taking 101 to 280 to 1. Highway 1 soon left the city behind; they topped a hill and Molly saw the Pacific Ocean on her right. A long way out the blue-gray water blurred into the blue-gray of the horizon; a huge tanker seemed stopped there, suspended between water and sky. Three large rocks stood like sentinels at the mouth of the bay. Spreading pine grew by the highway, squat and low to withstand the wind.

She had never taken this road before, was amazed at how abruptly the city ended. They passed through a small town of four stoplights and then Highway 1 narrowed down to two lanes and began to twist back and forth. Mountains reared up on one side; on the other the land fell away sharply to the sea.

They were driving faster than she liked now; her old Honda Civic began to rattle in protest. She downshifted to take a curve and then went back into fourth, nearly standing on the gas pedal to keep up with Samuel's Buick.

Ahead of her Samuel rounded another bend and she downshifted again. The Honda fishtailed; she had to struggle to get it back on the road. When she came out of the turn the Buick was nowhere to be seen.

She braked quickly and pulled into a turnout overlooking the ocean. The road ran straight in front of her, completely empty. As she watched a few cars drove up from the south.

There was a small hollow between the mountains to her left. Was that a trail? It seemed to resolve itself as she looked at it: an entrance trellised with roses, a dirt road barely wide enough for one car.

She waited until the traffic cleared, then swung across Highway 1 and drove through the entrance. A gate stood there, wide open. She went past it and down the unpaved road.

Almost immediately her car hit a pothole. Something underneath it scraped loudly, something else pulled it sharply to the right. She fought with it, cursing.

Trees appeared to the right and left, tall eucalyptus at first and then leafy oak and shadowy pine. Flowers grew among them, dots of color, white Queen Anne's lace and purple irises. The road narrowed; the trees seemed to close in. Branches scratched the car on both sides.

The path ended. A large wooden house stood ahead of her among the trees. Nothing led up to it; there was no middle ground between forest and house. It was as if someone had cleared away just enough land to set a house on and no more. She parked the car and walked toward it.

The front door stood open. The doorknob was brass, fashioned to look like a smiling sun. The door knocker, a brass alligator fastened to the door by its tail, stared down at her superciliously, its nostrils wide.

The front room was large, its length at least double its width. Windows running along one side looked out over a garden. She went inside.

At first the room seemed too cluttered for her to take it all in. Chairs with lions' paws for feet and lions' heads growing out of the arms; tables like rooted trees; the fireplace poker, shovel, and brush disguised as forest animals, a fox, a ferret, an owl. The coat rack was another tree, intricately carved down to the green leaves on its branches, and a woman's head peered down at her from above the fireplace, her hair brushing the mantel. The light fixture was another smiling sun. Even the light switch had undergone a magical transformation, the switch itself a long pointed nose, the screws on the plate eyes and a round open mouth. She almost expected everything around her to start dancing, like in an old cartoon.

"Hello?" she said. "Is anyone here?"

No one answered. She ventured farther into the room. "Hello!" she called. "Anyone home?"

Samuel put his head around a doorway. "Hello, Molly," he said. "Glad you could make it."

"You—you knew I was following you—"

"Of course I knew," Samuel said. "I brought you here, didn't I?"

"What do you mean, here? What is this place?"

"What do you think of it?" Samuel asked.

She turned, trying to take it all in. "It's all designed to look like something else," she said.

He nodded. He seemed a little disappointed in her response, and she wondered just what he had expected her to say.

His head disappeared; Molly heard him walking away. She hurried after him. She found herself in a hallway; here too the light switches had been fashioned to look like people, plants, animals. Doors opened out on either side, and a flight of stairs led to a second story. A large carved cat sat at the end of the banister.

Samuel stopped at one of the rooms and looked in. A kitchen, Molly saw. The faucet in the sink was a swan, the hot- and cold-water knobs its wings. Branching metal ivy grew up the refrigerator door and the kitchen cabinets. A short muscular man stood with his back to them, mixing something on the stove.

He turned. He was balding, and coarse gray hair sprouted from his ears. "You've brought her, then," he said. He smiled, showing gapped teeth. "Hello, Molly."

"Hello," she said automatically. Who was he? One of the family, of course, but she had seen him, or at least his picture, somewhere before. "Is it—Callan?"

"It is."

"You're not dead."

"Neither are you."

"Sorry—I didn't mean that. I mean my aunt told me you'd died."

"And what have you learned?"

Verey's question, she thought. They changed people's lives, she had said to Peter. Performance art. But it was different when it was *your* life being changed, when you were the one they had caught up in their act.

Callan went to one of the cabinets and opened it, using the ivy as a handle. "I guess I learned not to believe everything I hear," Molly said slowly. "That things aren't always what they seem."

Samuel and Callan said nothing. Callan didn't even turn around but poured something from the cabinet into his concoction on the stove. Molly smelled trout and rich spices.

She felt as if she had failed some sort of test, without even knowing what the test had been. "Well, what the hell do you want me to say?" she asked angrily. "Why didn't you ever get in touch with me? Would it have been so hard to call or write?"

"We didn't know you existed," Samuel said. "Your mother Joan left us — I never knew where she went, or that she'd had a child."

"But John told you about me weeks ago. Why didn't you say anything?"

"That's not the way the family works," Callan said. He seemed about to say more, but just then the swan-faucet lifted itself off the kitchen sink and flew heavily to his shoulder. "Corrig," Callan said without looking around him.

Molly turned. A young man with curly reddish-blond hair stood in the doorway to the kitchen, leaning against the doorjamb. But this couldn't be Corrig, Lanty's son. Corrig would be as old as Callan by now.

"Show Molly to her room, would you, Corrig?" Samuel asked.

Corrig nodded and beckoned to her. She didn't want to leave the kitchen — she had a thousand more questions to ask — but somehow she found herself following him.

They went up the flight of stairs and Corrig showed her to a room. "You can't be the original Corrig," she said. "Are you his son? Lanty's grandson?"

Corrig put his finger to his lips, then pointed into the room, then looked at her quizzically.

"It's fine," she said. "I don't like pink, but it'll have to do."

Corrig grinned. When she looked back at the room the bed-spread had turned blue, the curtains purple, the carpet light green. Trees grew from the four bedposts, shading the bed with green leaves. Corrig waved, and a red banner unfurled from the ceiling. She went closer to see what it said. It was blank.

When she turned around Corrig had gone.

TEN
The House in the Trees

She left her coat and purse in the room and went back downstairs. The kitchen was filled with people now, all of them talking loudly and carrying plates of savory-smelling food into the dining room. "Take these out to the table, would you, Molly?" someone said, handing her a set of salt and pepper shakers. One was an alligator woman, bright green, wearing a red hat and clutching a red purse, the other an alligator man dressed in blue overalls.

In the dining room someone was lighting a green and gold candle shaped like an avocado. More people crowded into the room and began to sit down. Molly took a seat next to a young man with a mustache.

"Hi, I'm Molly," she said to him. "What's your name?"

"Alex. You must be the long-lost cousin Samuel's been talking about—it's good to meet you. Listen up, everyone, it's Molly."

She'd been wondering if these people had any manners, if anyone would ever introduce her. Now she thought she would never be able to remember any of them. "My brother Matt," Alex said. "We're Lanty's great-grandchildren. My mother and father. My cousin Jeremy, and his parents—Lanty was his great-grandmother too. Samuel and Elizabeth, and their kids, Kate and Elizabeth. You've already met Callan, I guess. And Corrig."

"Alex — Allalie?"

"Endicott."

"The magic show!" Molly said.

"We do a magic show, that's right," Alex said. "The Endicott Family."

Molly shook her head. "No, I — I know some people who met each other at your show. The Westingates. Charles and Kathy — he's from England. A lord."

If the name Westingate was familiar no one in the family admitted it. Molly went on. "They said you called them up to the stage. You were trying to make amends to Lady Dorothy's descendants, weren't you? Introducing Charles to Kathy, so he could afford to buy the manor house back?"

"I don't remember them," Alex said. "It must have been before my time."

Molly looked down the table at Callan. "That was your doing, wasn't it?" she asked him. "Introducing them?"

Callan said nothing. Corrig passed her a platter, the trout she had smelled earlier. *One of these fish is going to wink now,* Molly thought, remembering Callan's account of their trip to England. She braced herself. But nothing happened as she took the platter from Corrig, served herself, and then handed it down the table.

"Could you pass the salt?" Alex asked.

The green alligator woman began to walk down the length of the table, her red handbag swinging. Molly backed a little in her chair. Alex took the ceramic figure and then passed it to her. "Salt?" he asked.

No one was watching her; no one said anything. Still, she knew somehow that this was a test. She reached out as calmly as she could and took it. "Do any of you know anything about Thorne?" she asked, looking down the table.

"She's Callan's sister, isn't she?" Kate said.

"But what happened to her?" Molly asked. "Does she ever come here?"

"Thorne?" Alex said. It was as if she had asked about someone in a history book, an obscure president or poet of the last century. "I've never met her, have you?"

Kate and a few of the others shook their heads. The talk turned to other things, plans for an upcoming tour, the music Callan wanted to use for the opening. Callan sang while Corrig beat his knife and fork together to keep the time. One of the cousins offered his own song, which Callan turned into counterpoint. It was only when Molly went back to her room after dinner that she realized that almost none of her questions had been answered.

She tried Callan again the next day, when he was in the kitchen cooking. "Do you know what happened to Thorne?" she asked.

"Thorne? Up until a few weeks ago I didn't even know what happened to Fentrice."

"That's not really an answer, you know."

"It wasn't meant to be. Is it my job to provide answers?"

Corrig came into the kitchen. He took three oranges in one hand and began to juggle them. They circled slower and slower around him, leaving arcing trails of gold, until finally one hung suspended in midair.

"How about you?" Molly asked. "Do you know where Thorne is?"

Corrig shrugged.

"Callan said in his diary that you might be the strongest of the family," Molly said. "Why do you spend your time on these tricks?"

He shrugged again.

"Why do I get the feeling you could tell me everything if you wanted to?" Molly said.

"He could," Callan said. "You should listen to him."

"Listen to him?" Molly said, frustrated. "He doesn't *say* anything."

Corrig threw her an orange.

She caught it and went outside, feeling angry and puzzled and even slightly amused all at the same time. A path wound through the trees, looping and turning in on itself. She followed it, brushing the overhanging leaves from her face as she walked. Voices and laughter and snatches of song came from up ahead.

She went on. To her right she saw a small green meadow among the trees. Kate was there, and Alex and Matt. They lay facing the sky, their heads close together, their bodies forming a star upon the grass.

"Hey, Moll!" someone called, Matt or Alex.

She left the path, sat down next to them. "What's up?" she asked.

"Corrig's up to his old tricks again," Alex said. Alex was the one with the mustache, Molly remembered.

You bet he is, she thought, but she didn't want to share her frustrations with the others. "Is Corrig my third cousin too?" she asked.

"Corrig?" Kate said. "He's Lanty's son, isn't he?"

"But then he'd be much older, wouldn't he?" Molly asked. "As old as Callan, at least."

"I suppose," Matt said.

"Is he immortal?" Molly asked.

"Immoral, maybe," Kate said, and they all laughed.

"Amoral," Matt said.

"Inamorata," Alex said, murmuring. The sun grew hotter, turning his light brown hair the color of polished wood. He made an effort to rouse himself. "But he's not going to get away with it this time. Not when he turns my bed into a horse."

"He turned your bed into a horse?"

"He did. I woke up in the woods somewhere."

"But why?"

"Because that's where the horse had taken me."

"No, I mean why did he turn your bed into a horse?"

"Because he can," Alex said. "I'd do it myself if I could."

Molly sighed. The air grew hotter. Kate lifted a hand to her yellow hair and pushed it off her forehead; it seemed heavy, like massy gold. A bee buzzed close to them and then flew away.

"We'll have to retaliate this time," Alex said.

Who? Molly thought sleepily, but Matt was speaking. "The trouble, of course, is that Corrig always seems to know what you're going to do before you do it," he said.

"Well then, we'll have to distract him somehow," Alex said. "Lure him out into the woods, maybe. Or put something in his coffee."

"I could use some coffee right now," Kate said. "Why do people say, 'Wake up and smell the coffee'? Shouldn't it be 'Smell the coffee and then wake up'?"

"Pay attention," Alex said. "I'm serious this time."

"Remember when he lined the floor of your bedroom with eggs?" Matt said. "And you ran in to get something without looking?"

"If he has so much power," Molly asked, "why does he only use it for practical jokes?"

"Well, that's the question, isn't it?" Alex said.

"Yes, it is," Molly said. "Are any of you ever going to give me a direct answer?"

"Yes," Alex said. "That was straight enough, don't you think?"

"I give up," Molly said, standing.

"I wouldn't," Kate said, not unkindly. Molly realized, surprised, that they wanted to help her, but that they were as constrained by the rules of the labyrinth as she was. She understood that she was supposed to learn something here, but she couldn't for the life of her figure out what it was.

She sat back down and listened to their soft, rambling talk. The shadows of the trees grew longer, drowning them in shade.

"Dear John," Molly wrote a few days later. "I'm writing you because I thought you might be wondering where I am. Though maybe not—we didn't exactly part on the best of terms. I hope things have worked out with you and Gwen.

"Anyway, I've learned a lot more about the case. I found Callan, for one thing. I know we thought he was dead, but it looks as if my aunt didn't tell me the truth about this. I'm here in his house, though house might not be the right word. College, maybe, or retreat.

"If you got the impression from the above that I don't understand everything that's going on, you'd be right. Lots of people live here besides Callan, other relatives, but I haven't sorted them all out yet: Samuel and his wife Elizabeth and his daughters Kate and Elizabeth, and some second or third cousins of mine named Alex and Matt and Jeremy and their parents. I think Alex said he and Matt are brothers—they look a lot alike, anyway.

"I called this place a college because I think I'm supposed to learn something here. I don't mean that there are teachers, because there aren't. But people keep speaking in these enigmatic phrases and then looking at me as though they expect me to understand something. I have to say I don't get half of what they're talking about. Well, more than half, if I'm going to be honest.

"This ties in with something I learned a while ago, something I never told you about. Peter and I went and took a tour of the Paramount Theatre. You should go there, if you're still on the case. Talk to a man named Jake Polanski. He was an usher in the thirties, knew the Allalie Family.

"Anyway, what he told me helped me understand more about how the family worked. They were teachers, as I thought, traveling the country and showing people truths about their lives. At the time I thought this was wonderfully exciting. Now, though, it looks as if I'm one of their students, and I have to say it's not as much fun when you're on the receiving end. What it is is frustrating as hell.

"I think the Allalies learned from their experience with Dorothy Westingate that you can't teach people by talking at them. You can put them on the path to wisdom, but they have to come to it by themselves. Emily's son did this to Emily, for example. Callan tried to do this with Polanski, but I think he failed there. You can show people the labyrinth, but they have to find the center by themselves.

"Now I think they're doing it to me, but I don't have the slightest idea what I'm supposed to learn. I have a lot of time to think about it, though, because everyone in this house seems wrapped up in his or her own concerns. Callan spends most of his time cooking. I wonder if that's a family trait—the older you get the more you withdraw from the world, the way Neesa did by playing pool.

"This is what I think so far. Samuel and Callan hired you to find me, so I would find this house. That's why I asked you if you were still on the case. They may have taken you off now that you've done everything they wanted you to do.

"And that's as far as I've gotten with this thing. Oh, and yesterday I found a book about Greek myths in the library. Did you know that Ariadne was the woman who led Theseus through the labyrinth? I guess I knew that once upon a time, but I didn't think it was important. Now I wonder who decided that that would be my middle name. Was it my mother, or Callan? And here's something we seem to have overlooked—there's a monster at the center of the labyrinth, the Minotaur. What am I going to discover if I do get there?

"The library is interesting, by the way, but more for what it doesn't have than what it does. I didn't find Callan's diary, for example—did you ever get around to giving it back to Samuel? And it doesn't have Dorothy's pamphlet, or that book on the occult we read in England. All I saw were rows of classics, all of them bound in the same color—Shakespeare, Dickens, Homer. Nothing you couldn't find at the Oakland Public Library.

"I'm writing this because, as I said, I have a lot of time to think here. And because so many people in this case have left written records, Emily and Callan and poor Dorothy with her crackpot theories. I don't know if I'm going to send it, or even if I can—

there doesn't seem to be a mailbox anywhere nearby. I'm not telling you where I am because I want to do this alone."

She folded the letter and looked through the drawers of the desk for stamps and envelopes. There was only more blank paper. She shrugged and put the letter in the bottom drawer.

She wondered where Peter was, what he was doing. Did he miss her? Should she have written to him instead of John? But she had been able to set everything down clearly, logically, in a letter to John, while a letter to Peter would be tangled up with all her feelings, all the things she wanted to say to him. It was too bad Callan didn't have a telephone.

The next day the old woman came. Molly had gone downstairs, lured by the smell of the dinner Callan was cooking. The others were already there, talking and laughing.

Someone knocked on the front door. "It's open!" Callan called, helping himself to thin slices of beef drowned in sauce.

The knock came again. Kate looked at Alex, one eyebrow raised. "Is this one of yours?" she asked softly.

Alex shook his head.

"Corrig's, probably," Matt said.

They heard the knock a third time. "Someone get that," Callan said. "Molly, would you?"

Molly stood. *This is one of Corrig's practical jokes,* she thought, and looked hard at him before she went to the front room. He grinned at her.

But when she opened the door she saw only a small old woman wrapped in a bulky shawl. The woman peered up at her from beneath her tangled, thick white hair. Despite her strange wild appearance she looked somehow familiar. "Can I help you?" Molly asked.

"I want to see Callan," the woman said.

Probably not a relative, Molly thought; she didn't have the gap between her teeth they all had. "We're eating dinner now," Molly said.

"No, it's all right, Molly," Callan said, coming up behind her. "What is it?"

"I want the book," the woman said. For the first time Molly noticed that there were only the familiar cars parked behind the old woman on the narrow dirt road, her own and Samuel's. How had the woman gotten here?

"The book?" Callan asked.

"You know which one. The book your sister Fentrice got in England."

"Fentrice? I haven't seen Fentrice in sixty years."

"You have the book, though. I'm sure you do."

"The scrapbook?" Molly asked.

The woman stared at her in disbelief. "No, not the scrapbook," she said scornfully. "What possible use would that be to me? Anyway, she still has the scrapbook. I want the book she got in England."

"I don't have any of her books," Callan said.

"Can I come in and look for it?"

"It's not really convenient right now," Callan said. "Some other day, perhaps."

The woman pushed past him. She went through the front room and down the hallway to the library, as boldly confident as if she had been there before.

By the time Molly and Callan caught up with her she was studying the shelves in the library, the rows of identically bound books. Her arms were crossed; her eyes snapped from one shelf to another. There were twigs in her hair, Molly saw, and more caught in her voluminous blue shawl.

"Huh!" the woman said. She opened what Molly had thought was a grandfather clock. There were shelves in its body instead of the wires and gears Molly had expected, each holding more of the identically bound books. She turned toward them. "You've hidden it."

"My life is an open book," Callan said, spreading his arms

wide. "You can search the entire house if you want. But you'll have to do it without me—my dinner's getting cold."

He walked back to the dining room. Molly stood a moment, her head filled with a dozen questions. "Who are you?" she asked. "How do you know Fentrice?"

The woman said nothing. Finally she turned away from the shelves and headed to the door. "You tell him I'll try again," she said. "I know the book's here somewhere."

"What book?" Molly asked, following her, but the woman closed the front door behind her. Molly opened it quickly. The old woman had disappeared; Molly saw only the trees, the path, the cars. She returned to the dining room.

"That was one of yours, wasn't it?" Matt was asking Corrig. "You sent her, didn't you?"

Corrig shook his head, his face perfectly innocent.

"Well, then, whose was it?" Jeremy asked. "Who sent her? Alex?"

"No, why would I?" Alex said.

"I don't think she had anything to do with your practical jokes," Molly said slowly. "She came here wanting something. She knows who Fentrice is. . . ."

"I still think it's Corrig," Matt said. "Don't grin at me like that, Corrig. I know you had something to do with all this."

"Look," Molly said, exasperated. "She wanted a book, a book Fentrice got in England." She turned to Callan. "You were in England in—when was it? 1935? Did you ever tour there again?"

Callan shook his head. Now he was grinning too; the similarity to Corrig was very marked.

"Remember in the diary when you say Fentrice disappeared for a few days while you were in England and then came back?" Molly asked. Callan nodded. "That's when she must have gotten the book. But what book? Was it—Oh, my God."

"What, Molly?" Callan asked.

"Maybe it was the confession Emily wrote. Maybe Fentrice went up to the Westingates' house, Tantilly, and looked in the library."

"Emily?" Matt said. "Which one was she? Changed her name, didn't she?"

"She was Neesa," Molly said. "She wrote a confession to Dorothy Westingate, an account of her life. It's in the library at Tantilly—I read some of it when I was in England."

"But if you saw it in the library," Callan said slowly, "then Fentrice couldn't have taken it."

"No, but she could have read it while she was there."

"Was there anything important in it? Something this woman would interrupt our dinner for?"

"I don't know. I only read part of it—some of the pages had been torn out," Molly said. Everyone around the table was looking at her now. "But there were strange disappearances around both Fentrice and Emily. What if those pages were about Lydia, Emily confessing what she had done to Lydia? What if Fentrice wanted to know what Emily did, because she wanted to do the same thing to Thorne? What if Fentrice went up to Tantilly because she wanted a way to get rid of someone that would never be traced to her?"

"What do you mean, get rid of?" Samuel said. "Do you mean kill?"

"God, I don't know," Molly said. Without realizing it she had started to agree with John: Fentrice was a liar, Fentrice had lied about a great many things. Why had Fentrice told her Callan was dead? She thought of the woman who had raised her, the strict but kind aunt who smelled of soap and starch.

"Lydia died in 1913," Callan said. "After Neesa came to the United States."

"I don't know what this family's capable of," Molly said. She looked squarely at Callan, but he didn't flinch. "Maybe Neesa killed her from the United States somehow."

"So you think Neesa's a killer? Your great-great-grandmother?" Callan asked. "And your aunt Fentrice? Is she a killer too?"

Could she be? Surely Molly would have guessed something, surely Fentrice would have let something slip, given something away. But the timing was right: Thorne had disappeared the same year the family had gone to England, the year Fentrice might have read Emily's book. "I don't know," Molly said again. "I don't know who anyone is anymore."

"That's certainly true," Callan said. "I think that woman at the door, the one who interrupted our dinner — I think she was Fentrice."

"What?" Molly asked, astonished.

"Sure. She used to love to disguise herself. She might have followed you here. You said there were pages missing from Neesa's journal. Maybe she thought you took them, maybe she wants them back."

"But why did she leave the family in the first place?" Molly asked. "What happened between you and her?"

"I don't know what she's told you," Callan said gently, "but I'm certain she didn't give you the whole story about the family. She was vain, she wanted the spotlight and would think up outrageous schemes to get it. I think she hated Thorne, her nearest rival, more than anything — hated her, and loved her too, of course."

"I got some of that from your diary," Molly said. "But Fentrice never told me anything, just that she'd been in a magic act when she was younger. She said you were dead, that I didn't have any other family."

"We never got along, she and I. She always wanted to be the most important person in the act, to be in control at all times. It was even worse than what I wrote in the diary. And when she couldn't get control she left." Callan paused. "And then she had you, to raise as her own when your parents died. You were just a child, you were someone she could control. But if that was her at the door — well, now she's seen that you're here with me. And if I know her she'll be furious about it. To her it would seem as if you've changed sides, you've betrayed her. I'd be careful if I were you, Molly — you could be in danger."

"Danger? What do you mean?"

Callan said nothing. She had been lucky to get as much as she had from him, Molly thought, the first straight answers to her questions since she had come here. Could he be right, could that have been Fentrice at the door? The woman, whoever she was, had seemed familiar. What would Fentrice do now?

As if in answer a wild wind swept through the room, toppling candlesticks and napkin holders and glasses. Molly grabbed for her water glass before it could spill to the floor. "Was that—was that Fentrice?" she asked, setting the glass back on the table.

Callan shrugged.

Later, back in her room, she took out her letter to John. "I said before that Fentrice never told me Callan was still alive," she wrote. "Now it looks as if there's a lot of things she didn't tell me—how she felt about Callan and Thorne, what she did in England when she disappeared for those few days. You were right—she is a liar. I've caught her out in too many lies to have any illusions on that score.

"But does that make her a murderer? Lots of people lie, but how many of them could kill someone? Still, what happened to Thorne? That's what we keep coming back to, isn't it?

"I guess I'm not going to send this letter after all. If Fentrice did kill Thorne I don't want to be the one to tell you. I couldn't bear seeing her go through the courts, go to jail, knowing that I was the one who had sent her there.

"Well, but she's probably innocent. Writing this in the safety of my room I find I can't really believe she could have done anything so horrible. This is my aunt after all, the woman who plays bridge with her friends once a week, who works in her garden, who bakes the world's greatest peach pie, with peaches she grows herself. When some brat in the third grade told me she was a witch and I came home crying, she was the one who wiped my nose, who told me how brave I was to stand up for her. I love her, and I know that she genuinely loves me. She doesn't seem very warm, but there's a lot of feeling beneath that prim starched surface she shows to the world. She could not have done what Callan said she did.

"No—let's be honest here. I was the one who thought she might be a murderer. I was the one who accused her of reading Emily's book and learning how to dispose of someone. So what do I really think? Was I telling the truth a moment ago when I wrote that I thought she was probably innocent?

"I don't know. I just don't know. All I know is that the thought of her killing someone makes me feel sick. It's as if I had never really known anyone, or anything, as if my entire life up to now has been a lie. I don't think I've ever been as miserable as I am this moment.

"Remember when I said that I have no secrets, in the restaurant at the airport while we were waiting for our plane? That seems so long ago now, back in a more innocent time. Since then I've learned that everyone has secrets, that no one's perfect. I wish my secret had turned out to be something less dreadful, that, for example, Fentrice was really my mother, even though she's much too old for that to be true.

"If I find out anything more I'll write it down. But my appetite for discovery, for being a private investigator, has completely gone. It'll be a while before I go prowling around the house and the woods again, looking for clues. You can't make someone explore the labyrinth if she doesn't want to."

Despite her last words Molly wandered through the house the next few afternoons. She told herself that she was looking for something to read or someone to talk to, but the house itself held a kind of fascination for her. *Everything here turns out to be something else,* she thought. *Tables are trees, lamps are stars. A mysterious old woman who comes to the door is really my aunt Fentrice.*

As if the thought had conjured her up Molly rounded a corner and saw the old woman through an open doorway. It was a shock coming upon her; Molly's heart began to race, her pulse pounded in her ears. She forced herself to step inside the room. "Who are you?" she asked.

They were in Callan's study, Molly saw, and the woman was rifling through the drawers of Callan's desk. She did not pause to answer Molly's question. "Are you my aunt Fentrice?" Molly asked.

"Huh!" the woman said. She opened another drawer.

"Callan says that's who you are. Does he know you're here? What are you looking for?"

"I told you. Fentrice's book."

"What book?"

"You know what book."

"Emily's confession?"

The woman straightened. "Yes, Emily's confession. Where is it?"

"It's at Tantilly, where it belongs. And it isn't Fentrice's at all. Emily gave it to Dorothy Westingate."

"Don't be so pious. You weren't above a little theft yourself. What did you do with those pages?"

"I didn't do anything with them. Someone named Joseph Ottig tore them out. What was in them?"

"Huh!" the woman said again. She turned back to the open drawer and lifted out a box of staples, another box of paper clips, a green stone, a handful of coins.

"I'm going to get Callan," Molly said.

"Good—I could use his help here. And what do you think he'll say when I tell him what you did in England? Stealing, interfering with a police investigation—"

"I don't care what he says."

"No? He'll throw you out of the house. Your education here will come to an end, that's for sure." She stooped to pull open the bottom drawer.

"Who are you?" Molly asked again. "Are you Fentrice? What happened to Thorne? Where is she?"

The woman straightened. She glared at Molly so fiercely that Molly took half a step backward. "Thorne isn't dead, whatever that wicked man Callan tells you. So don't you go thinking those evil thoughts about your aunt Fentrice. You owe her more than you'll ever know."

"But—"

"Don't ask questions!" The wind rose again, fiercer than before. Papers and books blew off Callan's desk; a paperweight clanged loudly against the wall. Chairs skittered sideways. Something struck Molly hard in the shoulder. She covered her eyes with her hands.

The storm subsided. She opened her eyes. The woman was gone.

Molly and Alex took leftovers from the kitchen and went out to the woods for a picnic. The sun was breaking from the clouds; it looked as if the heat of a week ago, after a spring of long rains, had been a true herald of summer.

"Tell me about the magic act, the Endicott Family," Molly said. "Are you touring this year?"

Alex said nothing for a while. Because his thick mustache covered his mouth he always seemed to be smiling; Molly had come to realize that she could have no idea what he was really thinking. "We'll be leaving in about a week," he said finally.

"A week?" Molly was surprised at how sad she felt to hear it. Everyone at Callan's house seemed to spend their time surprising and exasperating her, but they were her family, after all. What would she do when they left? How would she get answers to her questions? She found she missed them already: Callan's cooking, Corrig's pranks, the company of the cousins. "Did you grow up here?" she asked. "What was it like?"

"It was fun, actually. Different from all the other kids at school. My brother Matt and my cousins, we were all sort of snobbish about our family. Kept to ourselves more than we should have, I guess. I wish I could have seen my parents more, though."

Someone screamed from up ahead.

"What was that?" Alex said.

"I don't know." Molly broke into a run and Alex followed her through the trees. "Help!" the screamer shouted. "Help!"

The meadow on their right had turned to quicksand. Some-one floundered in the mud, arms and legs thrashing. It was Matt.

Molly held a branch out to him. Alex knelt beside her, and when Matt grabbed it he helped her hold on. Together they pulled Matt to safety.

"Who did this?" Alex asked. "Was it Corrig?"

Matt was shivering too hard to speak. He shook his head. Alex draped the picnic blanket over him.

"No, not Corrig," Matt said finally. "He would never do any-thing to hurt us. I nearly—I nearly drowned."

"Well then, who was it?" Alex said impatiently. "What hap-pened?"

"It was that old lady we see around the house sometimes. The one with the blue shawl, who goes through the books in the library. She asked me—" A great shiver went through him. "She asked me where Fentrice's book was. I said I didn't know. She said she'd make me tell her."

Molly put her hand to her mouth. Alex and Matt didn't seem to notice. "You think she would have killed you?" Alex said. "For a book?"

"Yes," Matt said. "Yes, I do."

"Callan claims she's Fentrice," Alex said. "In disguise."

"My aunt is not a murderer," Molly said, with more convic-tion than she felt.

"No?" Matt said. "Then what happened to Thorne? That's what you came here to find out, isn't it? Callan's got to stop giv-ing this woman the run of the house. She's dangerous."

"If I know Callan, he'll welcome her with open arms," Alex said. "Then he'll trap her into revealing herself."

"By that time one of us could be dead," Matt said. "No, I'm going to talk to him, tell him what that crazy woman did today."

"You know what he'll say, don't you?" Alex said. Matt shook his head. "He'll say, What have you learned?"

Verey's old question, Molly thought. *So they still ask it among themselves.*

"I'll tell him I learned to stay away from lunatic women in

blue shawls," Matt said, wiping the mud from his clothes.

As Alex had predicted, Callan did nothing. They all came upon the woman from time to time, rummaging through the pots in the kitchen, taking down books in the library, digging in the garden with her bare hands. "Why doesn't Callan just call the police?" Molly asked. "At the very least he should put a lock on the front door."

"Callan's a lot smarter than you think," Alex said. "He won't let anything happen to us."

But that evening, when Molly went back to her room after dinner, she found the old woman going through her desk drawers. "Get out of my room," Molly said.

The woman turned. She held Molly's letter to John in one hand. "Why do you write these lies to this man?" she asked. "Hasn't he done us enough damage?"

"What do you mean, us?" Molly said. "I still don't know who you are. But you seem to know all about me—you even know who John is."

"Of course I know him. I never trusted him—his eyes are too close together."

"You are Fentrice, then. That's what Fentrice said—what you said—when you met John."

"I'm not Fentrice."

"How do I know that? How do I know you aren't lying to me? Again."

"I've never lied to you."

Molly sighed. Somehow she felt that the woman was telling the truth. Fentrice would be incapable of drowning anyone. Hell, her aunt's innate politeness would even keep her from coming into a house uninvited.

I should be able to figure out who she is, Molly thought. *Everyone in my family has the Gift. She's familiar, but she's not Fentrice. Not a relative, I think. But she's met John . . .* "Lila?" she said.

The woman shrieked like a siren. She spun around several times. Her face blurred, but Molly thought she could make out the housekeeper's face, smell the familiar cigarette smoke. Then she disappeared.

Someone knocked at Molly's door. She stared at the place where the old woman had been. A wisp of dirty gray smoke fell slowly through the air. The knock came again. She went to open the door.

"Molly?" Callan said. "What have you learned?"

"I learned who that woman is," Molly said. She felt an enormous relief. "She isn't Fentrice. She's the housekeeper, Lila. Fentrice is innocent. She never killed anyone."

"Then why did she send her housekeeper here?" Callan asked.

"She didn't send her. Lila came herself."

"Are you sure of that?"

"Yes, I am," Molly said. "I know you and Fentrice never got along. But she wouldn't do something like this, wouldn't spy, or — or murder. She's innocent. If you had a phone I could call her right now and prove it to you."

"But we do have a phone," Callan said.

"You do? How come I've never seen it?"

"It's not a secret. It's in my study downstairs."

"Great," Molly said. "I'll call her right now."

They went downstairs. In the study Callan pulled out a phone from behind a stack of books. There were two wide eyes on the receiver, one at each end, and the rotary dial looked like a round, astonished mouth. Molly called her aunt.

The phone rang four times, five. Could she have been wrong? Could Fentrice be here, in California? Six rings. Someone picked up the phone. "Hello?" a trembling voice said.

"Aunt Fentrice?" Molly said. Static crackled through the line. To Molly it seemed almost as if the fiber-optic technology of the past years had never happened, as if her aunt were talking from somewhere in the midthirties.

"Molly. Hello, dear. Do you know what time it is here?"

"Oh God. It's two hours later there, isn't it? I woke you up, didn't I?"

"Don't worry about it. I'm always happy to hear from you. Is something wrong?"

"I just wanted to know how you were. You and Lila. Is she there?"

"Lila? Now that's a funny thing. She went away on vacation. Forty years she's worked for me, never asked for a day off, and then suddenly she says she has to visit her family. I didn't know she had a family, did you?"

"No. Did she say where they live?"

"Out west somewhere."

"How are you getting along without her?"

"Fine. Though I can't say I won't be relieved when she comes back. How are you, dear? I didn't get a letter from you this week."

There was no reproach in Fentrice's voice, but Molly felt guilty just the same. "No, I—I'm sort of on vacation myself. I'm pretty isolated here—It's hard getting letters out. I'll call you, though. I'll call you again a week from now and see how you're getting along."

"That would be wonderful. I'll talk to you later, then."

"All right. Go back to sleep, Aunt Fentrice."

"Good night, dear."

"Good night."

"There," Molly said to Callan after she had hung up. "Lila's out west—It's Lila who keeps coming here and bothering us. Fentrice is in Illinois."

"Is she?" Callan asked.

"Look," Molly said, suddenly angry. Ever since John people had been making the most outrageous accusations about her aunt. She had even started to believe them, before she had learned the truth. "I know you don't like her—you told me so yourself. You've told me your side of the story, but she never got a chance to tell me hers. I'm sorry, but everything tells me to believe her. She raised me, after all. I think I would know if she was some kind of criminal."

"Would you?"

"Stop asking me questions, dammit!"

"How are you going to learn anything if you don't ask questions? Only people who know all the answers don't need to ask questions."

"And I suppose you know all the answers? Are you sure? I've read your diary, you know. You weren't this wise old man back then. Now you're putting on this act, you're trying to convince everyone you've found inner peace or something—"

"Inner peace? Anyone who says they've found inner peace is dead. Would you feel peaceful in the face of illness, of death?"

His daughter had died, Molly remembered. He had survived more sorrow than she could imagine. Still, his certainty angered her. "Maybe you've been wrong about Fentrice all these years, have you ever thought of that?" she asked. "Maybe she isn't as bad as you thought. What have you learned tonight?"

Callan laughed, long and delighted. Molly left the study in disgust. What the hell was so funny, anyway?

A few days later she woke to loud noises: something being dragged down the hallway, two or three people laughing. She got up and looked outside her door. They were packing; the dragging sound had been made by a trunk like the one Fentrice had. She had nearly forgotten that the family was going on tour.

Arrangements went on all day. People slipped in and out of costumes, tuned and played musical instruments. Jeremy called a bird to his wrist and let it go, and then suddenly the room was filled with birds, their white wings beating. Flowers grew from Alex's hands and then disappeared. Kate and her sister Elizabeth drew eggs from each other's ears, noses, mouths, armpits, until a small mound of them stood at their feet. Matt cursed because he couldn't fit into his tuxedo. Samuel's wife Elizabeth took it from him and hurried to the sewing room.

That evening after dinner they gathered in the living room. It was not exactly a rehearsal, Molly saw, more a reaffirmation of who they were and what they did. Someone had dragged out an old rickety piano from somewhere; Elizabeth played and everyone sang. Callan touched the candles around the room and they blossomed into orange flames.

"I didn't know you still performed until Alex told me," Molly said to Callan. "Emily said something about investments in her journal."

Objects around the room began to rise to the ceiling, books and pillows and even candles. The piano shuddered and lifted slowly off the floor. "Corrig!" Elizabeth said, still playing. "Stop that!" The piano thumped back down.

Callan threw back his head and laughed. "Investments!" he said. "Where's the fun in that?"

Outside the room rain hit the windowpanes and wind shook in the trees. Inside it was warm, a fire burning in the grate. Elizabeth started on another song. Someone pressed sheet music into Molly's hand and she sang along with the rest of them.

"Got a dog, got a cat, got a car, got a flat. . . ." Corrig played a clarinet, Callan passed around champagne. They all applauded themselves when they finished.

"Listen," Callan said. "Listen up, everyone." The family quieted, looking up at him. "We won't all go touring this year. I've decided—I'm staying home. So are Corrig and Alex and Matt. The rest of you—good-bye. And have fun."

"What do you mean?" Matt said. He looked a little hurt. "Why can't I go? I've already got my tuxedo and everything."

"Things are going to happen here," Callan said. "How about you, Alex? Do you mind staying on?"

"Oh, no," Alex said. "I like surprises."

Callan grinned. "Good," he said.

"What about me?" Molly asked.

"Oh, you'll be here with us, Molly," Callan said. A great relief flooded her; she would not have to go back just yet. "Nothing's going to happen without you."

Vans came to take the family to the train station early the next morning. It was raining hard. The family packed up in silence, exhausted from the celebration of the night before. Molly, Alex, and Matt waved out the front windows, and then the family was gone.

The woman in the blue shawl never came back. And when Molly called Fentrice a few days later her aunt told her that Lila had returned from her vacation. Molly was more certain than ever that the woman had been Lila.

Now that she knew where the phone was she tried calling Peter's hotel several times, but he was never in. She gave the phone number and elaborate directions to Callan's house to a bored-sounding receptionist, who assured her in a languid voice that he would pass them on. And she continued writing her letter to John, which had turned into a kind of diary.

"Why would Lila come all the way out here just for a book?" she wrote. "Maybe Fentrice told her something about the Allalie family and she became intrigued, wanted the kind of power she thought that they had, that we have.

"I don't know. In just a few weeks I've met relatives I never knew I had, I've learned that my family is far larger than just two people. I've had to stretch my brain to accommodate that, and then I've had to entertain the idea Aunt Fentrice might be a murderer, and then, just as I was beginning to despair, I realized she was innocent after all. If Callan asks me what I've learned I can answer, truthfully, that I've learned a hell of a lot, but I don't see where any of it gets me. I still don't know what happened to Thorne, for example.

"Lila said Thorne is still alive. How does she know? Could Fentrice have let something slip? Or what if—oh, my God—what if Lila *is* Thorne? Both sisters were good at disguises, Callan's diary says so. Should I tell Fentrice? Is Fentrice in danger from her?"

ELEVEN
Visits and Letters

Molly lay in bed late the next morning, looking up at the leaves of the trees and wondering if she should go to Callan with her suspicions. But what would Callan do? He didn't even seem to like Fentrice very much. Would he come to her defense?

What a family, she thought. You couldn't blame Fentrice for running away.

She heard someone knock on the door downstairs, and then footsteps going to answer it. "Molly!" Alex called. "You have a visitor!"

Oh, shit, Molly thought. *It's that woman in the blue shawl again. She's back.* She dressed quickly and went down the stairs. Peter stood at the door.

For a moment she was speechless. They she reached out and held him tightly. He put his arms around her, tentatively, as if unsure of his welcome.

"You got my directions!" she said.

"And about time, too," he said. He pulled away and grinned, the old easy smile that made her melt. "I thought you'd disappeared off the face of the earth. What are you doing here? Did you find out anything more about the Allalies?"

She found herself hesitating. She couldn't tell him the suspicions she'd had about Fentrice; he might not believe in Fentrice's innocence. "I found out I have a lot more relatives than I thought. My grandfather Callan lives here, and some cousins and second cousins . . . What about you? What are you working on?"

"Nothing. All my book proposals were bounced. I'm broke — living off my savings. I need monnney," he said. Then he laughed. "You going to ask me in?"

Once again she hesitated. "Let's get some breakfast," she said.

They took Peter's rental car up the highway to the small town Molly had seen, Pacifica. Peter drove to a café by the beach. When they had been seated and ordered breakfast Peter asked, "What did you mean about your relatives? How many of them are there?"

In answer Molly took out her genealogy. "Good God," Peter said. "Look at all these people. Not bad for someone who thought she only had a great-aunt. Who was that guy who answered the door?"

"Alex."

"What was he smiling about?"

"Oh, he always looks like that. It's his mustache — you can never tell what he's thinking."

"Alex Allalie?"

"Why are you asking all these questions?"

"I'm curious. It's an interesting story, you and your relatives."

Their breakfast came and they ate in silence for a while. Peter reached for the genealogy and turned it over. " 'Magicians Dazzle at the Paramount,' " he read. "What's this?"

"It's the article that got me wondering about my family," Molly said. "John Stow gave it to me."

"Mmmm," Peter said. He studied it a moment.

After breakfast they walked down to the beach. Fishermen stood or sat by the water, the ends of their poles buried in the sand beside them. Surfers rode the waves, bobbing black dots. Fog lay on the ocean farther out, and in the valleys between the hills by the shore. Peter picked up a rock and flicked it underhanded into the water, but the ocean was too choppy for it to skip. A gull cawed overhead.

"Are you going to invite me back to the house?" Peter asked.

She felt uneasy. Somehow Peter and her newfound family did not seem to mix; it reminded her of the times Fentrice came to her school on parents' night, and how strange it always was to see her there. Still, she'd missed him.

"Sure," she said.

After his visit Peter headed north, driving through San Francisco and continuing across the Bay Bridge. In Oakland he parked in front of the downtown library and went inside, climbing the stairs to the periodicals room.

The Oakland *Tribune*, he thought, standing in front of the filing cabinets of microfiche spools. April 9, 1935.

He found the spool he wanted quickly. He threaded it onto the machine and read it through and then, as Molly had done, he went to the telephone directories and looked up Andrew Dodd.

Unlike Molly, though, he decided to visit Dodd without calling first. Dodd lived close to the library; Peter put more money in his parking meter and then walked to the address in the phone book.

The receptionist at the apartment building made him wait while she called Dodd. "You can go up now," she said when she got off the phone. *Amazing,* Peter thought, *the way people will see total strangers. What if I were a burglar?*

He took the elevator to the third floor and rang the bell. Nothing happened for a long time. He rang again and then a third time, holding his finger on the buzzer. *Come on,* Peter thought. *The old boy's got to be home.* He tried the doorknob, and it opened.

He went inside. Now he could hear sounds coming from the bathroom, a toilet flushing and then running water. A sheet of paper lay upside-down on the desk in front of him and he moved toward it. He did not need to turn it around; he had learned to read very nearly anything from very nearly any angle.

"Dearest Bess," someone had written in shaky penmanship. "I have been very unhappy since you died. We went through so much together, we knew each other so well, that it sometimes seemed as if I knew what you were thinking. Now I can't imagine what you might be thinking, or even if you're thinking at all. You've changed utterly, you've gone on without me. I feel angry a lot of the time. I can't help but wonder why you've abandoned me.

"When the hospital called to tell me you'd died all I could say was 'What?' I'd heard them, of course, nothing wrong with my hearing, but I wanted to give them the chance to say something else. What they said was somehow wrong, obscene, was something that shouldn't have been said. But they just repeated, 'She died during the night. There was nothing we could do.' And I felt as if I fell through a hole, and as if there was a hole after that, pit upon pit, falling and falling. 'Mr. Dodd?' they said. 'Are you still there?'

"I have a question for you, Bess. If there is a heaven you must be in it—there's no one I know who's a better person, or more deserving. And in heaven, of course, everyone is happy all the time. But how can you be happy knowing how miserable I am? You were always so caring, so concerned.

"This sounds terribly selfish, I know. I hope you're not unhappy, of course. I hope you're busy playing your harp, or whatever it is they do there. I try to imagine it, but I can't. It's almost as if there are two of you, the living, lively Bess I knew and the one who is dead, and there are no points of congruence between the two whatsoever.

"Here's something I learned about sorrow—you can cry and brush your teeth at the same time. You can cry and do any number of small household chores, washing laundry or making sandwiches or doing dishes."

✾ ✾ ✾

A door opened somewhere in the apartment. Peter stepped back quickly. He had read enough of other people's mail to know that this was something unusual, extraordinary. He did not think he had ever read the sentence "I have been very unhappy since you died."

An old man — a very old man — moved forward slowly, pushing his walker into the room. His hair was white and reached to his shoulders, and there were patches of white stubble on his lined cheeks. "Who the hell are you?" he asked.

"I'm Peter Myers. The receptionist told you I was coming up."

Peter took out a business card and handed it to Andrew Dodd, but the other man ignored it and sat heavily on the couch. "What do you want?" Dodd asked.

"I'd like to ask you some questions about an article you wrote. The Allalie Family."

"She told me not to talk to you," Dodd said.

"Who did?"

"That woman. Fentrice. No, wait. Molly — her name was Molly."

"Molly was here?"

"Sure she was. Looked exactly like her aunt Fentrice, too, 'cept she didn't have the gapped teeth. She sure didn't act like Fentrice, though — she was a nice kid, straightforward. I appreciate that."

"Wait a minute," Peter said. When had Molly talked to this man? Had she gotten anything from him? He couldn't imagine that she had. "Molly told you not to talk to me?"

"That's right. She said if that detective comes around, that what's-his-name, not to talk to him."

"John Stow?"

"How am I supposed to remember? That might have been it. I don't know."

"I'm not John Stow, Mr. Dodd. My name is Peter Myers."

He offered the business card again, and this time Dodd took it.

"I don't give a damn what your name is. I don't want to talk to you."

"Why did you let me up, then?"

"Oh, I don't know. My wife just died—I'm not thinking very clearly."

"Bess?" Peter asked.

Dodd's head jerked up. "How did you know that?"

"I'm a reporter. It's my job to know."

"Reporters have certainly changed since I was a pup."

Peter looked at the letter on the desk. "Did you know the Order of the Labyrinth claims to be able to contact the dead?" he asked.

"The Order of—what was that now?"

"The Order of the Labyrinth."

"Never heard of them."

"It's an occult group Fentrice's grandmother started. Emily Wethers, also known as Neesa Allalie. Ever hear of her?"

Dodd shook his head.

"She received messages from a dead man named Lord Albert Westingate."

"What's your point, young man?"

"If she could do it then maybe her descendants can as well. Fentrice, or Molly. Maybe you could talk to Bess again."

Dodd sagged against the couch. His lips moved, murmuring something.

"The thing is, I called Fentrice," Peter said. "She won't speak to me. Maybe you'll have better luck. They liked you, the Allalie Family—I could tell that from the article you wrote. They put on a show just for you, to teach you something. Maybe you can go out to Illinois and ask Fentrice about the Order. And about Bess. After all, you were a reporter too."

"I haven't seen Fentrice in sixty years."

"I'll give you her address, and I'll pay your way out there. All you have to do is answer a few questions for me now, and then ask her some things."

Andrew closed his eyes wearily. He moved his lips again. "Maybe," he said finally.

A while later Peter let himself out. He went down the street to Tangled Tales Bookstore, and spent a long time in conversation with the pale man in the turban.

A few days later Molly went to Callan's study. A doorstop in the shape of a rock held the door open. *Maybe it really is a rock*, Molly thought. This house would drive her crazy before she was done.

She lifted the phone out from behind a pile of books. It seemed surprised to see her, its mouth an *O* of astonishment. *What do I tell Fentrice about Lila, about Callan?* she thought.

She forced her questions aside and dialed quickly. "Hello," Fentrice said.

"Hi, it's Molly."

"Molly, how wonderful. I was just thinking about you. Are you still on vacation, dear? Are you having a good time?"

"Yeah. It's great here, very quiet." Fentrice hadn't asked where she was; she never would. Still, Molly felt guilty. What would her aunt think if she knew Molly was with Callan? "How are you?"

"Just fine."

"And Lila? She didn't go off on any more trips, did she?"

"No, she's right here, upstairs in her bedroom. I'm a bit worried about her, though."

"Worried?" Molly said. Her fears for her aunt, never far from the surface, returned stronger than ever. "Why?"

"She's acting a little strangely. She seems angry about something. Do you suppose I should talk to her?"

"Angry? With you?"

Fentrice hesitated. "Not with me, I think. With her family, with something that happened on her visit." She paused again, longer this time. "Maybe she is angry with me. Maybe I slighted her in some way, without meaning to. Oh, dear."

"Can I talk to her?"

"To Lila? I don't know that that would be such a good idea. I shouldn't want to disturb her. Why, dear? What are you thinking?"

"Aunt Fentrice, what do you know about Lila? Where does she come from? How did you hire her?"

"I met her through an agency. A long time ago—I'm sure they're out of business by now. She'd worked for a family in Chicago, but they couldn't afford to keep her any longer. I wrote to them and they gave her excellent references."

"Do you still have their address?"

Fentrice laughed. "Oh, no. That was what—forty years ago?"

"What's the name of the agency?"

"Professional Housekeepers, something like that. Do you think she's done something criminal? She can't have, not Lila. I've known her for years, after all. She's just unhappy about something. It'll pass."

Should she worry her aunt? After all she had no hard evidence, just a strong guess. But what if Fentrice was in danger? What if Thorne, in disguise, had wormed her way into Fentrice's confidence? Who knew what might happen, given the sisters' complex and stormy history?

"Be careful, that's all," Molly said.

"I will, dear. Thanks for your concern."

They said good-bye. She could smell Callan's cooking through the walls, chicken and sausage jambalaya. She dialed directory assistance in Chicago and asked for the number of Professional Housekeepers. There was no listing for them; she hadn't thought there would be.

She went outside with Alex and Matt after dinner. The evening was cold, the sky overcast. She turned and looked at the sun setting over Callan's house.

"Hey," she said. "The house only has two stories, right? What's all that extra space under the roof?"

"That's the attic," Alex said.

"The attic?" Whenever she thought she had made some momentous discovery it seemed that someone in the house already knew about it. "No one ever told me there's an attic."

"Callan would say that you have to know the right questions to ask. Though I don't think you'll find anything very interesting there—only old clothes and things."

"Neesa's clothes? And Verey's and Lanty's?"

"I guess."

"How do we get up there?" she asked, heading toward the house.

"There's a closet on the second floor," Alex said. "Maybe you've seen it—it looks like a broom closet. You open it and there's a ladder leading to the attic. Molly, wait a minute. We'll have to get a flashlight first—there's no light up there."

They went into the house and she followed him as he got the flashlight. The flashlight, not surprisingly, was in the shape of a candle, the light coming from the flame. They climbed the stairs to the second floor and stopped in front of a narrow door.

Molly took the flashlight. She opened the door and began to climb the ladder. At the top was a trapdoor. She pushed it aside.

She shone the light into the attic. At first she could see nothing but dark, bulky shapes. Then her eyes became accustomed to the dimness and she began to make out cartons and wardrobes and racks of clothing. The air smelled dry, like burnt paper.

She pulled herself up into the room and Alex followed. She looked around, playing the flashlight over everything. "This is terrific," she said.

A tattered pool table. An ashtray from the San Francisco International Exhibition in 1939. A stuffed fox. A high school diploma for Matthew Endicott. A birdcage. A harp with no strings. A dressmaker's dummy. A menu from the Cliff House in San Francisco, turning brown at the edges.

"Is that Neesa's pool table?" Molly asked.

"I think so," Alex said.

She ran her fingers over it, feeling the accumulation of thick, furry dust.

"Give me the flashlight for a minute," Alex said. He turned the light on a box of black-and-white photographs. "Look at these people."

"Who are they?" Molly asked.

"I don't know."

"Would Callan?"

"Probably. Would he tell us? I doubt it."

She looked through a few of the photographs—dancers, jugglers, dog acts. "Look at that—it's W.C. Fields, isn't it? 'To the Allalie Family, with my greatest admiration.' And this one." She held out a picture of a man in a straitjacket dangling from the top of a building. " 'To the Allalie Family, the best disappearing act in the business. Harry Houdini.' "

The next picture showed a man and woman dancing; it was nearly covered with rows of X's and an illegible signature. Then a black man with an oval face and a crown on his head. *To Verey and Lanty,* " this one said. *"With love, King Oliver."*

Alex was busy sorting through another group of photos. "Is that the Allalie Family?" Molly asked, looking over his shoulder. "They look familiar, don't they?"

"No one smiled in pictures back then," Alex said. "You can't tell if they had gapped teeth or not."

A woman stared boldly at the camera, smoking a cigarette. She had bobbed hair and wore a straight white dress with no waist. Another woman, this one wearing heavy black glasses, stood next to her. "That could be Fentrice," Molly said, pointing to the one smoking. "Look how pretty she was."

"She looks a little like you," Alex said.

Molly lifted out the rest of the photographs. A bundle tied with a faded red ribbon lay beneath them. She pulled it out.

"What's that?" Alex asked.

"Letters, I think." Molly untied the ribbon and opened the first one. "No envelopes, though. No return addresses. Here's a date—March 20, 1937."

She began to read aloud. " 'My dear brother. You think you can usurp my position but you're wrong. You know as well as I do that the direction of the family has always been the responsibility of its oldest member. You think you're safe now but I promise you I'll return, and when I do I'll take my rightful place at the head of the family.' "

"Who wrote that?" Alex asked.

Molly turned the page over. "It doesn't say. It's typewritten, and there's no signature. Thorne, maybe."

"Thorne?"

"Yeah. She was the oldest, then Fentrice, and then Callan."

"But Thorne left, didn't she? She abdicated her position. Maybe Fentrice wrote it."

"Fentrice left too. She got sick of the whole thing."

"Well, someone has to have written it. A sister writing to a brother, in 1937—it has to be either Thorne or Fentrice."

"Wait a minute," Molly said slowly. "All we know about that time comes from Callan's diary. He was the one who said Thorne left, and then Fentrice. What if he somehow made them leave? What if he threatened them, got rid of them, so he could take over the leadership of the family?"

"Callan?"

"Yeah, why not? He even gave me the diary to read, through Samuel. He wanted me to think he was innocent. But look here— 'usurp,' it says. What did he do?"

"I don't think he did anything—it's not in his character. You don't know him the way I do. I grew up with him. He's a wise man, a good man—"

"He gives that impression. But look at his house—everything here looks like something else. Everything's an illusion. Maybe even this pose of his, the wise old man."

"Molly, you can't think—"

"Why not? Everyone here is so quick to accuse my aunt Fentrice. Callan even said she was the woman in blue. Only she wasn't—the woman turned out to be Lila, Fentrice's housekeeper. You might have grown up with Callan, but I grew up with Fentrice. She never pretended to be wise, but she was good. She was a good moral woman, forced out of her rightful place, forced to live separate from the rest of the family."

"This letter doesn't sound very moral at all. It reads to me like a threat—You think you're safe now, but I'll come after you."

"It sounds to me like someone who's been wronged. She's bitter, sure, but she hasn't given up. She's going to claim her rightful place, see that justice is done."

"What do the rest of them say?"

Molly opened the next letter. They were all on thick rag paper the color of cream. She held it up to the flashlight; the watermark showed what looked like a pair of spectacles, crossed at the temples. *Turn your spectacles around*, she thought, *and look at the backs of things*. Someone had said that to Emily on the streets of London in 1910.

" 'May 29, 1938,' " she read. " 'My dear brother. You have no right to the position you've usurped. Surely you know that, surely you understand that the place you've made for yourself is built on sand. I promise I will return one day and claim what is mine.' "

"It sounds a lot like the last one," Alex said.

"But more than a year later," Molly said, turning the letter over. "No signature, no return address."

They looked through the rest of them. There were five more; each spoke of wrongs done to the letter writer and each made the same vague threats. The last was dated August 13, 1970.

"Why did she stop?" Alex asked. "What happened in 1970?"

"It's the year my parents died," Molly said. Alex looked at her. "No, that can't be it."

"Why can't it? Is that when Fentrice started raising you?"

"Yeah."

"Well, maybe she lost interest in her feud with Callan then. She was busy with you instead."

"Maybe." She hesitated. "Unless it was Thorne who sent the letters."

"But if it was Fentrice, then why didn't she tell you we were here? You said she'd told you Callan was dead."

"Because they'd wronged her, taken her rightful position. Because she felt bitter." She shook her head. "Can't you see it from her point of view?"

"Maybe," Alex said. He sounded doubtful.

TWELVE

Illusion

Andrew Dodd was the last person off the plane at O'Hare Airport in Chicago. A flight attendant came out into the terminal with him, helping him with his walker and his small bag.

A man at the gate held up a sign with his name on it. So Peter Myers had been as good as his word, Andrew thought. Here was the driver of the car to take him to Fentrice's house.

They headed down one of the main highways leading out of Chicago. He had dozens of questions spanning sixty years, everything from what had happened backstage at the Paramount to whether Fentrice could truly speak with the dead. He had hoped to arrange his thoughts during the drive; instead he found himself fighting against sleep. He woke as the car stopped, his heart pounding.

"Here we are," the driver said.

Where? Andrew thought, panicked. *And where was Bess?* The driver went to the trunk and took out his bag and walker, giving him enough time to remember where he was, what he had to do.

He made his way slowly to the front door and knocked. An old woman in black answered.

"Andrew Dodd," the woman said. "Well, this is indeed a surprise. I'd say you haven't changed, but you know I'd be lying."

"Fentrice Allalie?" he asked.

"The same," she said. "Don't tell me you were expecting a young woman in a kimono."

He had been, for a moment. He had been expecting someone who looked like Molly. He shook his head. "Fentrice Allalie," he said, amazed. "The last disguise."

"What brings you here?" she asked.

"I have some questions for you."

"Do you? Your deadline was sixty years ago, if I'm not mistaken. And what makes you think I'll answer?"

Behind him the hired car reversed out of the driveway. Why should she answer, after all? He had hoped to surprise her, hoped to find an aged woman ready to give up her secrets. She had surprised him instead with her apparent health, her sharpness. Why on earth had he thought himself still fit to do a reporter's job?

"Why shouldn't you?" he asked.

She laughed. Another woman came to the door. "Who is it, Fentrice?" the woman asked.

"His name's Andrew Dodd," Fentrice said. "He used to be a cocky young man—now he's a cocky old man. Andrew, this is my housekeeper, Lila." She laughed again. "Look at him, how he watches us. I think he's afraid we'll disappear before his eyes."

"I am," Andrew said. "Can I come in?"

"It's customary to call first," Fentrice said. "Oh, very well. Lila, could you get us some tea and biscuits, please?" She opened the door and showed him in. "Have a seat."

He made his way to a stiff horsehair sofa in Fentrice's living room. Fentrice sat gracefully in a chair opposite him, smiling; now he could see the marked gap between her teeth. Lila came back into the room and set tea and biscuits on the table between them, then took a chair near Fentrice.

Andrew opened his brand-new spiral notebook, remembering as he did so the blank pages after his last interview with this woman, his desperate search for something to write about.

He thrust the old memory aside. He had not taken a drink in sixty years. "Well," he said. "What have you been doing since I saw you last? Confuse any other poor saps?"

"I don't know what you mean."

"You don't? You seem to remember me. Do you remember the tricks you and your family played on me, the way you had me so turned around I didn't know if I was coming or going?"

"I don't, no. You did drink somewhat in those days, Mr. Dodd."

Was that all it had been, the drink, the extraordinary champagne? And why had he started his interview in such a hostile manner? Surely he had learned better in all his years as a reporter. "I'm sorry, Miss Allalie," he said finally. "I wanted to ask you about that interview I did with you backstage at the Paramount. Sixty years ago, you said it was."

"I remember it, yes. You must have made quite an impression on us—we did such a lot of interviews in those days."

"I did a lot too, though from the other side." Suddenly he felt a kinship with this woman. They had both been through so much, a depression and then a world war, they had seen the world change utterly. No one these days could possibly understand what it had been like, not Molly, certainly not that punk reporter. Hardly anyone even read interviews anymore; they all got their news from the television. "The Palace closed that year, didn't it?" he said. "Vaudeville was dying—the talking pictures were taking over. What happened to the act?"

"I don't really know," Fentrice said. "I retired around then."

"And Thorne and Callan? Did they retire too?"

"Callan went on for a bit longer. I don't know what finally happened to him—we've lost touch over the years." She glanced at the housekeeper for a brief moment. "I don't know where Thorne is."

"When was the last time you saw her?"

"The last time . . . somewhere around the last time I saw you,

I think. And what happened to you after that? Molly said you got married."

"I did." For the first time the thought of his dead wife did not cause him pain. "You know, I seemed to see clearer once I stopped drinking. I'd met her before—she lived in my apartment building—but she never seemed to . . . to come into focus. After I stopped drinking I saw how beautiful she was, and how sweet." He smiled a little, remembering. "So I asked her out, and to my great surprise she accepted."

"Did you?" Fentrice asked softly. "Do you remember Playland at the Beach? That long wooden slide, and the Big Dipper roller coaster?"

"Of course. We must have gone there dozens of times. That horrible mannequin, Laughing Sal. She had gapped teeth too, if I remember."

"They tore it all down, didn't they?"

"Yes, they did. Just memories now." He looked at his notes, wondering how they had come to be talking about a long-gone amusement park. "Could you tell me anything about your grandmother? Emily Wethers, or Neesa Allalie."

"Grandma? What do you want to know about her?"

"What did she have to do with the Order of the Labyrinth?"

"The Order of the Labyrinth? I don't really know—that all happened before I was born. There was a great fad for spiritualism in those days."

"She claimed to be able to contact the dead. A man named Albert Westingate, for one."

"If you say so."

"Can you . . . can you contact the dead as well?"

Fentrice started to laugh, then stopped abruptly. "Oh. Oh, I see now. Oh, I *am* sorry. It's your wife, is it? What did you say her name was?"

"Bess." Few of his friends had wanted to talk about Bess since her funeral; it was as if she had done something shocking, never to be spoken of, by dying. He was surprised at the sharp joy he felt in simply saying her name. "Bess," he said again.

"You poor man. How are you coping? Do your children come to visit you?"

"Children," Andrew said. To his horror he thought he might be about to cry. "They don't do anything but visit me, it seems. They won't leave me the hell alone. All I want is to be by myself, just me and my grief . . . Well." He wiped his eyes quickly on his sleeve. "They mean well, I guess."

"And you want me to contact your wife for you," Fentrice said.

Andrew nodded.

"I'm so sorry. I can't do that, any more than Grandma was able to talk to Lord Albert Westingate. We deal in illusion, Mr. Dodd. It's all trickery—none of it was ever real."

"Oh." Andrew closed his eyes briefly. A great tiredness washed over him, partly from the plane ride but mostly because of his wasted errand, his lost chance. "He said you could."

"He? Who?"

"That man who came to visit me. Wait a minute, I have his card here. Peter Myers, that's it."

"Peter Myers? Molly's boyfriend?"

"Is he? He knew Molly, that's right."

"You're here because of Peter?"

Was he supposed to keep that a secret? He couldn't remember now. He felt as confused as he had that day long ago when Thorne and Fentrice had changed places backstage.

"Is Peter writing a book about us?" Fentrice asked.

"I don't know. He said he was a reporter."

"I'll have to warn Molly. I knew that man was wrong for her. Would you excuse me for a moment?"

She stood, gathering her skirts around her, and went down the hallway into an alcove. Her strong voice came back to them, as loudly as if she were still in the room.

"Hello, may I speak to Molly, please. Molly, dear, this is Aunt Fentrice. No, nothing's wrong here. Listen, it's not important how I got this phone number. I'll tell you all about it later. I have something to tell you—please listen. That Mr. Andrew Dodd came to visit—yes, the reporter. He told me an extraordinary thing. Your friend Peter is apparently writing a book about us. . . . Well, that's what he says, dear. He says Peter paid a call on him, asked questions about the family. . . . Oh, dear. Oh, I'm so sorry. Yes, just a minute."

Andrew heard her set the phone down and then return to the living room. "She wants to talk to you," Fentrice said. "The phone's down the hall."

"To me?" He stood and pushed his walker slowly to the alcove. "Hello, Molly."

"Hi. Is it true? Did Peter come to talk to you?"

She was trying not to cry, Andrew realized. He remembered the day she had come to visit him; she had seemed so strong, so forthright, a tough young woman who had reminded him of women he had known in his youth. Reminded him of Fentrice, for one. Now he saw that she was vulnerable after all. "Yes, I'm afraid he did, Molly."

"Did he say he was writing a book?"

"He was writing something. Said he was a reporter."

"He told me—" She was silent for a moment. "God, I feel like I've been kicked in the stomach. He used me, didn't he? God, I've been such an idiot."

"I know how you feel," Andrew said. He had been fooled once too, back when he was young. When was it? The Allalies, that was it. But had they really tricked him? Or had he tricked himself, befuddled with wine and enchantment?

"Thanks for telling me," Molly said.

"I knew I shouldn't have trusted him," Andrew said. "Him and that pretentious beard of his. Good-bye, Molly. Take care."

He went back into the living room. "We'll have to go to California," Fentrice said as he sat down. "We'll have to visit Callan, after all these years."

"Callan?" Andrew said. "I thought you said you had lost touch with Callan."

"I know where he lives, of course. I just called his number. He's in the old family home in California. Oh, dear. I'm not looking forward to seeing him again, not at all." She sat up straighter, looked at Andrew. "When are you going back to California?"

"Tomorrow."

"May we come with you?"

"Sure," Andrew said. He grinned at her. He had come to Fentrice seeking answers and had somehow acquired an ally instead. Molly had been right; Fentrice wasn't nearly as terrible as he had thought for all these years. He should have paid this visit long ago, gotten things straightened out. Without noticing when it had happened he had changed allegiances, gone over from Peter's side to Fentrice's.

"Lila, could you please phone the airlines, make the arrangements?" Fentrice asked.

The housekeeper nodded silently.

Molly put the phone down, her eyes filled with tears. She looked up at the study, not seeing it.

"Molly?"

She wiped her eyes roughly. It was Callan. "Molly, are you all right?" he asked.

"That was Fentrice," she said. "She told me Peter's writing about the Allalies. About us."

Callan came over to her, held her. Molly felt his muscled arms around her, smelled a sharp spice she couldn't identify. She stood there, letting him hold her, feeling protected. "He lied to me," she said. "He was using me, all this time."

"It'll be all right. Don't worry."

"I trusted him. I even thought he might be coming to like me, to feel the same way about me I felt about him. And all the time . . ." She took a deep breath. "Maybe she's wrong. Maybe Fentrice is wrong. She's been wrong before."

"What do you think, Molly?"

"God, I don't know." But she did know. She knew the way Emily had known about the lords and ladies who asked her questions, the way Callan had known about his vaudeville audience. It seemed that she had always known, and that she had tried to force the knowledge away. "Why?" she asked. "Why would he do something like that?"

Callan shook his head. "I only saw him once, when he came to visit you," he said. "But he seemed a lot like some of the people who came to our shows, the ones who wouldn't be fooled no matter what. He seemed very knowing, Peter did. He was clever, he wasn't going to be taken in. But you miss so much that way. You miss all the magic in the world."

"I thought you said there was no magic. I thought you said it was all illusion."

"Did I?"

"Oh, God, you're going to ask me questions again. You're going to ask me what I've learned."

"Well, what have you?"

"I learned—I learned that illusion is a way to truth. That illusion can reveal truth, a deeper truth. That there are things beyond or beneath or on the other side of what most people—of what Peter thinks of as reality. I learned . . . Oh, God. I've made another turning of the labyrinth."

Callan laughed, and after a moment she joined him.

She took out her letter to John after dinner the next day. "Ironic, isn't it, that your girlfriend Gwen thought I knew so much about people, about relationships. I know nothing at all about people. All this time Peter was using me to write his damn book, and I had no idea. I'd managed to convince myself he liked me, maybe even loved me."

The alligator door-knocker banged against the door downstairs. "Molly!" Alex yelled. "You have visitors."

Peter? she thought. No, not Peter. That turning of the labyrinth was behind her. She went downstairs.

Three people stood outside, the trees behind them, the last three people in the world Molly would have expected to see: Fentrice, Lila, and Andrew Dodd.

"We know it's customary to call first," Andrew said. He was grinning at Fentrice, as if they shared a secret. What was going on here?

"We were worried about you, Molly," Fentrice said.

"Aunt Fentrice," Molly said weakly. "It's good to see you."

"Fentrice," someone said. Molly turned around quickly; Callan had come up quietly behind her. "After all these years. Come, let's go inside." He opened the door and motioned them into the crowded living room. "Sit down, please. Can I get you anything? Tea and biscuits?"

"This isn't a social call, Callan," Fentrice said, spreading her skirts and settling in one of the carved chairs.

"No, I don't suppose it is. What does bring you here after so long? Though it wasn't that long really, was it?"

"What do you mean?" Fentrice asked.

"That was you, wasn't it, prowling through my house a few weeks ago? Looking among my books and things?"

"I told you, that wasn't my aunt," Molly said. "It was — " She turned to the housekeeper. For a moment she had forgotten Lila was there, she was so unobtrusive. "It was you, Lila, wasn't it?"

Lila looked from one to the other impassively, first Molly, then Callan, and finally Fentrice. "Yes, that was me," she said.

"Why?" Molly asked. "What did you want with Emily's journal?"

"You know what I wanted," Lila said. "You wanted it too, or you wouldn't have gone to England to get it. I wanted Emily's secret."

"Emily's secret?" Molly said.

"Oh, don't play innocent with me," Lila said impatiently. "You're an Allalie, you know very well what I'm talking about. Emily knew how to enchant people to make them do her bidding. That was how she got rid of Harrison's wife Lydia."

"What?" Molly said.

"Don't tell me you hadn't guessed," Lila said. "You weren't nearly this dull as a child. How else could a laundress have taken Lydia's place as the head of the household? She enchanted Lydia,

put her into a sort of trance. Lydia did anything Emily wanted her
to. She backed away from Harrison, let Emily take over."

"No," Molly said. "No, she wasn't like that—"

"How do you know she wasn't?"

"I read her journal, for one thing." Suddenly Molly remembered the final words of the journal: *"And I did the one last, necessary
thing I told you of . . ."* Could Emily's last act in England have been
to loose the enchantment, to restore Lydia to her normal life?

"Ah, but you never knew her, did you?" Lila said.

"No, did you? You did, didn't you? You're Thorne, aren't
you? Emily was—what? Your grandmother?"

Lila gave her strange choking laugh. "No, of course not. I'm
no Allalie, I'm a housekeeper your aunt hired. I learned a few
things from Fentrice over the years, things she let slip."

"Is that what happened?" Molly asked Fentrice. "You told
her about the family, and she wanted Emily's power?"

"I suppose so," Fentrice said. She looked drawn, tired. "After
you left there was only Lila for company. I may have mentioned
something."

Callan moved his hands suddenly, and spoke a few words.
Lila looked unchanged, was still the sullen, taciturn housekeeper,
but Molly understood that Callan had put her under the same enchantment that had silenced Lydia. She would not say anything
more as long as she remained in his house.

He can do it too, Molly thought. *He'd said so in his diary, when he
made that jerk in the audience shut up, though the enchantment would last
only while the man remained in sight. Can I? How much can I do?*

"Well," Callan said. "Here we are. You and me, Fentrice, and
Andrew Dodd, a reunion of sorts of that day at the Paramount.
The only one missing is Thorne. And I wonder whether, if we put
our minds to it, we can't figure out what happened to her."

"I'd say you owe me an apology first," Fentrice said. "Did you
truly think I would come here, push my way in, disrupt your house
like that? What on earth would I want with Grandma's journal?"

"There's the small matter of your disappearance in England,

when we toured there in 1935. You went up to Tantilly to see if you could find the journal, didn't you?"

"Nonsense. And if I found the journal then, why would I want it now? Be sensible, Callan. That was always your trouble, wasn't it? All those wild, fanciful ideas you had. It got so you couldn't tell the difference between what was real and what was illusion."

But illusion is important, a way to the truth, Molly thought. *Isn't that what I learned? Or is Fentrice right?*

"I thought you came here because you wanted to know whether I had the journal," Callan said. "Whether Molly had brought it to me. That would have been a terrible blow, wouldn't it, if Molly had given it to me instead of to you? And if I had it, I'd know what you did with Thorne."

"That wasn't me who came here. You heard her — it was Lila. I didn't do anything to Thorne, and I resent your insinuation that I did. She left with that trumpet player, that Tom."

"Did she? I've always wondered. And who wrote me those letters?"

"What letters?"

"I've still got them, up in the attic. Threatening me, accusing me of usurping someone's place. Did Thorne write them or did you, Fentrice?"

"Don't be ridiculous. Why would I write to you? I wanted nothing more to do with the family."

"Didn't you? Why are you here?"

Fentrice stood. "I won't stay here and listen to this. Molly, dear, I came because I wanted to be sure you were all right. I'll find a motel room in town, and you can come visit me. I won't stay under this roof another minute."

"Wait," Callan said. He gestured with his hands again.

Fentrice said a few words in reply. Callan stood, spoke over her loudly. Their voices clashed like thunder.

Molly stood. "Stop it, stop it!" she said. "What are you doing?"

Another loud clap of thunder drove her back into her chair. "Listen to me, both of you!" she said again. "Callan! Fentrice has the right to leave your house if she wants to. Stop it!"

The thunder rumbled, subsided. Callan and Fentrice stood facing each other. Fentrice had gone very white, the tip of her nose pink.

Callan laughed. "Now I'm the one who owes you an apology, Fentrice," he said. "I'm truly sorry—I didn't mean to get so angry. Of course you're free to go if you want to. But I had hoped you'd stay here as my guest. We could work out the mystery of Thorne's disappearance together. And we have so much to catch up on."

Fentrice said nothing for a moment. "I'm glad I didn't grow up in your family," Andrew Dodd said, breaking the silence. "Were all your arguments like this?"

"No, of course not," Fentrice said. "We had Verey and Lanty to keep us in line."

"So what do you think?" Callan asked. "Will you stay?"

"I don't know," Fentrice said. "I don't trust you, Callan, you know that."

"Please stay," Molly said. "It's been so long since you've seen one another, and there were so many misunderstandings—we could be a family again."

"Oh, very well," Fentrice said. "But I warn you—if I hear one more reckless accusation I'll leave."

"Great!" Molly said.

"Is it?" Callan asked softly.

THIRTEEN
Disillusion

Molly and Alex sat outside Callan's house the next day, watching the sun rise through the fog. "What on earth was all that about yesterday?" Alex asked. "I heard shouting, and then what sounded like thunder . . ."

She told him a little about Fentrice and Lila and Andrew Dodd. "So Lila was the woman in blue, just like I thought," she finished. "She even admitted it."

"Where's Thorne then? Do you think Fentrice knows?"

"No, why should she? She hasn't had anything to do with Thorne for years. Why is everyone here so quick to assume my aunt is guilty? Did Callan turn you against her when you were growing up?"

"No, of course not. He barely mentioned her."

"Do you know what it must have taken for Fentrice to come here? She was the one who made the first move, she had to humble herself to Callan after all these years of not speaking to him. What if he had turned her away? And she did it for me, to make sure I was all right."

"Callan was certainly right about one thing," Alex said. "Things are definitely happening here. No wonder he asked us to stay behind."

"Do you know what's going to happen next?"

Alex shook his head. "I'm not as good at that as Callan is," he said. "What about you?"

"No. I keep trying to see it but there's something blocking me, something in the way. I don't know what it is."

A rose appeared in Alex's hand. "This is what I do in the act," he said. He gave her the rose. "Listen, Molly, I want to—oh, it's ridiculous! I want to ask you out on a date, but I can't, can I? I mean, we already live together, don't we?"

She looked at him in surprise. "I always thought you were laughing at me," she said. "It's that mustache."

"Do you want me to shave it off?"

"No, it's—Is this why Callan asked you to stay here? Did he know this would happen?"

"I don't know. Maybe."

Molly shook her head. "I just don't trust that man. I can't go out with you if he's behind it, if he's planned our every move."

"Maybe after all this is over. Maybe when we find out what happened to Thorne."

"Do you think we will?"

"Oh, yes," Alex said.

"A lot has happened since I last wrote you," Molly wrote to John. "Aunt Fentrice and Andrew Dodd have come to visit. Something's happened between them—they keep grinning at each other as if they share a secret. Well, she can be very charming when she wants to be—no one knows that better than I do.

"And Lila's here too, though I haven't seen much of her. Either she's under Callan's enchantment or she's off sulking about something. She seems to know an awful lot about the Allalies, but she learned it all from Fentrice. She's not Thorne in disguise, which is something I thought before she came here.

"Lila says Emily enchanted Lydia do her bidding, and that she explained how she did it in the book she wrote for Lady Dorothy. If she's right this would certainly answer a lot of questions—why all those people were looking for the journal, Joseph Ottig and that awful man with the sharp face who followed us in England.

"It would also explain what happened to Lydia. But would Emily do something like that, would she essentially take away someone's life? Because that's what enchanting Lydia would have amounted to. It's almost like murder.

"I wonder if this is what Callan meant. I said it was great to have my aunt visiting, and he said, 'Is it?' He was wearing what I've come to think of as his wise-old-man look, that exasperating expression of his that says, You'll see that I know more about this than you do. Everyone wants to learn more about their ancestors, but what happens if you find out something really unpleasant about them? Was he suggesting that I'm going to discover something like that about Emily, or even Fentrice? Or was he trying to direct my suspicions somewhere else, away from him?

"And meanwhile there's what I learned about Peter. I can see now why people are so eager to get their hands on Emily's journal—there are days when I fantasize about enchanting Peter. It would be great if I could make him stay here with me instead of gallivanting all over the country, if he could be persuaded to stop doing harm to my family. If he saw how much I loved him, and finally came to love me in return.

"But I don't think I could murder Peter like that, no matter how much I'm tempted. What I have to do is try to forget him, realize that he's used me, that he's every bit as bad for me as Robin Ann said he was.

"It's very difficult. Sometimes I wake up in the morning and think about him for what seems like hours. I remember the excitement I felt being with him, the way he seemed to know everyone and be connected to everything. That's something I wanted all my life, a connection, a place in the world. Was it my family I was looking for all this time?"

She reread what she had written. There was something important in it, some clue that she had missed. The man with the

sharp face. No, before that. Joseph Ottig. Joe. "This is the third
tour Joe's missed," Jake Polanski had said at the Paramount.

Could Joe be Joseph Ottig? Could he have missed the tour
because he was dead? Ottig might have made the connection between Emily Wethers and Neesa Allalie, might have gone on to
read Andrew Dodd's article. And if he had he would have known
that Callan considered the Paramount Theatre the most beautiful
place in the world. Maybe he thought that Callan had hidden
something away there, maybe he had gotten a job there as a tour
guide so he could have access to every corner and cranny. Maybe
he had mailed the missing pages from Emily's journal from England to himself at the Paramount. He hadn't mailed them to his
house; John had said he had checked Ottig's last known address.

It was very far-fetched. She reached for an answer, trying to
feel her way toward it as Emily had done with the audiences at her
seances. Something was in the way, some unopened door or un-
turned corner. She was afraid of what she might find.

Well, but if she stayed here she would only get more enigmatic questions from Callan, more shrugs from Corrig. She got her
purse and went out to her car.

As she drove along the ocean on Highway 1 she found herself thinking not of Joseph but of Alex. Did she want to go out
with him? She barely knew him, had never thought of dating him.
But there was no denying that his question had sparked an answering interest in her. She thought of his burnished-brass hair,
his stomach as concave as a greyhound's, his lean thighs. His kind,
courtly manners, the way he had conjured up the rose.

One date with him and her future would fissure off into
unguessed directions. Maybe she would even join the family on
tour, become part of the act. She shook her head. It was just a date,
after all. And it was no good thinking about it until all the mysteries were solved.

She headed east on the lower deck of the Bay Bridge, then
turned off toward downtown Oakland. It was noon when she
pulled up in front of the Paramount Theatre. There had been fog

by the ocean but here, farther inland, the sun was shining.

The Paramount was closed. A notice on the door said that tours were available on alternate Saturdays. She studied the hundreds of light bulbs shooting out from under the marquee, the green and pink and black tiled floor.

A man came up to the front door and began to unlock it. "Excuse me," Molly said. "My—my uncle Joseph Ottig worked here as a tour guide."

"Joseph, of course!" the man said. Molly felt triumphant. *John Stow should see me now.* "Whatever happened to him? We've been calling and calling."

"I'm afraid it's bad news," Molly said. "He's dead."

"Dead! How?"

"Someone shot him. In England."

"England? We didn't even know he was away. Well, come in, come in. Do they know who did it?"

"Not yet. I'd like to pick up his mail, if that's possible."

"Of course." The man led her through the great front lobby and under the high black staircase, then unlocked a small office. "It's funny, a letter did come for him. We were going to send it on to his house but we never got around to it. We did think it was odd he got mail at this address, instead of at home." He looked a question at Molly, but she said nothing. *Because he was afraid his house would be searched,* she thought. *And it was.*

The man rummaged through the piles of paper on his desk. "Wait a minute, wait a minute . . . Yes, here it is."

She took the envelope from him. It had a British stamp and was just big enough to hold three or four sheets of paper. "Thanks," she said. "Thanks a lot."

"Sure. If there's anything I can do, any help we can offer the family . . ."

"I'll let you know," Molly said, fighting the urge to run from the theater, to tear open the letter right there. "Thanks."

She walked as slowly as she could out the lobby and toward her car. She sat in the driver's seat and opened the envelope. Then, her fingers trembling a little, she took out four pages ripped down one side.

"Of course Harrison and I did make love to each other again, many times," Emily had written in her round clear hand. "('To make love,' when I was young, meant to pay court to, to favour with attention. I have more than once been brought up short by this expression when it is used in the modern sense, as I use it now.) While Lydia was away we managed to meet several times, and after she returned I used my Gift to make certain that she remained unaware of our trysts.

"I became pregnant. Harrison felt strong guilt, even embarrassment. In those days, as I have said, pregnancy was never discussed; it was too obvious a reminder of lust and pleasure, both of which were kept discreetly hidden. But he was also proud, and delighted that the barrenness in his marriage was not his fault.

"When the child, which proved to be a boy, was born, I named him Henry. The name was far enough from Harrison not to arouse suspicion, but close enough to remind us both of his origins. Harrison hired a nanny to look after him, and she continued on with us after Florence was born.

"You are no doubt wondering, my old friend, what Lydia thought of this arrangement. And I owe you that explanation too, as I owe you so many other things. The truth is that Lydia was no longer part of our little group. She had gone to live with her sister. No one in the Order ever alluded directly to our situation, Harrison's and mine, but of course they were aware of it and I know that there was gossip when we were not present. And more than one person, as you know, resigned from the Order in disgust.

"Well. That is a part of the truth, and it is accurate as far as it goes. That is the truth you know, or suspect: that Lydia left us, that she and Harrison were estranged. Oh, why am I finding it so hard to come to the point? I am deeply ashamed, more ashamed about this one thing than I am over all the money I ever took from you. Because I did do you some good, Dorothy—you know I did.

"I enchanted Lydia to do my bidding. There, I have said it.

I turned her into a dull creature, someone with little wit or will or understanding of her own. I told her to leave Harrison and to go live with her sister. I told her never to attempt to see Harrison again.

"Why did I do it? I disliked her, of course, had done ever since I first met her and she dismissed me so peremptorily. And I love Harrison and he loves me, far more than he had ever loved Lydia. And this was the only way I could have him, and it seemed so *unfair* that she had become his wife only by an accident of birth.

"I laid my plans after she had finally angered me past bearing. I encountered her in the upstairs hallway, a day after a meeting of the Order. By this time she recognised me, of course, knew that I was both servant and adept, though I don't think she suspected all that had passed between Harrison and me. She was carrying a pot of ink and several pens and a sheaf of paper; she was on her way to her morning room to answer her correspondence.

"She brushed against me and spilled her ink all over the newly cleaned bedding I was carrying. 'You stupid, clumsy girl,' she said. 'You'll have to wash that all over again, won't you?'

"I saw that she had ruined the sheets on purpose. Anger overcame me; I wanted to kill her, to end the life that she knew. But I was not strong enough. I could enchant her while she remained in my presence, but the moment she left me she would return to what she was.

"I bided my time, waiting until we went up to Tantilly. At the manor house I whispered to her to come with me to the Labyrinth, told her that it was time for her to reach another grade in the Order. She suspected nothing, though I was only a servant; she had seen evidence of my Gift.

"She followed me willingly enough. I traced the passages of the Labyrinth I knew so well. We passed rooms of jewels and flowers and animals, came to a vast blue lake holding a pale drowned moon. Lydia slowed; I urged her on. Corridors twisted like rivers, walls grew up like briars.

"And all the while I felt my power grow at every turning. Finally I found myself at the top of a ring of mountains, looking down on a great forest far below me. Wind shook the trees, tossed our clothing.

"I knew that now I was strong enough to do what I wanted. I saw Lydia's thoughts as I always had, saw her hatred for me. I saw her life whole, and then I saw how I could end that life. It was as simple as that.

"When we returned to Dorothy's parlour, Lydia was silent, docile. That night she repeated to Harrison what I had suggested to her, that she wanted to go live with her sister. I never saw her again.

"Would she still be Harrison's wife and the mistress of his house if she had been better to me? If she had shown me kindness instead of spite that day? But there is no excusing what I did. I give you my word, Dorothy, that I will free her before we leave."

Molly sat a moment in the car, thinking of what she had read. So Lila had been correct; Emily had enchanted Lydia Sanderson, and had explained in the journal how she had done it. The labyrinth had been the key. But who else had read the journal?

Molly put the pages in her purse and drove slowly back to Callan's house.

She pushed open the door, Callan's front door which was never locked. She was about to call for the family, wanting to tell them what she had learned, when someone stepped out from the shadows in the corner. Peter. A pale man came with him, hunched in his jacket as if against chill weather.

"Hello, Molly," Peter said.

"Peter!" Molly said. "What the hell are you doing here?"

The other man looked a little familiar, but out of context somehow. Was he a friend of Peter's? But Molly had never met any of Peter's friends; he had always been careful to keep the different parts of his life separate.

"Visiting you," Peter said, smiling.

"Oh, no, you don't," Molly said. "I know all about you now.

You're writing a book about the Allalies, aren't you? Andrew Dodd told me."

"I've learned some interesting stuff about the Order of the Labyrinth," Peter said. "I thought you might want to hear it."

"Oh, please," Molly said. Where was everybody, the rest of the family? "Don't lie to me. You've got a contract for a book, don't you? You promised me you wouldn't do this."

"I'm interested in your family, that's all. Look, Molly, can't we talk this over? I'll tell you what I learned and you can show me Emily's journal."

"Emily's journal? What do you know about that?"

"You told me about it, after you came back from England. I'd like to see it."

"Why?"

Peter sighed. "Because it's interesting, that's why. Because, all right, because I might want to write a book about the Allalies. There's no law against it. In fact the First Amendment—"

"Don't talk to me about the First Amendment! I've read your books—I've even typed some of them for you. You turn everything you write about into some kind of sleaze, you make everything sound much worse than it is. Well, you're not going to do it to my family."

"You sound as if your family has something to hide."

"Of course we don't! It's just that—"

"Then why don't you show me the journal? That way I can judge for myself. And the pages that were torn out, too. You've got them, don't you?"

"The—pages?"

"We saw you going to the Paramount," the pale man said, speaking for the first time. "We knew Ottig worked there, but he never told us why."

"Did Ottig tell you he'd mailed the pages there?" Peter asked.

"I figured it out for myself." Even now, Molly thought, Peter couldn't believe that she had a mind of her own, that she could be a player in the game.

"All right," Peter said. "Enough of this. Just show me the pages and we'll go."

"Absolutely not," Molly said. "I'm not going to help you hurt my family."

The front door opened again. Molly and Peter turned quickly to look at the newcomer, a sharp-faced man in a leather jacket. He took a gun out of his jacket pocket and pointed it at Molly. "Give me the journal," he said. He had a British accent.

Suddenly Molly recognized him, and the pale man as well. "I know you, don't I? John and I met you in England, in Applebury. You wanted the book, Emily's journal. You threatened to go to the police unless we gave it to you. And you—" She turned to the other man, studied his blue eyes and milk-white skin. "You were the clerk at Tangled Tales Bookstore. You were wearing a turban the last time I saw you. What is all this? How do you all know each other?"

"They're members of the Order of the Labyrinth," Peter said.

"It still exists?" Molly asked. "It's been—what?—a hundred years."

"Eighty-five since Emily disappeared," the sharp-faced man said. "He's lying, though—these two are no more a part of the Order than you are. I'm from the true Order—we've held to the faith while these pretenders in America went whoring after false gods."

"Liar!" the pale man shouted. The other man's gun turned toward him. "You were deluded, you never understood the real purpose of the Order. You thought Arton would return and lead you to wisdom, but there never was an Arton, don't you see? It was all lies invented by Emily, lies to cover up her true purpose . . ."

"What would you know about it?" the sharp-faced man said. "I'm the great-great-grandson of one of the original members, Jack Frederick. And I've read Dorothy's pamphlet—"

"So what? We've all read the pamphlet. Poor Dorothy was deluded too, she believed everything Emily told her . . . Emily's journal is the important thing. I'll bet you haven't read that."

"No, have you?"

"No, but—"

"And you never will, either. I'll take it and be gone. Where is it?"

They were making enough noise to rouse the entire family. Would someone come and help her, or was this something they thought she should do by herself? Surely they couldn't all be sleeping through this mad theological argument.

"I don't have it," Molly said.

"I don't believe you," the sharp-faced man said. "I heard you talking before I came inside. Where is it? In your purse?"

He moved toward her, toward the purse hanging from her shoulder. The pale man stepped in front of him.

"Don't," Molly said. "He's already killed at least one person."

The sharp-faced man scowled. "What would you know about that?" he asked. He sidestepped the pale man, lunged toward her purse. The other man reached for the gun. There was a loud bang. Someone shouted. Molly hit the floor. When she looked up the pale man was clutching his shoulder.

"Keep away from me," the man with the gun said. "And you, Molly, whatever the hell your name is—hand it over."

Corrig came down the stairs. *Great,* Molly thought. Of all the people in the family, he was the one least likely to be of any practical use. The sharp-faced man looked up at him and then dismissed him and turned back to Molly. "Give me the book."

Corrig reached into his baggy overcoat and handed the man a brick.

"I said book, not brick!" the man said angrily. "The bloody journal. Where is it?"

Corrig dropped the brick and drew out a large bird mask.

"What the fuck?" the man said.

"Beak," Molly said. "Corrig, please—"

"Give me the book, you stupid—"

Corrig reached out. His hands were empty and back at his

sides by the time Molly realized that he had slipped the bird mask over the man's face. "What the hell!" the man said, struggling with the mask. "I can't get the damn thing off!"

Suddenly Corrig held the gun. He studied it, turned it over, closed one eye, and looked into the barrel. Then he twirled it around his index finger, faster and faster, until it blurred to almost nothing. He stopped, spread his hands. The gun was gone.

"Great," Molly said. "Let's call the police."

Corrig reached into one of his pockets and retrieved the gun. He shrugged and handed it back to the sharp-featured man.

"Corrig, for God's sake!" Molly said.

"All right," the man said. "Give me the book or I shoot you."

Corrig shrugged again. Molly watched, horrified, as the man took aim at him and pulled the trigger. A bouquet of flowers shot from the barrel.

The man looked at the gun, stupefied. Molly reached for it. Something moved through her mind, picking its way across her memories, her jobs, her loves, her life.

Suddenly she was overcome by an urge to take the four pages out of her purse and give them to Peter. *No,* she thought. *No, I won't let him win, I've come so far. . . .*

She was holding the gun now, though she didn't know how she had come to take it. Everyone was watching her, waiting to see what she would do next.

She reached out for Peter's mind. She saw his greed, his self-importance, the feelings of insecurity that made him strive for success with his dreadful books. Her hand began to move toward her purse; she watched it impassively, as if it belonged to someone else. Soon she would give him the pages and he would go write his book, would turn her family history into something sleazy and cheap.

Wait, she thought. *There's something wrong here. What is it? Peter. Peter can't be doing this, he isn't part of the family. Someone wants me to give Peter the pages because it'll be easier to take them from him than from me. Who? Who is it? Who can be calling to me like this?*

She looked around the room. The rest of the family were finally coming down the stairs. Fentrice, Callan, Alex, Matt: Emily's descendants. Behind them came Lila, and behind her, walking slowly and clutching the banister, Andrew Dodd.

She reached out into their minds, cautiously.

Peter and the other two were silent. Someone—Callan? Corrig?—had frozen them into immobility so they could not do any more mischief.

Corrig's mind was a riot of color and sensation, of the laughter he saw underlying everything. He could easily stop the compulsion calling to Molly, but he didn't see that it was important. Very little mattered to Corrig.

Callan's thoughts were more complex, mysteries and their answers, tragedy as well as comedy. His life had been hard: his daughter and son-in-law had been killed, he had thought his granddaughter lost to him forever. Yet he had come to a hard-won equilibrium, and, yes, to wisdom.

Alex, to her great surprise, saw her as a rose, beautiful and self-contained. And Fentrice—

Fentrice was a stone. Something kept Molly from her great-aunt's mind, pushing her away.

She turned to Lila, went into her mind. She saw her as a young woman, her parents impoverished and unable to provide for her, saw her come to the offices of Professional Housekeepers looking for a job. She saw her meeting Fentrice, saw their friendship blossoming slowly over forty years, saw Fentrice begin to confide in her. And she saw which member of the family had sent Lila to Callan's house.

She didn't have to go on. She could stop now, could move away from Lila's mind and never tell anyone what she had found there. No one would ever need to know the truth.

But she had wanted answers. She was traversing the labyrinth blindly, her hands outstretched, moving without a plan toward the center. She turned to Fentrice. "You sent Lila here, didn't you?" she asked.

Fentrice stood up straighter but said nothing. The pressure to surrender the pages grew stronger.

"You'd found Emily's journal in 1935," Molly said. "Callan

said you left the family for a few days while they were touring in England—you must have gone up to Tantilly and read the journal, found out how to enchant people. You enchanted Thorne, you made her leave the act so that you would be in charge.

"And then I started asking questions about your past. I even went to England, started poking around at Tantilly. You were afraid I'd found the journal, that I'd guessed what you'd done and that I'd come to Callan because I was disillusioned with you. You knew all along that I was here at Callan's house—look how quickly you found me when you wanted to. You always knew more about me than I wanted you to.

"But you didn't know how I felt about you. You sent Lila here to see what was going on, you worked your magic through her. You told me she was angry with you so I'd suspect her, think that she wanted power and hadn't gotten it. You wanted to draw my suspicions away from you."

No one spoke. Molly reached again toward Fentrice's mind, was stopped again. It wasn't only Fentrice stopping her, Molly realized. It was herself, the fear she had felt ever since she had begun her quest. The fear of what she might find out.

She took a deep breath, pushed outward past her terror. Suddenly she was in Fentrice's mind, she saw all the complex mix of envy and hatred and scorn and love that Fentrice had felt toward her sister. "What did you do with Thorne?" she asked. "Where is she?"

Fentrice stood stiff and straight, a woman made of onyx. Molly went farther into the labyrinth of Fentrice's mind, saw a bridge game, a garden of flowers, purple stars and cigarette smoke and a cork shooting off a bottle of champagne. Laughing Sal roared at Playland.

"You enchanted her," Molly said. "You lured her into the labyrinth somehow and turned her into someone you could control. You enchanted her, took her life away. You murdered her. The kids at school were right—you are a witch. You and all those weird friends of yours, that bridge club."

The pressure on her mind grew stronger. Fentrice was trying to silence her as she had silenced Thorne. Molly pushed back, terrified. And then suddenly the pressure eased, and Molly saw something she had missed earlier. Fentrice loved her, cared about her as she had never cared about anyone. She was Fentrice's daughter, they were bound together by their shared history. No matter how badly Fentrice had treated the rest of the family, she still wanted to justify herself to Molly. She was ready to confess.

"It wasn't . . . it wasn't murder, Molly," Fentrice said. "I went up to Tantilly to look at Emily's journal, but I swear to you I was just curious. I wanted to know why everyone was so afraid of the Westingates, and so worried about the Order . . . I didn't even think about what I read until later, when Thorne took Tom away from me and left the act. I was so angry with her. I invited her to come to England with me, showed her the labyrinth. I just reached out the way Emily had, and . . . and she didn't expect it."

"You took her life away," Molly said again. She went farther into Fentrice's mind, feeling her way toward the answers. "That's why you left the act," she said. "Corrig knew what you were planning. He told you so, he asked you not to harm Thorne." She turned to Corrig, who nodded. "You became terrified whenever you had to do that scene with the golden statues. You never knew whether Corrig would bring you back to life or leave you frozen forever. But finally your hatred of Thorne got the better of you and you took her to England. Corrig wouldn't stop you—he didn't care enough. He knew what you'd planned to do, though, so you could never return home after you enchanted Thorne. But you always felt that your rightful place was at the head of the family, and you kept sending Callan threatening letters." She looked straight at her aunt. "You'll have to release her now," she said.

"No," Fentrice said. "Molly, no."

"Yes, you will. You have to give her back whatever life remains to her."

"No. She'll be so angry."

"You have to. Where is she?"

Molly pushed toward the answer. Something blocked her way. Fentrice was guarding her last secret.

"It's wrong, don't you see that?" Molly said. "It's as if you murdered her. You have to make amends."

"Do you think I don't know that? Do you think I haven't felt remorse every day of my life for what I did? I thought of releasing her—every day I thought it. But it was too late, always too late . . ."

"It's only too late when she dies. Where is she?"

"No, I won't—I can't—" A tear fell down her cheek, coursing through her soft pink face powder. "Molly, please, can you ever forgive me?"

"It's not up to me to forgive," Molly said. "It's up to her."

Fentrice squeezed her eyes shut. "All right," she said softly. "All right, I'll do it. But I need your forgiveness too, Molly. Molly, please . . ."

Molly said nothing. Could she forgive her aunt? Murder was the worst crime, she had always thought; a murderer took away something that could never be replaced. Thorne had lost sixty years of her life.

"Where is she?" Molly asked. "What happened to her?"

Fentrice shook her head.

"All right," Molly said. "We'll have to—" To what? How could she make sure her aunt kept her promise? "We'll have to meet in England, in Applebury. Bring Thorne. We're going to walk the labyrinth together, and I'll see that you release her."

"Very well."

Molly looked at Callan. Callan nodded, and Molly relaxed. Callan thought that it was safe to let Fentrice go.

Fentrice walked down the stairs. "Good-bye, my brother," she said to Callan. "You were right all along. I would have been a poor choice as the head of the family."

"Thank you, my sister," Callan said. "I hope you'll come back."

"Perhaps I will," Fentrice said. "Come along, Lila."

Everyone watched as the two old women made their way to the door, walking past Peter and the men from the Order. The men were still frozen, Molly saw. Blood had started to flow down the pale man's shoulder and then stopped.

"We'll have to call the police," Callan said.

"What on earth are we going to tell them?" Molly said.

"We won't have to tell them much," Callan said. "This one" — he pointed to the sharp-faced man — "still has powder burns on his hand from shooting the gun, the same gun that killed a man in England. And this other one is wounded with a bullet from that gun. They came in here, tried to rob us, started quarreling among themselves. They'll probably keep arguing all the way to the police station."

He turned to Alex. "Would you get some rope and bind them, please? And Corrig, would you take off that man's bird mask? Molly, you can call the police. As for me — I think I'll go make dinner."

FOURTEEN
Journey's End

Callan gave Molly the money for another trip to England, and a few days later she was back in London. She caught the train to Canterbury and spent the trip thinking about her aunt.

Fentrice had asked for forgiveness, and Molly had said that it wasn't up to her to forgive. But even if it was, she thought, she didn't know if she could. Fentrice had lied to her all these years, lied not just about the rest of the family but about her terrible crime. Some things were too dreadful to forgive.

She took a cab to Applebury, rang the brass doorbell at Tantilly. Kathy Westingate answered the door.

"Hello," she said, leading Molly into the chilly entryway. "That other woman—is she your aunt? She's already here."

Molly looked into the drawing room. "Where is she?"

"Oh, she's already gone down to the labyrinth. I have to say I'm not quite sure what you're trying to do—"

"The labyrinth?" Molly said. "She was supposed to wait for me."

"I don't—" Kathy looked flustered.

"Never mind. Down the hall, right?" Molly hurried through the drawing room to the unmarked door that led to the labyrinth.

Kathy followed. "Did she bring someone with her?"

"Yes, she did. Strange-looking woman—"

Molly barely heard her. She pushed open the door and went down the stairs. Someone had already turned on the light. Fentrice, probably.

She ran through the cluttered anteroom and into the labyrinth. The lights were on here as well. "Fentrice!" she called. The name echoed off the walls.

She turned right at the first door, remembering the Victorian man sitting at his desk. But the room had changed since she had last seen it. She was in the deli she had gone to with John Stow, the place where all her adventures had begun. Mannequins stood behind the counter, serving other mannequins lined up for sandwiches.

She left that room and entered another. Now she was in Andrew Dodd's apartment, looking at his wooden office chair, his battered desk, his gold-and-red patterned couch. An aluminum walker stood in the corner.

"Fentrice!" she shouted again. "Fentrice, where are you?"

She moved faster down the halls and rooms. She passed Fentrice's kitchen, the scrapbook open on the round oak table, passed Tangled Tales Bookstore, passed the Great Hall at Tantilly with its stained glass windows sparkling blue and yellow and red in a nonexistent sun.

The next room was the empty storefront in Camden Town, the dead man, Joseph Ottig, slumped where she had found him months ago. She had been half expecting him, but still the sight of him against the wall made her gasp and put her fist to her mouth.

Then she was in the great lobby of the Paramount Theatre, its amber light coming up through the yellow fountain, shining gold on the frieze of women along the walls. And here was Callan's confused, jumbled living room, all the cartoon animals changed into chairs and tables and lamps.

She was nearing the end now. "Fentrice!" she called. She thought she could hear footsteps and voices, around the next bend, maybe, or the next. She turned a corner, another. The voices drew closer.

Two women stood at the end of a hallway, shadowy in the dim light. "Fentrice!" she said again.

One of them turned. And then the other, and as Molly came closer she thought the second woman looked familiar. Heavy black glasses, heavy jewelry, a gray dress like a sack.

"Estelle!" Molly said. "Estelle is . . . is Thorne?"

Estelle said nothing. *Of course,* Molly thought. The glasses she had seen in some of the old pictures, the teeth so even they had to be dentures, replacing the gapped teeth of the family. The woman's docility, her slowness. "Estelle?" Molly said again.

"She can't say anything," Fentrice said. "She's deep in enchantment now. Come—I have to take her to the center."

Molly followed Fentrice as she negotiated the turnings of the labyrinth. Sometimes she caught glimpses of rooms off the corridors, flashing pieces of Fentrice's life: the deck of an ocean liner, Laughing Sal at Playland, a garden shaded by a peach tree. "Do you know how to get there?" Molly asked.

"Hush," Fentrice said.

They took another corner. Strange bright lines appeared in the gloom, connecting her and Fentrice, Fentrice and Thorne, connecting the rooms to one another. She was growing stronger with each turning, Molly realized, stronger and more aware. Beside her she felt Fentrice grow stronger as well.

Fentrice went through a doorway. The room was empty, but somehow Molly knew that they had reached the center, the final turning. And the Minotaur, the dreadful monster at the end of the maze—she had brought the Minotaur with her. Fentrice.

Fentrice was silent, concentrating. The lines of force drew together, warping around her and Thorne.

Suddenly Thorne stumbled back. "Where—" she said. "Fentrice! My God, what happened to you? You look so old."

Thorne looked down at her hand, turning it back-to-palm in the darkness. "I—I'm old too. Wait, I remember. I remember something. Wait. A bridge game. An old woman, Estelle. You enchanted me. My God, you enchanted me for sixty years!"

Loud thunder cracked out. Fentrice staggered.

"You bitch!" Thorne shouted over the noise. "You took my life away, you enchanted me! I'll kill you, you bitch!"

But Fentrice had walked the labyrinth, gathering power to herself. Thorne had been enchanted during the journey to the center, had been Estelle. Molly felt Fentrice push back. Thunder shook the room for a long minute.

The silence, when it came, was nearly as shocking as the noise. "Hush," Fentrice said. "I enchanted you, yes. And I'll do it again if you try to harm me. I brought you here to make amends."

"Amends for what? For sixty lost years? What kind of amends can you make for that?"

"I don't know," Fentrice said.

"I'll kill you. I'll walk the labyrinth, become as strong as you. I'll take your life away."

"You already have. Did you think I could live with myself after what I'd done? I left the act, left the family, took you with me to a small town so I could watch over you. And every week I saw you at our bridge games, every week I repented what I'd done. But I felt trapped, committed to what I had chosen. Thorne, I'm so sorry. I can't tell you how sorry—"

"Your sorrow won't give me sixty years."

Fentrice shook her head. Tears fell down her lined cheeks. "You're right. I can't make amends. I was wrong, I made a mistake. I can only say how sorry—"

"I don't care," Thorne said. "Live with it. I hope it makes you unhappy for the rest of your life." She left the room, began the long walk to the beginning. A glowing thread followed her back.

"Can she find her way out?" Molly asked.

"I think so. Molly—"

Molly shook her head.

"I can't bear to have both of you hate me," Fentrice said. "Molly, try to understand. You wanted to enchant Peter—you said that in the letter you wrote to John. Wouldn't you have done it if you could?"

"How do you know that? Did you read my letter?"

"Lila read it. But I know you, Molly. I raised you, after all."

"All right, I wanted to. But I wouldn't have. I draw the line at murder."

"Do you? If you could have gotten away with it? If you could have him always with you, always at your beck and call, willing to do whatever you told him?"

Molly said nothing.

"It's a terrible power we have," Fentrice said. "Grandmother found that out, when she enchanted Lydia. She warned me, but I didn't listen to her. We can do anything we like. The only limits are our own desires."

Molly nodded. *What would I have done if I'd known the extent of our power? I was so angry with Peter, at least as angry as Fentrice was with Thorne. To have him always where I wanted him, doing what I wanted him to do . . . I might have. Maybe I would have.*

What am I capable of? I've walked Fentrice's labyrinth, but what would happen if I walked my own? What would I find at the center? What sort of monster is lurking there, what horrible emotions do I have that I keep hidden away, that I never look at?

"I don't know," Molly said. "Maybe. I don't know anything anymore."

Fentrice moved closer to her, put her arms around her, held her wordlessly.

They said little on the trip back to Heathrow Airport. Once there they went to their separate flights. "Good-bye, Molly," Fentrice said.

"Good-bye, Aunt Fentrice. I—I'll write you."

Fentrice smiled. "Thank you, dear," she said.

Alex Endicott was waiting for her at the San Francisco airport. "Is it over?" he asked.

Molly nodded.

"How do you feel?" he asked.

"God. God, I don't know."

He drove her to Callan's house. He asked her a few questions and she answered them, but her mind was still on the labyrinth, on all the rooms that made up her life.

She went to her bedroom at Callan's house and slept for a long time. When she woke she took out the letter she had written to John. She reread it and brought him up to date, telling him what had happened as briefly and unemotionally as she could, giving him directions to Callan's house. Then she got in her car and drove to Pacifica to mail the letter.

She spent the next few days in her room, coming down only to eat Callan's huge meals. Andrew Dodd was still there, she noticed. He and Callan spent a lot of time together, talking about the deaths of people they had loved. It seemed to do them both some good, and when Dodd finally went back to Oakland he promised to visit again.

A few days later a knock came at the door. "Molly!" Alex called.

What now? she thought. She did not think she could face anyone. She went downstairs. John Stow stood there, his arm around his girlfriend Gwen.

"I got your letter," John said simply.

She said nothing.

"Come on, let's go out to eat," John said. "I've got some questions for you."

"All right," she said. She turned to get her coat; Alex was still standing by the door. "Do you want to come with us?"

"Sure," Alex said.

The drive to Pacifica cheered her a little. "So you two are back together," she said to John and Gwen.

"Yeah," Gwen said. She seemed happier than Molly had ever seen her. "I think he learned something from you."

"Well, he's not stupid, after all," Molly said. Gwen grinned.

They went to the restaurant where she and Peter had eaten,

so long ago. "So, what do you want to know?" she asked. "I thought I wrote you all about the case."

"Oh, it's not about the case," John said. He looked at the other diners, abstracted. "How are you? You don't look very good."

"He *has* learned something," Molly said to Gwen. "He pays attention to other people now."

"And he doesn't like to be talked about in the third person," John said. "You're avoiding the question, Molly."

"How do you think I am?" Molly said bitterly. "My aunt, the woman who raised me, turns out to be a kind of murderer. And when I accuse her she tells me that I would have done the same thing, I would have enchanted Peter if I could. And the scary thing is I think she's right."

"No one's perfect," John said. "You said that in your letter to me."

"Why does everyone keep quoting my letter?" Molly said. "Anyway, is that supposed to make me feel better? No one's perfect, right. So I want to enchant Peter, to take his life away. I'm no better than Fentrice. I'm just like her."

"Hey, we'd probably all like to enchant someone once in a while," John said. "A couple of weeks ago I sure would have liked Gwen to do my bidding."

"Thanks a lot," Gwen said dryly.

"But you didn't do it," John said to Molly. "Peter's still walking around."

"He's in jail, actually," Molly said. "Breaking and entering."

"Well, whatever. The important thing is that he did it to himself—you didn't do it to him."

"But I—I have this power. I didn't want it, I don't know what to do with it. I could kill someone, the way Fentrice did, or Neesa."

"But you didn't," Alex said.

No, she thought. *No, I didn't. I didn't walk Fentrice's labyrinth as I thought, but my own. I've come to the center. I've seen the Minotaur. I've recognized my monster; I know its habits. I've learned a hell of a lot more*

*about myself. All my life I'll have to watch out for my desires. I'll have to
be terribly careful. But Alex is right. I didn't kill anyone.*

"What did you want to ask me?" she asked John.

"What do you plan to do with your life?" he said.

"Do?" Molly said. "Hell, I don't know. I never did know."
She paused. "First I'm going to write to Fentrice. I don't know if
I can forgive her, but at least I can tell her I understand what she
did. And she raised me, after all, she was good to me, if not to
Thorne. . . . That has to count for something."

"Do you think you'll move again?"

"I—no, I don't think so. I've got a family here. I never knew
I had a family."

"Not just family," Alex said. "Friends. Remember what I
asked you, that day on the porch? It's all over now—do you think
you can give me an answer?"

"I suspected you, you know," she said to Alex. "I suspected
Callan, Lila, everyone, and all because I didn't want to admit the
truth about Fentrice. Oh, I was so unhappy—it made me suspicious. But you—you didn't do anything, did you?'

"No," Alex said.

"Ask me again."

"Would you like to go out with me, Molly?"

She looked at him. Why not? He couldn't be as bad as
Peter—no one could. She had loved Peter passionately, and all
it had ever gotten her was misery. She didn't love Alex, not yet
and maybe not ever, but she liked him a lot. She could have fun
with him.

"All right," she said.

"Great," Alex said.

"It's about time for me to leave Callan's," she said. "I think
I've learned what I had to learn, at least for now. I need to put some
distance between me and him or he'll take over my life. The family will, and I'm not ready for that yet. I'll move back to Oakland,
find another temp job. You can come get me there—we'll have a

real date." She turned to John. "Does that answer your question?"

"Sort of," John said. "I have an offer for you, a job offer. Would you like to be my partner?"

"Your partner?"

"That's what I said. I've gotten a couple of new clients and I can't handle them all. And I thought, well, a talent for mind reading would come in handy in my business."

No more temp jobs, Molly thought. No more restless moves from state to state. A family, a job, good friends. A place in the world. "Sure," she said. "Why not?"